Matthew Ravden is in his early forties and is married with two young children. In 1985 he joined a fledgling PR agency, which he helped to develop into one of the most successful PR groups in the world. Recently, after spending four years in Australia, he returned to the UK to start a new career as a writer.

BlokeMiles

Matthew Ravden

An Orion paperback

First published in Great Britain in 2006
by Orion
This paperback edition published in 2007
by Orion Books Ltd,
Orion House, 5 Upper St Martin's Lane
London, WC2H 9EA

An Hachette Livre UK company

1 3 5 7 9 10 8 6 4 2

A CIP catalogue record for this book is
available from the British Library.

ISBN 978-0-7528-8152-2

Typeset by Deltatype Ltd, Birkenhead, Merseyside
Printed and bound in Great Britain by
Mackays of Chatham plc, Chatham, Kent

The Orion Publishing Group's policy is to use papers, that
are natural renewable and recyclable products and made
from wood grown in sustainable forests. The logging and
manufacturing processes are expected to conform to the
environmental regulations of the country of origin.

*To Sophie, Callum & Owen for your love and indulgence,
and to all men who inhabit dog houses for large tracts of time.
May this book help you find your way out.*

Part One

ROB

but this time unfailingly picking out the chap's most unfortunate attributes. He's tall, but skinny, arguably even quite weedy, and the beginnings of a bald patch are clearly visible through the thinning hair on his pate, like a copse of trees in early winter. Poor bastard. And I'd wager he's probably receding at the front, too.

The girl seems taken aback. Her body language retracts like an anemone protecting itself from a passing fish. Her eyes look stern, her face turns away – just fractionally, but it's a clear signal. Or at least it is from where I'm sitting. My sense of relief is palpable, which is strange as I didn't realise I was quite so uptight. Ho hum. Anyway, quite right too. Presumptuous git. Who does he think he is?

'Don't worry, Rob. It's you she fancies,' says Brian, and I just catch the twinkle of a piss-take in his dark eyes before they disappear behind the rim of his pint glass.

It's a game we've played since we were students: sitting in pubs, or huddled on the edge of a dance floor, spotting talent and brandishing our brittle machismos. To each other, mostly, in a spectacular implosion of hormonal energy.

Now, somewhere in that same dark, dusty space in my brain where the male instinct is now yawning and wondering whether to get up or go back to sleep, I can feel the prickle of rivalry. The thin bloke hasn't gone away, the beautiful girl hasn't slapped him and, in fact, there is clear evidence of a deep thaw. She's turned her hips a few degrees towards him, and is now sporting a coy smile, betrayed only by a veil of wariness around her big brown eyes.

'The bugger's buying her a drink!' It's Donald. The third in our triumvirate.

I look over at him, and wonder how on earth he can see what's going on. As they so often do, his huge black glasses have slipped down his nose, presumably through simple force of gravity. The lenses must be at least half an inch thick. We're all thirty-somethings, but Donald probably looks forty-something. He's lost a fair bit of hair, both from the top and at the front, his forehead extending upwards like a huge cliff. To continue the tree analogy, Donald is suffering some relentless deforestation. He's become a little doughy physically as well, thick around the middle without exactly being fat. But his weight doesn't seem to bother him, and the boyish smile and impish sense of humour are clear signs that he, like Brian and me, is just a kid in a middle-aged man's body.

The scene unfolding in front of us is true to type. We have each enjoyed a modicum of success with the fairer sex down the years – I continue to cling to the conviction, possibly deluded, that I've had arguably more than my fair share – but by our own admission, we've never exactly been . . . how can I put it? . . . prolific.

Looking around the pub, I notice I'm not the only one perplexed by this unassuming guy who clearly has something I lack. There are several other posses of men, drinking and checking out the bloke's progress. Some are sitting with women, their eyes flitting across to the couple at the bar as they sip their drinks, trying (and failing) to be subtle. I can't help but chuckle to myself, marvelling at the robotic inevitability of male window-shopping. Men, of course, will always window-shop. Single, romantically involved, married, divorced, gay – well, perhaps not gay – but no red-blooded bloke can stop himself looking once he's zoomed in on an attractive woman.

The couple are now engaged in conversation – I am forced to concede that a couple is what they have become, at least in terms of the primitive, biologically driven ritual being grudgingly witnessed by the male population of the pub. The thin man looks relaxed now he knows he has an invitation to hang around a while. And the woman is carefully lowering her guard. In truth, she probably has no intention of letting this man get anything other than the pleasure of buying her a couple of vodka tonics before the female infantry arrives, but she's enjoying her power, and he's happy to indulge her. He is probably the kind of guy who does this all the time, just playing the percentages. Win some, lose some, and get a great deal more than blokes who just sit around on the sidelines.

Like us. Like dozens of others in the pub. Like most blokes.

Because most blokes aren't like the thin guy. Most blokes talk a good game but hate the pressure of the performance and the fear of rejection. We are onlookers, fantasising, arguing lamely about who she (whoever she might be) fancies, and drinking steadily in the hope that we might be able to summon the courage to do something, or at least say something. And while we contract into tight little balls of angst, the rogue walks right up to the object of our desire and just starts talking to her. She responds positively, and the onlookers are left thinking 'that could have been me, if only I'd had the guts'. We drink a little more to ease the pain, and immerse ourselves in our collective camaraderie. It's a cop-out, but it's comfortable.

Truth is, much as I occasionally attempt to deny it, I'm a team player, more at home nestled in the bosom of my male friendships than exposed in the harsh, unforgiving world of dalliances with the opposite sex. Rogues like this guy tend to work alone. Teams cramp their style. It's unlikely that men like him have many male friends. They probably don't have many female friends either, but they have a gift. It pains me to say it, but they do.

Does it make them happy, these lonely, soulless bastards? Probably.

I get back from the pub around half past eleven, creeping in through the back door as quietly as I can, aware that my movements are likely to be clumsy and I'm probably making far more noise than I realise. Sure enough, I trip spectacularly over a pair of misplaced boots – my boots – and my keys clatter across the kitchen floor.

I pour myself a glass of cold water; it's a tokenistic attempt to kid myself into thinking I'll feel less washed out in the morning. I know it won't work, at least not at 6 a.m., or 6.30 a.m., or whenever it is little Ralph decides he's ready to start his day.

Clare's in bed. I knew she would be. After all, she's got a job to go to in the morning, and anyway, why would she want to wait up for her half-cut husband, smelling like a passive ash-tray, only to observe him fall asleep on the sofa, snoring like a warthog, mouth catching flies? But despite the logic, I can't help wishing she'd been up, watching telly and

6

drinking a glass of red, and we could have cuddled up, had a snog and, who knows, maybe had sex. But no, she's tucked up in bed having held the fort and put the kids to bed. There's a kind of undemonstrative stoicism in her silence.

I feel guilty. I would say she makes me feel guilty, but that's probably not fair. I'm making myself feel guilty. Clare is OK about me going out with the boys. In fact she positively encourages it. But there's always something in the air when I get back. A whiff of damaged vibes. I know I haven't done anything wrong. I have nothing to feel remotely bad about – hell, the worst I did was ogle a woman being chatted up at the bar – and yet the awful, heavy stench of guilt is unmistakable. It doesn't really matter what I did or didn't do – or what Clare does or doesn't think of it, and in this case I know for a fact she wouldn't be the slightest bit bothered. Guilt seems to have a mind of its own.

I swig down the rest of my water and refill the glass from the tap. I'm desperately adopting self-preservation mode, but it's way too late for that. The fridge starts singing Yankee Doodle Dandy to me – a strange choice of tune for a Korean appliance – so I slam it shut so it doesn't disturb Clare's slumber.

Once upstairs, I can hear her rhythmic breathing. I wonder if I should check on the kids, but a) I know she'll have done that before she went to bed herself, and b) it's one of those girly things she's done ever since Emily was a baby and we checked to see if she was still breathing. Now the paranoia's gone, but the sentimental gesture lives on.

As I undress, carefully lobbing my clothes over the back of the chair, proud that I can do it in the dark, I realise I can't hear Clare breathing any more. She's awake.

'You awake?' I whisper.

'I am now,' she says, and rolls over towards me in the blackness.

'Sorry. I thought I was being quiet.'

'You were, until you slammed the fridge door. It's all right. I haven't been in bed long.'

There's silence as I slip out of my underpants and crawl into the bed next to her. She turns her back, not to snub me so much as to offer her warm backside as the prelude to a non-sexual cuddle. And anyway, she's wearing her pyjamas, just in case I had any ideas.

I feel another nip of irritation. I'm naked. She's clothed. What's all that about? There was a time when our two nude bodies happily intertwined at every available opportunity, but now there's this barrier. Her pyjamas make a statement. *No sex.* But more than that, they say, 'I have more important things to think about.'

I reach round and cup her breasts through the thick cotton. She doesn't pull away. Bugger it. I sneak up under her pyjama top and put my hands next to the skin. Now that feels real. I nuzzle closer. She doesn't respond and I sense a tiny sigh has just exited her mouth.

'Did you have a nice time?' she mumbles, in that slurring speech pattern that occurs when sleep is about to take over.

'Yes, thanks.'

'What did you talk about?'

The words are tailing off now, and I'm quite sure Clare has no interest in hearing my answer. And besides, she knows perfectly well that blokes don't really talk about things in that way. I rack my brain for a second to see if I can disprove my theory. Did we talk about anything? Can I actually recall a topic of any note? Any twinkling pearl of conversation in a bed of empty shells? Nope. Thought not.

'I hope you're not too pissed 'cause it's your turn tomorrow,' she says softly, and her breathing settles into that wonderful, natural, nocturnal rhythm, unfettered by the stresses and strains of conscious life.

'My turn' means I'm on Ralph duty. Bollocks. I knew as much, but managed to push it from my mind as my second, third and fourth pint came and went. So much for self-preservation. Now I don't just feel guilty, I feel stupid. I will most definitely, indubitably, 100 per cent feel like crap tomorrow morning. I'll have a dry mouth, dry eyes, a headache and I probably won't sleep properly because I'll be on edge waiting for my son's plaintive cries to come singing out of the monitor.

I suppose I could have asked if Clare could cover for me,

but I know she has to be off at the crack of dawn anyway. Christ, I can't wait for the kids to get up by themselves, fix us a cup of tea, put their own clothes on, and wait patiently while we take a leisurely bath. Surely one day? But in the meantime, it's my turn, it's Clare's turn. It's bloody shift work.

I don't say any of this stuff but the thoughts flow through my brain, transported by hot, beer-soaked blood around my temples. I always rehearse speeches when I'm worked up about something, and there's one going on now.

I slowly withdraw my hands from my wife's breasts and roll over to face the other way. I glance at the clock and note it's past midnight. If I'm lucky, I'll get five or six hours' sleep. Perfect. Fucking perfect.

And before my eyes close and weariness takes over, I think of my friends, and wonder what sort of greetings they'll have had from their respective wives? Like me, Brian and Donald have probably crawled unquestioningly into the great meta-phorical kennel of male life. Clare, Tanya and Judy have happily sanctioned our night out, there are no hard feelings whatsoever, and yet we still slink off to sleep in the dog house. It's the male condition, it's entirely self-induced, and we're comfortable there.

From the depths of a blissful slumber, I'm surprised and somewhat startled to find I'm in a Disney cartoon, and something pretty awful is happening. I'm not absolutely sure if it's *Lion King* or *Lion King* 2; I've seen them both so many times. But Zeera is there – the ringleader – and she is the evil one in the sequel. I am huddled behind the huge figure of Simba. The dark-maned lion – Kovu – is loitering, his eyes full of grim intent.

'It's time, Simba,' growls Zeera in her gravelly, jazz diva voice, her teeth bared. 'The lionesses will take things from here.'

'Go home, Zeera,' says Simba.

I feel he'd stand more chance if he had a deep, powerful James Earl Jones voice rather than his light, adolescent tenor. Or maybe if he had an English accent like Scar. Truth is he sounds about as threatening as Barney, that nauseating purple dinosaur.

'I am home,' Zeera snarls. 'And you and your stupid shaggy-maned friends had better leave. NOW!'

Christ, I'm in the movie. But something's different. It's not one pride against the other. Simba glances across to his daughter Kiara for reassurance. She holds his gaze while she moves slowly, deliberately, across the parched earth to stand alongside Zeera. Simba does one of those cartoon double-takes, blinking and pulling his head back in shock. And Nala? Simba's wife and lover? She avoids his gaze, slinking low to the ground away from her husband to join the new matriarchy. It is lions against lionesses, and the males are outnumbered five to one.

Zeera steps forward a few menacing paces. She eyeballs Simba.

'You don't hunt, you don't bring up the young, you just *stand* at the top of that ridiculous rock and expect everyone and everything to treat you like a king. And for what? Simba, you and your kind are lazy, selfish fools. Go. Go now!'

Simba blinks again. Then he lowers his magnificent head submissively and turns away. I can feel panic welling up inside. No! Surely not. This is madness!

'SIMBAAAAAAAAAAA!' I scream.

I open my eyes. Clare is standing over me, bestowing me with a look of sympathetic amusement. She's wearing her Jigsaw power suit.

'Darling, you were dreaming. It's OK.' She strokes my furrowed brow. 'Simba has gone.'

I wriggle into a sitting position, propped on my elbows. How fucking embarrassing. I had a *Lion King* dream. The lionesses . . .

'And Ralph has just started up. Can I leave him with you? I've got to run.'

She stoops to kiss my forehead, then she's gone.

And there you have it, in a nutshell. The plight of the modern bloke. My wife's gone to work wearing a suit designed to mimic her male colleagues and clients whilst simultaneously showing off her fantastic legs, and I'm at home in a scummy, ill-fitting, moth-eaten pair of tracksuit bottoms and a maroon sweatshirt that never quite recovered from the Repetitive Vomit Syndrome (RVS) it was subjected to during Ralph's first couple of months on the planet. Pretty clear who's wearing the trousers in this family.

But hey. I wouldn't swap it for anything.

Chapter Two

I start the day, as I do most days, in the company of my six-month-old son, Ralph. Like his father, Ralph is a tad slow to wake up and appreciate the world's startling beauty, and the two of us grizzle in Little and Large male harmony for half an hour or so while Little sucks angrily from a bottle and Large stares, in a state of trance, at the morning news on the TV mounted on the kitchen wall.

I've poured myself a Berocca, tropical fruit flavour no less, to try to pep myself up and shed the hangover, even though the damned stuff has a quite shocking effect on the colour of my urine. I'm looking at the earnest, concentrated face of my wee boy. He looks like a miniature Churchill preparing for a major oration, and I can feel the clouds of early morning grump part for a moment.

I've come to savour this time alone with Ralph now those fraught early weeks have passed and he's more of a knockabout shape. With both my kids, I was petrified of dropping them when they were very small, but now I know Ralph would more or less bounce straight back into my arms I'm considerably more relaxed. The little man is watching the news, probably taking it all in, and I marvel at his fierce blue eyes, his impressive mop of dark hair – complete with bald patch at rear – and tweak his strong, sausage-like fingers, letting each one thump back into its grip on the bottle.

All the books say it's important to bond with your children by having time alone with them, and at times like this, I have no doubt there's some sort of connection being hard-wired between me and Ralph. I wouldn't say I really know his personality yet, but there's plenty of time for that. Ralph smiles all the time, giggles, gurgles and seems more or less unflappable, and for now that's plenty good enough.

There's a shuffling sound – slipper on tile – and Emily emerges from the twilight into the glare of the kitchen. She stops in the doorway, resplendent in her brand new *Dora the Explorer* pyjamas, squinting as her eyes adjust to the unkind ferocity of the kitchen's halogen lighting and clutching her cuddly toy, Wilf – a hybrid bear/dog creature – to her face in such a way that she can pop her thumb in her mouth at the same time. Clare has been harsh on thumb-sucking just recently, determined to help her daughter break the habit and using the traditional threat of teeth sticking out at right angles for the rest of her days if she carries on. I've been less vigilant, though I daren't admit as much to Clare. I figure there are going to be bigger battles ahead – you know, boyfriends, teenage tantrums, sex . . . oh, and if she thinks she can put her boy-band rubbish on my Linn hi-fi (I'll have one by then), she can think again, and I'm damned if I'm going to tolerate her gratuitously flaunting her midriff. So if she wants to suck her thumb . . .

Emily has just turned four, and is – has always been – an absolute angel. She's got curly blonde hair – strange, as we're both dark. She's smart, articulate for her age, and amazingly sensible. Quite literally, she keeps us on the straight and narrow sometimes, with that precision logic that young kids seem to have. It's as though their lack of deep knowledge and experience helps them to see things far more clearly than us confused adults.

'Morning sweetheart,' I say, yawning, and force myself creakily to my feet, trying to maintain Ralph's milk-drinking posture whilst in transit to the fridge. I pour my daughter a glass of milk, shove the carton to the back of the top shelf and flip the door shut before the damned thing can start crooning at me.

Emily shuffles to the table like a lobotomy patient, wordlessly accepts the glass and empties it in several loud gulps. She looks up at me, panting slightly with the effort, her entire top lip coated with milk, and proffers the glass to me with both hands.

I give her the old raised-eyebrow treatment.

'More,' Emily gasps.

My eyebrows go up another few millimetres.

'More milk.'

Another few. They'll pop clean off soon.

'More milk, please.'

My face is starting to hurt, but I force my eyebrows to their fullest possible vertical extension. Emily could probably climb into one of the crevices on my forehead and hide there for a while.

Her face cracks into a grin. 'More milk please Daddy DARLING!'

'Lovely man?'

'Lovely man!'

I scratch my chin, pondering my daughter's request.

'Er, no, actually,' I say, keeping a straight face.

'DAAAAAADDY!'

'Oh, all right then. Since you asked so nicely.'

This time I can put Ralph on the floor, since he's finished his bottle. I reach over and ruffle my daughter's hair before refilling her glass.

Today is Thursday, which means Donna, the family nanny, will be taking Emily to school. On Wednesdays, I do it, and I have to admit I find the whole thing extremely stressful. Getting two small children fed, cleaned, dressed, making the packed lunch . . . oh, and let's not forget the small matter of finding time to get *myself* dressed – rarely finding time for a shower and a shave, let alone anything else beginning with 'sh' – I've done it for more than a year now and it's still total and utter chaos. I sometimes wonder if Clare would make a better fist of it. Surely it can't just be male incompetence? But I don't complain, and certainly not to Clare. She'd just laugh at me and give me her own version of the raised-eyebrow look, which is considerably more withering than mine.

I fix Emily's breakfast, having conceded that *Noddy* makes more appropriate viewing than the news for the current audience demographic, and the two of us chew on our Weetabix while Ralph wriggles around on the floor and bangs bits of Lego together.

'So what are you doing at school at the moment, darling?' I say.

Emily giggles as Mr Wobblyman goes on a drunken, spiralling rampage around ToyTown, howling in a Python-esque falsetto.

I clear my throat.

'Er . . . hello?'

My daughter shovels some more cereal into her mouth, allowing the milk to drizzle down to the bottom of her chin before wiping it on the sleeve of her pyjamas.

'Emily,' I say, loudly. 'What are you doing at school at the moment?'

'France.'

'France, really? Are you speaking French?'

She nods.

'Are you good at it?'

Nod.

'What's French for hello?'

'*Bonjour.*'

'What about bye bye?'

But Mr Plod is arresting Sly and Gobbo, and my scintillating conversation just can't compete.

There's a sound of keys in the door. Emily ignores it, redoubling her efforts to polish off the bowl of Weetabix, but Ralph is immediately on alert. He's stopped in mid grovel, his neck arched skyward like a giant tortoise sniffing the wind. And then he gurgles with delight as Donna marches into the room and slings her keys on the kitchen counter.

Donna is rather larger than life; a big girl from Swansea with a booming mezzo-soprano. I find her somewhat over-bearing, truth be told, but she's a lot better than the previous one, Lindsay. She was a right job's-worth, doing the kids' washing up and pointedly leaving my beans-stained plate in the middle of the kitchen table. Apparently adult detritus fell outside her contract. For some bizarre reason, Emily was quite fond of her. Thought she was cool, and as a result is still decidedly offhand with Donna, despite her being with the family for a good three months. But to make up for it, Ralph thinks she is quite the goddess, and the two of them have formed a very happy relationship.

Sensibly, Donna focuses her attention on the little chap, who at this point probably wishes he could jump up and throw his arms round her neck, but can only dribble and make silly gurgling noises.

Donna turns to Emily.

'Right, young lady, are you ready to go and get dressed for school?'

Emily shakes her head. Why use words when a curt, dismissive gesture will do?

'Aw, come on, you!' says, or rather sings, Donna, whisking Emily away by the hand.

And the three of them breeze from the room. I feel like the last survivor of a great hurricane. I switch the telly off and sip my coffee, enjoying a moment of comparative silence. But before I can get too settled, my children are swept past me once again, dressed now. Their little faces are placed in front of mine, puckered lips on which to plant my goodbye kisses, and they are out the door and gone.

I sigh and look at my watch. It's 8.30. I've got time for a shower and shave, and who knows maybe more, before I hit my work. Clare left at about 6.30, so it's only been two hours alone with the children. It's nothing really. Nothing at all.

So why do I feel so drained already?

My name's Rob Pearson. Most of the time, I think I've got things pretty well sorted, and my friends certainly take that view. I've got a lovely wife and two beautiful kids. Now, before we go any further, I have to clarify something. I really do have a lovely wife. So many people say they have a *lovely wife*, or maybe others tell them they have a *lovely wife* – 'have a nice Christmas with that lovely wife of yours' – when in fact they aren't lovely at all. Now, obviously it wouldn't be advisable to be too blunt here – 'say hello to that awful minger of a wife, won't you?' That wouldn't go down well. And the trouble is, the word 'wife' on its own doesn't sound very attractive, does it? Try it: 'wife'. Hmm. There's something about it.

Anyway, what I'm trying to say here is that people always talk through a contented filter about their own lives. 'Happily married' – there's another suspect phrase to add to 'lovely wife'. There are millions of people who once found their partners attractive, but things have changed. Perhaps that person has become less attractive – put on weight, lost hair, generally gone to seed – or perhaps something less tangible, like falling out of love.

But either way, you can be pretty sure ninety-nine per cent of blokes would say, even to close friends and family, they are 'happily married' and have a 'lovely wife'. And lots of them are kidding themselves. Disasters are waiting to happen.

I often find myself looking at my wife and thanking my lucky stars. In a society where relationships seem as fickle as the weather in March, I regularly swear to myself that I must never, *never*, take her for granted. Clare is my beautiful little dynamo. She's only five foot two, with dark brown hair and bright blue eyes. She's built like a gymnast: impossibly neat, with military-straight posture and a strong, supple body. I fell in love with her the moment I saw her and, two kids later, I'm still just as attracted to her.

The thing about me and Clare is – at least from my point of view – it doesn't matter what life throws at us, our partnership is at the heart of things. What I mean is, even though we now have two kids and can lay claim to being a 'family', the *reason* for all of it is me and Clare, and our relationship. The reason I live where I live is because of her. The reason our two kids are on this earth is because of her. I'm in this whole thing because of her and, after ten years together, that's what really matters to me most of all. Clare. Us.

I said to her once that if we became less of a relationship – less close for some reason – through having children, then it was a net loss for me. She was shocked, but why shouldn't I say it? People hide behind their children to mask the fact that their relationships are crumbling. And they pretend that having kids was the best thing that ever happened to them, because they can just focus all their love somewhere else and no one will notice. My kids are a by-product of my relationship with Clare. That's what made this happen and by God that is the thing that needs the most tender loving care. Easier said than done, as you can imagine, but a nice idea all the same.

As regards me, well, I'm not exactly a house-husband, but I'm at home most of the time. I get up, have breakfast with the kids, and then retire to my little shed of an office at the bottom of the garden, and I write. Technically, I'm a journalist, but I have dabbled with some other things and I'm halfway through a novel, so I prefer to think of myself as a writer. I've found that very few people like journalists, so this suits me better all round.

By default, I've always been a very hands-on dad. I suppose I chose to have it that way, but I'm sometimes not quite sure. Did I have a choice? I'm sure I'm closer to my kids than many other dads are to theirs, and I'm thankful for that.

It's odd, though. Most people look at my situation and think I'm the luckiest man alive, and yet I don't really feel that way. I'm not sure why. I look at the guys who schlep into London, leaving at the crack of dawn and getting back in time to peck their kids on the cheek if they're lucky. Part of me thinks 'you poor bastards' and part of me is insanely jealous. I can't really explain it.

Clare has just gone back to work, and although I didn't tell her, I let out a huge sigh of relief. I don't think she enjoyed her maternity leave much and, I've got to say, neither did I. The whole thing was a monumental struggle between mothering hormones and the feeling her brain was being starved of intellectual oxygen. She was dying to get back to work, and desperate not to at the same time. The net result? Not a happy time.

Clare is a director at a fast-growing PR firm. She joined it six years ago when there were only five people, and now there are forty-odd. She is clearly one of the stars of the show. I've listened to the speeches the MD has made, I've watched her go through the incredible rollercoaster of stress and exhilaration of pulling in new accounts, but most of all I know my wife has star quality. She's just one of those people. She's an achiever, and she's a leader, too.

But that's also where having babies has been tough for Clare. With Emily, she approached it like a business project: determined, methodical, organised, leaving nothing to chance. But Emily didn't play ball. She didn't sleep when she was supposed to, or eat when she was supposed to. The routine Clare was banking on didn't materialise, and she suddenly found herself utterly powerless.

I would find her sobbing in the kitchen.

'I can't do this,' Clare said on one occasion, crying fresh tears onto my shoulder.

'Course you can,' I said, patting her back gently.

'I'm no good at it.'

There wasn't much I could say. Is anyone good at it? Does anyone have the faintest clue what they are doing with their first child? What does 'good' mean? No, I knew that Clare was applying the wrong set of metrics. Or rather, she was wrong to apply a set of metrics at all.

'Darling,' I said. 'You've got to forget about being good, and just be yourself. That will be plenty good enough. Be there for her, that's all, and I'll be there for you.'

I knew it was trite, but it seemed to do the trick at the time. Clare relaxed for a while and went with the flow, and things got better.

And when Ralph was born, the big difference was that we both knew that things do, in fact, get better, and that you just have to hang in there and eventually, bright, robust, lovely little children emerge and parenting becomes less an ordeal and more a joyous journey of discovery.

There's no question in my mind, though, that the ridiculously high standards Clare sets herself in her work life were the root cause of her early issues with motherhood. She doesn't suffer fools gladly, so when she herself felt a fool, she was insufferable. But now she's back at work, pulling in new accounts again, she's become a quite brilliant part-time mum. She's winning on both sides of the fence.

Result.

Chapter Three

'The boys' – my mates, Donald and Brian – have come round to watch England play France in the last warm-up game before the Rugby World Cup starts in earnest in October. They've got passes. I haven't. Or at least, I've got a pass to watch the game – Clare knows better than to deprive me of my rugby – but not unfettered with fractious, bored, hungry, tired children, desperate for attention.

Clare has gone out. Getting her hair cut. Or is it highlights today? Either way, it's going to take three hours. I can never quite understand why women spend so long getting their hair done, when most blokes can rarely tell the difference. Of course, I always make a point of saying, 'Wow, that looks lovely,' after years of Cold Tongue Pie (CTP) punishment for failing to acknowledge the investment. In all honesty, I can spot the cut – especially if she comes in looking like a brunette Sinead O'Connor – but the highlights just pass me by:

'I thought you were getting your highlights done.'

'I did, but only the ends this time. Roots next time.' Right. Of course. How could I be so daft?

So, as usual, it's tit for tat. Quid pro quo. She spends the quids and I get the quota of children. I am allowed to watch the rugby with my friends, a tradition going back as far as I can remember, and drink cans of Stella in the middle of the day. But in return, I have to tolerate – or perhaps 'humour' would be a more charitable word – my two kids, who think rugby, and sport in general, makes for the most pointless, mind-numbingly boring entertainment possible.

It all starts off quite well. Brian has brought the beers and Donald the pizza, and we're already tucking in as Wilkinson kicks off. The first sip of beer, the roar of the crowd, the comfortable camaraderie between the three of us and all feels extremely well with the world. Ralph is on my lap, back ramrod straight, and for the time being, at least, seems fairly gripped by the action. I am absent-mindedly jigging my knee, my left arm wrapped around my son's midriff, while my right travels rhythmically to and from my mouth, can in hand. Occasionally the can is replaced by a slice of Meat Feast pizza.

I've packed Emily off to the family room and put her *Mary Poppins* DVD on. I reckon this should do the trick. She's nothing short of obsessed with *Mary Poppins* at the moment, and has been since her fourth birthday party a fortnight ago, when she and her wee friends, all wearing tutus, watched the film from start to finish *twice* instead of playing with all the expensive presents that had been lavished upon her. Like the bike I spent days choosing.

Anyway, favourite film or not, I know it's only a stay of execution, because for some reason her enjoyment of movies comes from sharing them with a parent, so she can ask the same questions at the same points in the movie, time after time after time. Repetition. Kids love it. Adults get headaches. But all is quiet for the moment.

Brian, Donald and I settle down and do what we do best, indulging ourselves and speaking the uniquely male language of the armchair sportsman.

'Aw, we're gonna muller them,' says Brian eloquently, rubbing his hands together with anticipation.

I look over at him. He's got short, brown, curly hair and a boyish face. He loves his rugby. We all do. He's like a kid at his own birthday party. We all are.

'It's only their B team,' says Donald, ever the pragmatist. His body language suggests he's waiting to be convinced. He is slumped back on our most comfy armchair, legs stretched in front of him and beer balanced on belly. His glasses are teetering on the end of his nose. With his thinning hair, he looks like a judge about to pass sentence. 'It's bloody stupid, really. We put our second string up against their first team in Marseilles and blow a fourteen-game winning streak, and they do the same at Twickenham. Daft if you ask me. Oop. Hello?' Donald sits forward animatedly and shoves his glasses up the bridge of his nose, where they are suspended, weightless for a moment, before sliding back down again.

England's backs are offside, or was it a hand in a ruck? I've been momentarily distracted by a series of tremors transmitting from Ralph's bottom across my thighs. I notice he's red in the face. Damn. We'll need to do a *live pause* soon. Merceron's popped the penalty over and France are ahead. Maybe we won't muller them after all. But now it's obvious that Ralph's straining has not been in vain. A sickly sweet odour creeps under my nostrils, and I'm concerned about the hazard this might soon pose to my friends.

'Er . . . Rob, I think your son might have filled his pants,' says Brian, without taking his eyes off the screen. He's sitting at the other end of the room's centrepiece, our maroon three-seater, and Ralph's noxious emissions have already reached him.

'Anyone mind if I live pause this for a second while I change Ralph's arse?'

'No, you bloody well will not!' snaps Brian, his passion massively out of kilter with my request. And I remember. He has a pathological hatred of any kind of tampering with live sport. He won't watch videos; it has to be live. And he won't even let me avail myself of my wonderful new Sky Plus capability. I think it's a technological marvel. I can actually pause the game, go and do the necessary with Ralph's nappy, and just press play when I get back. And if the half-time analysis is boring, I can just fast-forward until we get back to real time. Fantastic.

But such is Brian's manic obsession with living in the moment, he won't even let me pause for a few seconds. I fling my arms in the air with exasperation. If I were French, I'd probably say 'bof'. Jesus, as if it makes any difference! As if our neighbours are going to shout out the score a few seconds before Brian sees it on the scoreboard. I am frozen in time for a moment, and one of my mute, angry speeches whizzes through my head. A lengthy diatribe, compressed into the blink of an eye, lecturing Brian on his short-sightedness and loss of perspective. Then I regain mine. I probably won't miss much. I hoist Ralph over my shoulder and we're off to the change table.

We pass by the family room, and Emily is standing, doing what appears to be some form of child aerobics to *Mary Poppins*, swinging her loose arms rhythmically around her body. It's not a good sign. She should be sitting on the couch, sucking her thumb. That would mean she was engrossed. Standing means she's bored. Next she'll turn the TV off, then on again, but she'll have mucked up the TV input and will see nothing but a blue screen. Then she'll scream for me, I'll get the DVD picture back, but the spell will have been broken. Smashed into tiny pieces.

'Fuck it,' I mutter to myself as Ralph and I flit swiftly past, hoping not to attract Emily's attention. I figure Ralph doesn't care about my language. Hell, he's only six and a bit months old. Obviously, I'll eat my words if Clare or I are bent over him one day, crooning, 'Can you say Daddy? Da-ddy? How about Mu-mmy?' And he grins and says, 'Fu-ckit'.

In my haste, I make a hash of cleaning Ralph up. I'm pretty proficient, usually – one of the advantages of being around to the share the load, so to speak – but on this occasion, everything goes to shit in every conceivable way. It's a particularly messy poo, spreading the entire length and breadth of his nappy, and tastefully garnished with un-digested sweetcorn.

'Christ, little fella,' I say, recoiling. 'You could poo for England.'

On cue, the sound of 'Eng-land, Eng-land' floats down the hall from the lounge. The crowd is singing in that two-tone, seesaw way they do at Twickenham. Something exciting is happening in there. I return to my son's mottled bottom, which currently looks as though someone has painstakingly pasted sweetcorn-encrusted Nutella all over it, and halfway up his back for good measure. I grab both his feet with one hand, and lift them so the totality of the soiled area is free from the surface of the change table. With my free hand, I fumble for wipes, pull one sharply from its flimsy plastic housing, and succeed only in yanking the pack off the shelf onto the floor. I narrowly avoid another expletive this time, instead emitting a low growl.

Damn. Now I've scared Ralph. His bright, happy face freezes, and his lower lip starts to curl downwards. His eyes have a betrayed look.

'Oh, sorry, little man!'

My heart melts in an instant, and my irritation dissipates into the pungent atmosphere. I tweak Ralph's double chin reassuringly, and his smile beams back as though someone's flicked a switch. As I retrieve a wipe at last, Ralph reaches down to fondle his balls. He's only recently discovered the whole waterworks area, and delights in pulling, squeezing and doing things that, frankly, make my own privates hurt just watching. The trouble this time is that his hand is now covered in shit. Next, his gums will itch and the hand ... well, it doesn't bear thinking about. This is not going well.

I frantically wipe his hand down, and pin both his mitts above his head with one of my adult-sized paws whilst wiping the offending – some might even say offen*sive* – area clean. It takes me six or seven wipes and he's good as new. Except there's poo on his little under-tunic. But only a little. The crowd is roaring again. Screw it. He'll live. I pop him back up and stride back to the TV room, carrying my son like a prop forward with a rugby ball tucked under his arm.

England are nine-three up. How did that happen?

'Aaaah, Christ, Brian! You arse!' I'm livid. A speech rears its ugly head, but instead I hand Ralph over. It's not a delicate movement, but then again, prop forwards don't pass very often. I enjoy watching Brian's face morph from mild guilt one minute to absolute, unmitigated horror the next. Ha. I just hope Brian's not immersed in a fantasy about being Jonny Wilkinson, in which case he's likely to punt little Ralph left-footed through the skylight.

I can understand his reaction, though. You see, blokes like us have learned what it takes to be comfortable and natural around kids, but only our own, for goodness' sake. We pretend to be interested in each other's offspring when that's the polite thing to do, but let's face it, those hard-earned bonds we've developed with our own kids just aren't there. Don't ever ask me to change someone else's child's nappy. Suddenly, poop would be poop, and I'd be sickened by the smell and appalled by the sheer, primitive, animal nastiness of it all. Women seem much better at it. Perhaps their mothering instinct is less exclusive than ours. Or maybe they are just better at faking it.

Anyway, when you've got a pass, as Brian and Donald have, why on earth would you want to spend it helping with someone else's childcare? Which is why I've taken particular delight in plonking my baby boy on Brian's unsuspecting lap, the lingering whiff of doo-doo still floating around his partially soiled clothing. Soon, though, Brian clicks into politically correct mode, and pretends he's perfectly at home with Ralph. Now he's jigging him energetically and playing a game of 'tease' with his can of lager.

I pick up my own beer and have a well-earned sip. And then I notice my daughter. She is standing directly in front of the screen, and her diminutive but determined presence dominates the scene in front of us. I glance over at Donald, and he raises an eyebrow. Brian, too, flashes me a knowing look, having recovered his equilibrium. They have clearly been wanting to manhandle my daughter, or yell, or threaten her with something awful. But good manners have prevailed, and now I'm in the room, she's my problem.

'Have you had enough of *Mary Poppins*, love?' I say, pointlessly.

Emily nods shiftily, not enjoying the full, unwavering attention of the three of us. Four of us, actually. Ralph seems to sense that something interesting is happening.

'Tell you what, come and sit next to me for a bit, OK?'

'I don't want to.' There's no defiance in her voice, but there's something non-negotiable about her demeanour.

'OK, well, can you just get out of the way of the telly, please?'

I'm aware I have failed to keep the rapidly rising irritation out of my voice. And behind Emily's neat little body, the visible action reduced to fragments of body parts hurling themselves at each other, England have scored a try. Ben Cohen. Under the posts. England are rampant.

Emily still hasn't moved away from the screen, although she's shifting uneasily from foot to foot. There's nothing malicious in her behaviour. She just wants someone to pay her a little attention.

My brain's working furiously. We need a workable strategy here. Or, more specifically, *I* need a strategy. I'm rapidly losing interest in the game. Unofficially, it's England A against France B and, really, it's a meaningless exercise. Nothing but a bit of jockeying for position – shadow-boxing – before the main event in a month or so's time. But the Twickenham faithful don't care. They want to see a one-sided rout so they can send their heroes off to Australia on the crest of a wave. To me, it's not a real game of rugby. Nobody wants to get hurt. The French, in typically French fashion, already look as though they'd rather be sipping pastis than having to tackle twenty stones of Phil Vickery on the hoof. So it's going to be one-way traffic from now on.

With that piece of subtle, mind-bending preparatory psychology, I stand and offer Emily my hand, feeling the comforting glow of a halo forming itself above my head. The nice thing about four-year-olds is that they are easily bought. In a couple of years, she'll know what she *does* want rather than just knowing what she doesn't, and life will become more challenging. For now, she meekly moves away from the TV and the two of us leave the room.

I look over my shoulder and hiss at Brian. 'If I'm not back in ten minutes, use live pause, OK?'

And I hear Donald's baritone laughter explode. 'Fat chance,' he guffaws.

I sigh. 'Call me if I miss something.' I'm out in the hallway now, wondering what I'm going to do to keep Emily occupied. There's another roar.

'You missed something!' shouts Donald. 'Cohen's scored again! Lovely try!'

'Fucking great pass from Greenwood,' yells Brian. 'Oops. Sorry, Ralph.'

I stop, caught in a moment's quandary. Can I be bothered

to go back and watch the try? No. To hell with it.

'Come on, chick,' I say gently to Emily. 'Let's find something for you.'

There's a skip in her step now.

'Do you want to watch another DVD, darling?' I'm scanning the impressive shelf of kiddie movies, but a bucket-load of self-hatred soaks me to the skin the moment my words have emerged. Don't be such an arsehole, Rob. She's just watched most of *Mary Poppins* on her own, after all.

Emily doesn't grace my question with an answer. Rather, she stands and looks at me with doleful eyes, taking my instant guilt and pouring on hot water.

'No, that's OK love, course you don't. So . . . what shall we play?'

'Can we . . . can we . . . can we . . .' She's sporting that beautiful, heart-wrenching little girl look, where she tucks her chin in tight to her chest, puts a finger in her mouth and smiles the coyest of smiles while rotating her hips gently.

'How about we do some jigsaws?'

'Yes!' Emily jumps on the spot to emphasise her approval.

Brilliant. It's a win win, because actually I find there's something quite aesthetically pleasing about doing jigsaws with my daughter. Although I am, technically at least, an adult, and the pieces are about the size of one of my hands, there's still something that satisfies the right side of my brain in the way they fit together. It's also quite a new development for Emily, and she's been showing a real aptitude for jigsaws, and puzzles in general. Clearly another genius in the family.

I pull down a pile of boxes. The word was put out prior to Emily's birthday that jigsaws were the next big thing, so predictably she received about ten of them from the extended family. Animals, buses, children, Bob the Builder, Noddy, Dora, Jungle Book, Lion King . . . some large, some small, some ridiculously easy, and some challenging to me, let alone a four-year-old.

Emily chooses the Bob the Builder puzzle. She's not a great fan of the famous handyman, but it's one she's done a few times already, so confidence is high. I pour the pieces on the floor and wait. So does Emily.

'Come on, Emily; turn the pieces over.' I have to work to keep the impatience out of my voice. She does this every damned time. It's some kind of power trip.

'You do it, Daddy.'

'No, you do it.'

Emily relaxes further into her Lotus posture and looks at the ground. I sigh and start turning each piece over. Immediately, Emily snaps from her stupor. Another little battle lost.

Emily is quickly absorbed by the Bob puzzle, but sadly I'm an integral part of her absorption. Were I to attempt a sly exit, all hell would break loose. Apart from anything, she needs me to get the pieces in roughly the right places so she can start putting them together.

Despite the sounds of the rugby in the other room, and the knowledge that my two best mates are in there, drinking beer, I am happy to be doing what I'm doing. Really, I am. I've long since realized that when you have lengthy periods of time to spend with kids, the best thing you can do psychologically is remove all conflict. Forget about trying to check your email, or buying some books on amazon.com, or even moving your tools out to the garage. And reading the paper, or watching some sport on the box? Occasionally, you might have a run at it, but don't bank on it. You see, when you're playing with kids but secretly pining for something else, you can't enjoy their company. You can almost resent it. And the fact is, with young kids at least, it is nigh on impossible to do anything other than concentrate on them. So go with it. Enjoy it. Savour it.

When I remind myself of this simple maxim, I find myself relaxing and really appreciating my children for what they are. Little people. Little miracles, sometimes. And most of all, little bits of me and Clare. They deserve my time. They need my time, and when I swallow my male self-centredness, I realise how much I need theirs. My kids keep me honest, I reckon. Stop my maleness from becoming too dominant, too ingrained, too stubbornly selfish. I realise I have to make sacrifices and achieve some sort of balance between the indulgences in life and taking responsibility for my place in the world.

So, as Emily and I work our way through her entire collection of puzzles, my perspective is refreshed once more.

Just as well, as the cheers from the other room come thick and fast.

'Whoa! Go on. Go, Go, GOOOOOOOO! WOOOOOOOOOOOOOOOO!'

'Awesome!'

There's a silence as my two friends catch their breath.

'Jason Robinson!' shouts Donald considerately in my direction.

'What's the score now?'

'Thirty-three – three,' says Brian. 'And it's not even half time! Shit, this could be embarrassing. What do you reckon, Ralph?' He's trying to imply he's not ignoring my son. Yeah, right.

I'm half helping Emily with a particularly tricky *Jungle Book* puzzle and half listening to Brian and Donald's running commentary, which is almost better than the real thing.

'Dawson's on.'

'Bracken didn't look fit to me.'

'No. And his pass is so bloody slow.'

'Actually, they reckon his service is better than Dawson's.'

'Yeah, but he's got a five-minute wind-up.'

'Fair point.'

'Half time.'

It's Waterloo all over again, as I expected. The French are sulking, supporting my view that this is a warm-up match too far. If we reach the semi-finals of the World Cup and play France again, I'll make sure the occasion gets my undivided attention. The thought is pretty unequivocal, but in practice? How the hell do I guarantee that? Got about a month to think of something.

Brian lugs Ralph in during the interval. He's looking a little ragged, the poor little fella. Might be a bit tired. I feel a pang of guilt as Brian passes him over to me, heightened as I realise he's overdue a feed.

'Shit,' I mutter. 'Mate, could you stay with Emily for a minute while I make up Ralph's bottle?'

'Yeah, sure,' sighs Brian, trying unsuccessfully to disguise a resigned sigh.

Donald wanders out to the kitchen as I boil the kettle, ostensibly to retrieve a fresh beer.

'Here. Do you want me to take him?' he says, arms outstretched.

For someone who professes to have no interest whatsoever in having children of his own, Donald is remarkably good with kids. In fact, he's probably more comfortable with my two than Brian is.

'Er . . . yeah. Thanks.' With two arms I'll be able to get this done a damned sight quicker.

Donald picks Ralph up and hoists him high, like a winning captain showing off the FA Cup, and Ralph gives him one of those irresistible smiles. Unconditional. Uncomplicated.

'Yeah, there you go, little chap!' says Donald, thrilled.

To an extent, I take back what I said earlier about us men not being interested in each other's kids. I mean, it's true, but when I look at Donald holding my boy and smiling, I can see he's not having to make an effort. The offer to take Ralph was spontaneous and genuine, and he really does seem to want to interact with him. It's nice to see. Maybe it actually helps that he doesn't have kids of his own. And then again, it is half time.

I spend the second half entertaining both kids whilst listening to the whoops, shouts, cheers, gasps and jeers coming from the other room.

'Go on . . . you BEAUTY!'

'Balshaw's scored, straight from the kick-off.'

'Just ran through them.'

'He's having a blinder.'

'Yeah. Hope they pick him.'

A few minutes later. 'Look. Johnson's coming off. And Wilkinson.'

'Yeah. Smart move. Game's won. No point in getting them hurt now.'

I feel vindicated, and smile smugly as I fit the second to last piece of a Barney jigsaw (we're scraping the barrel now). Gotta leave the last piece to Emily or she'd flip her innocent little lid. This is no game of rugby. It's a bloody procession. I am content in the knowledge that I'm saving my serious rugby viewing for the serious rugby, although that nagging thought of how on earth I'm going to gain Clare's approval for four or five consecutive weekends of untainted armchair spectating just won't go away. But this is the Rugby World Cup. And not any old Rugby World Cup, but one where England really do have a realistic chance of winning. No way am I going to miss any of that. No way.

I notice that Ralph has stopped manically cavorting in his baby bouncer. He's heard keys in the front door, and in comes Clare. I look at my watch. Good Lord, yes, it really has been three hours! Now, what was it . . . highlights? Highlights.

'C'mon, let's have a look at you,' I say, the moment she steps inside the house.

She knows, from years of experience, that I don't really care what she does to her hair. I always like it. She always looks great. She can wear it short, long, dark, blonde, permed – no, second thoughts, I draw the line there – and I'm happy. But that's not what she wants to hear now, is it, especially not after spending eighty quid or whatever it is. It sounds apathetic. So I have to enter into the spirit of this being a big deal, as though she were wearing a brand new ball-gown for the first time.

'Wow,' I say in a measured way, not rushing it. 'It looks . . . *great!*'

I'm simply responding to my wife's body language. She's got that look on her face that suggests she is not entirely convinced.

'Do you think?' she says, sounding child-like and gingerly fingering her hair. 'I'm not sure.'

'Yeah.' I'm being quietly reassuring now. Strong in my conviction, even though actually they've given her something of a bouffe. 'You look lovely, babe.' I've got eye contact with her now, and she smiles knowingly. Knowing, but not saying, that it's all lost on me.

'Anyway, what are you doing in here? You're not watching the game?'

'Er . . .' I give her a long-suffering smile, and nod my head in Emily's direction. She's doing her usual thing of feigning complete lack of interest in her mother's return. In minutes, she'll be wrapped around my wife's legs, and it will take the two of us to prise her off.

'Aw, c'mon! They're little angels,' says Clare, kneeling to embrace Ralph, who bounces into her arms like a pogo-ing Cheshire cat, his face radiant. If you ever need to feel loved, hug Ralph.

'You weren't any trouble, were you?' Clare squidges one of his ample cheeks between her thumb and the crook of her forefinger, and gives the ripe flesh an affectionate tweak.

Emily has decided to join in, and now all my family bar me is enjoying a one-piece cuddle.

'What about you, Em? Bet you've been a good girl?'

Emily looks at me without moving her head and nods complicitly.

'You didn't stop Daddy watching his rugby, did you, darling?'

Now the head shakes, still eyeing me sideways on.

I feel like the outsider in some kind of conspiracy. Clare doesn't seem to care that she's asking leading questions. She's obviously not bothered what really happened but is keen to apply a cooling balm to any potential guilt she may feel for having left me in such an untenable position. She must have known I couldn't enjoy the rugby and look after the kids at the same time; the two things just don't go together. Doing *anything* and looking after the kids – other than actually looking after the kids – is a physical impossibility. She allowed me to look forward to the match all week, with my juvenile male enthusiasm for hanging out with my old friends building steadily, and then threw me a dipping curveball at the last minute. She gaveth, and she tooketh away.

Oh dear. It's another speech, zipping past my autocue eyes in fast-forward. So much to say. So little said.

It's 8.30 and the kids are in bed. Clare and I are enjoying a glass of Chilean Sauvignon blanc and allowing the debris of the day to settle. I'm sitting at one end of the sofa with my arm around my wife, who is curled up with her feet under her body. My fingers idly play with her hair, tucking it behind her ear and then untucking it again.

I know she's right. Our two children are no trouble at all. Quite the reverse. They are brilliant value. Cute, funny, loving, lovable, original and, above all, part of the two of us. Our creation. It's a thought I never cease to find entirely mind-blowing.

But still, at this point of every day, when one of us has popped Emily's book shut with just enough finality that she knows not to ask for another story, marched her to bed and said our goodnights, when the lights on Ralph's monitor flicker gently in time with his contented snores . . . I inwardly sigh with relief. I'm not sure if it's a bloke thing, but I still find the children incredibly hard work to be with. It saps my strength. I'm not stressed; I know how to handle them, know what to do in virtually any eventuality, but there's a part of me that continues to feel as though I've been locked out of a hotel room stark bollock naked.

Maybe that's because my comfort zone is so utterly incompatible with the notion of hanging out with a couple of young nippers. My comfort zone is work; head down, yes sir no sir, making decisions, feeling in control. Pals, drinking, talking crap, playing golf, squash, footy, watching TV programmes about natural disasters, or killer sharks, or whatever; listening to music, buying expensive electrical items, reading the accompanying manuals line by line, comparing cars . . . Some of it interests me a lot, and some of it doesn't, but it all goes into the essential cocktail of clichéd male content. Stuff we're at ease with. Stuff we can do – or talk about doing – for hours, days, years, without breaking sweat.

But kids? They suck us dry. Gone is that relaxed state of self-indulgence in which most of us men spend the first thirty or so years of our lives.

So, as the curtain falls on another day, and a window of opportunity appears – not much bigger than the eye of a needle – for Clare and me to truly appreciate each other's company, the chilled wine softly lowers us to a new plane. It's like the eerie silence after a rock concert, when the ears continue to ring for a while.

My mind has stopped buzzing, but it's still humming quietly to itself. I've been thinking about today, and how something is still troubling me about it.

'Babe,' I say, with a very particular down and up intonation that tells Clare there's something I want to discuss.

'Mmm?' She employs the same tone.

Our eyes meet and she's looking at me suspiciously. Amazing how much two people who really know each other can communicate with so few words.

'You know . . . well, you've probably forgotten . . . the Rugby World Cup starts in a month.' I leave the words hanging, full of implication but, by themselves, trivial.

'Ye-es?' The word is stretched out sardonically, inviting me to get to the point.

'Well . . .' Damn. I haven't thought this through properly. 'I know it sounds stupid, but I'm really looking forward to it. It's . . . really important to me.'

Clare's eyes are burning brightly at me across the top of her wine glass. She seems to enjoy these little stand-offs. They make me nervous.

'And your point is?' I see a hint of a smile at the corner of her mouth. She's not going to make this easy for me.

'I want to watch it. I mean, not all of it, obviously, because there's shed-loads of games and they're all on telly, but definitely the England games. Well, the home nations. I'd like to see how they get on, but they'll all be gone by the semi-finals and . . . and I'm not too bothered about watching every minute of England playing Georgia or . . . Namibia or whoever the other crap one is . . . but, you know, England South Africa is huge. *Huge*. And if we win that, we're pretty much in the semis.'

Bollocks. What am I? I'm a silly little schoolboy in a grown man's body. I'm excited in that infantile, bladder-tingling way that a young child is. And I've confessed as much to my wife who, unlike me, seems to have grown up. I don't know if she gets as dribblingly thrilled about things as me – I doubt it – but if she does, she has the dignity to conceal it.

There's a pause. There needs to be. I've shot my bolt and I'm now staring into my wine. No bluffing with this boy. I've just put my cards on the table and all I can do now is wait for her response, like a guilty man in the dock.

'I know all about the Rugby World Cup,' Clare begins. 'It goes on for about six weeks – maybe more – there are games every weekend and some during the week, and I am *not* going to just vacate my own house for half a day every Saturday so you and your mates can drink beer and watch rugby.'

'The games are in the morning,' I interject.

'Right. So it's the first half of the day, not the second. What's the difference?'

I get the impression this has come out a bit harsher than she intended. She lowers her wine glass and looks at me with those big, beautiful, blue eyes. God, she's lovely. And her hair looks super, I have to say, now that she's rewashed and blow-dried it herself. For a fleeting moment, a moment as breathtaking and transient as a shooting star, the Rugby World Cup doesn't seem important. Whoosh. Lovely. Gone.

'Look, I know you're excited about it, Rob. And that's fine. Of course you can watch it. But we have to give and take. I have things I want to do as well. And maybe I'll want to watch some of it.'

Hmm. I hadn't thought of that. Give and take. Compromise. We always seem to be striking deals with each other. But . . . dammit, this isn't going to be one of my speechless speeches.

'We always seem to be doing deals, Clare. I can have half a day here if I give you half a day there. It seems like we're constantly bribing each other.'

'But that's exactly what it is like, love. The best thing about you and me is that we're equal. We share.' She lowers her voice. 'I know you get frustrated. You've given lots of things up, you've hardly played any golf . . . you are brilliant. You're brilliant with the kids and I really appreciate it. And I want you to do your own thing – play golf, watch rugby, whatever – but you're right, it does have to be equal. If you want to bugger off for a day and get pissed with Brian and Donald and watch England play on a big screen somewhere, then . . . to hell with it, that's a day you owe me.'

It's her turn for a stream of consciousness and, like me, she's got a bit carried away. She has an exasperated look.

Of course, I don't particularly like what I'm hearing, but once again I know she's right. I'm not sure I'd have put it in quite such black and white terms, but there you have it. We trade 'me time' with each other. It seems awfully unfair on the kids, but then again, we're just being honest. It's not that time with them is a penance. More that time for self-indulgence is a reward.

I smile wistfully. 'So . . . I need to earn credits. You know, like AirMiles, between now and the Rugby World Cup.'

She chuckles. 'BlokeMiles.'

'BlokeMiles,' I parrot.

'Take me out for a slap-up dinner, organise the babysitter and the taxi, and you get 150 BlokeMiles in your account.'

We both laugh. I like it.

'Which I can redeem against Rugby World Cup matches?'

'As you see fit.'

We both enjoy the idea in silence. I think Clare's comfortable that we've reached some kind of understanding. But my imagination is going banzai. BlokeMiles, written just like AirMiles, trademarked. BlokeMiles™. www.blokemiles-.com. I have this entrepreneurial instinct that surfaces every once in a while. Nothing ever comes of it because I'm all dreamer and no finishing skills, but I am instantly convinced that the idea of BlokeMiles has legs. Donald's a bit of a techno-whiz – maybe he could do the website?

'OK, so I'm going to open a BlokeMiles account tomorrow. We're going to come up with a list of different ways I can earn points. We're going to work out how many points I need per game of rugby . . .'

I look up at Clare. She's watching me quizzically.

'Well?' I say.

'It could work.'

Something's popped into my head. I'm not at all sure if I should say it or not.

'I'm going to price up some big items as well. You know, where I have to earn stacks and stacks of BlokeMiles.'

'Like what?'

'Like . . . Oh, I dunno. I'll think of something.'

I have thought of something, but I can't say it. It's too impractical, too big, too dangerous, and much too soon.

Chapter Four

Something strange is happening to me. I seem to be fading in and out of consciousness, suggesting that perhaps this is another one of my vivid dreams. But no, on reflection, I do appear to be awake, although my short-term memory is blank. I'm in bed, but I feel hot, my skin is prickly and my heart is racing. There's a smell, vaguely familiar but difficult to pinpoint. My breathing is laboured. Christ, maybe I'm having a heart attack?

I shut my eyes tight and try to focus my mind. There's a nagging pain in my right tricep, which appears to be cramping. In fact, come to think of it, my arms are hyper-extended and are actually supporting my entire body-weight, which accounts for the discomfort. I'm facing downwards and there is Clare, her eyes closed and her hair dark as night against the white linen of the marital pillow. She clearly isn't asleep, though. In fact, her breathing is coming in short gusts, each slightly more rasping than the last, and she too appears to be finding the room uncomfortably warm.

My increasing levels of awareness spread from top down. My hips are on the move, slowly, rhythmically in time with those of my wife.

Good Lord, we are having sex, no doubting it now. We are snatching a moment of rare intimacy in the dying embers of another fretful day, and what's more, at a time when we almost *never* have sex. In our sexual heyday, we decided sex late at night was overrated, so we'd pile into bed, sleep blissfully and make relaxed, slow, original love the following morning. And at weekends, we'd do it again after passing an hour or two reading the papers and drinking coffee in bed. But that was another time. A time long gone.

I can feel a climax fast approaching, like a Tube train bustling into a station in a hurry, and as usual it's accompanied by a rush of panic. Clare seems to be having a nice time, but she doesn't appear on the verge of an orgasm. Shit, bollocks, got to hold back. In one of life's great ironies, the great surge of sensation that rockets through my body is tainted with disappointment. Once it's over, it's over. Gone, finished, empty, no bullets left. I'm suddenly impotent and weak instead of armed and dangerous.

Clare's eyes open and she smiles benevolently at me. She pulls me down and we hold each other tight, our breathing slowing in unison. There's a lot of important unspoken communication going on. *That was nice. It's OK. It's nice to be intimate together. I love you. I love you too. Why don't we do that more often? It's so easy, isn't it? We're lucky to have each other.*

I slip out of the bed and carefully dispose of the condom, wrapping it in layer upon layer of toilet roll before putting it in the bin.

'God, I hate condoms,' I mutter, as I slide back into bed next to Clare's warm body.

'Me too,' says Clare, rolling over towards me and draping an arm over my chest. 'But needs must.'

'Suppose so.'

There's a small, contemplative silence between us.

'Unless you want to have the snip, darling?'

'I thought we went through that?'

'We did. You said you'd look into it.'

'Did I?'

'Yes, you did.'

'Oh.'

Another pygmy silence.

'It's OK. I know you don't feel comfortable with it.'

'Mmm.'

'I'm not either.'

'Why not?' I prop myself up on an elbow and peer into the whites of Clare's eyes, which is all I can see of them in the gloom. My reticence is to do with the pain, and the idea of having testicles the size of melons for a week after the op. I doubt that's what's worrying Clare.

'Oh, I dunno. It's just so . . . final.'

'It's reversible.'

'Yeah, but don't they say you're not supposed to think of it as reversible? You can't guarantee that . . . and anyway, what if I got hit by a bus tomorrow? You might want to have children with someone else.'

'Oh, don't be so daft.'

'No, seriously. Or . . . what if we decided we wanted a third?'

'I thought we discussed that, too.'

'We did.'

It's a circular conversation we've had on many occasions. We know we don't want a third child, but can't help but conjecture every now and again. Rather in the same way we can't convince ourselves to say yes to a vasectomy, we can't quite say no to child number three.

'Clare,' I say, softly, once she has finished plumping up her pillows and getting herself in the optimum slumbering position.

'Mmm?'

'Were you close to orgasm back then?'

'Umm . . . no, not really. But that's OK.'

'Why is that OK?'

'Oh, I don't know, Rob. I just . . . don't need one. Not every time. It's just nice to make love, to be close. It was lovely.'

'But . . . I mean, I lasted quite a long time, didn't I?'

'Yes, love. Rob, it's not about that. It's about where I'm at. Where we're at. We can't just have sex the way we used to.'

'Why not?'

'Oh, come on. You know why. We don't have the time to relax in the same way. We don't have the same energy. We just have other priorities in our lives right now.'

I wriggle across the bed and spoon myself to Clare's foetal form.

'Do you think it will come back? I mean, the way we used to make love?'

'Course it will, love,' she says gently, stroking my hand. 'It's just a phase, that's all.'

And that's good enough for me. I can't handle the thought that my youth has withered on the vine. I want to be carefree and young and stupid when I'm sixty.

'Clare, there's something you should know,' I say with mock seriousness.

'What's that, love?' she says, sleepily.

'I did manage an orgasm just then.'

'You clever boy,' she says.

I may get stupidly nostalgic from time to time for the pre-children sex life Clare and I used to have, but actually I'm just incredibly relieved and happy that sex is back in our lives again. All the things people say about sex; how it's the great healer, how it's a vital glue between two people, well it's all true. But it's also a crutch for me as a bloke. It helps support my self-esteem.

And there's no doubt in my mind that the worst thing, by far, about having kids, is the pressure it puts on your sex life. I used to think it was the relentless brutality of the early-morning wake-ups, but slowly realised that the real victim was our ability to be intimate together. Even as our default waking hour moved from a savage 5 a.m. to a more civilised 7 a.m., the idea of a lie-in, with its inherent potential for natural, relaxed spontaneity, was clearly a non-starter. Apart from anything, Clare and I are both sleep addicts, which I suppose begs the question what on earth were we thinking about having sprogs in the first place? What did we think, we'd go from eight hours a night to very few overnight and just get used to it? Four years later, and neither of us is remotely used to it.

It's not that sex sits permanently atop the agenda. For long periods, we're pretty much anaesthetised – groggy, almost – oblivious to the cheeky promptings of frustrated libido. It's as though someone has slipped a bloody huge condom over our entire lives. Apparently, some women get unfeasibly horny during pregnancy, but it didn't happen to Clare, nor Tanya, Brian's wife. They just lost interest. Another urban myth is that men can get sexually hot under the collar for pregnant women. Not me. Not Brian, nor Donald for that matter, and his view is considerably more objective. It's not that pregnancy is unattractive, just that it's about as sexually alluring as a freezing cold bath. Aw, come on! Just look at the simple body language. What is it saying? It's saying Bugger Off and Don't Even Think About It! I've been HAD, can't you see?!

Notwithstanding all that, nine months is a long time. And it's not simply the physical issue of sex or no sex, more that it's awfully bad for the male ego for sex to be so far off the agenda. It's OK to be lazy and not to bother for weeks on end, but to have it taken away from you . . . that's an entirely different matter.

I remember a moment, shortly after Emily was born, when I thought thank Christ for that and half-expected Clare to jump all over me. How bloody naïve. First, Clare's body was battered and bruised. Second, every waking hour, and every available kilojoule of energy was spent working out what to do with this tiny person. How to keep it alive, basically. And every non-waking hour – or perhaps it's more accurate to talk in minutes – was spent trying to sleep.

So if pregnancy is barren, postpartum is a nuclear wasteland.

But it was still mutual, at that stage. Sex was quite honestly the furthest thing from our minds. It's just as well she didn't jump on me, because I don't think I'd have been up to much, to tell you the truth.

Then, after, say, three or maybe six months, things started to change. A routine emerged; we began to feel we knew what we were doing; Emily appeared to be less prone to imminent death (though I always felt we were more likely to die than her), and thoughts began to wander beyond the cocoon of our new life, to elements of our old one. Sex. I wonder if . . . do you think . . . how is she feeling . . . perhaps now's the time to . . .

I made my first tentative overture one night after I'd given Emily her ten o'clock bottle of expressed milk. Clare was asleep but stirred when I slipped into bed, so I thought I'd chance my arm before she woke too fully. Obviously, the maternity bra had to go. I found the clasp and lifted the thing off. Wow. I hadn't realised how much I'd missed my wife's breasts. I mean, fair play, they'd had more important things to do, but nevertheless . . .

As I ran my fingers lovingly around Clare's breasts, she opened her eyes and looked at me sleepily. She smiled, softly, but with a twinkle of amusement. Bloody ha bloody ha, I thought. I noticed a drop of clear liquid appear on the tip of a nipple, wiped it gently with a finger, and made to put it in my mouth.

'Mmm.'

'Er, Rob.'

But I was enjoying myself by now, and feeling horny to boot. It had been a while, and I was sure that now was the time.

'Rob.'

I was into it now, my face buried in my wife's brand new cleavage.

'Darling. Stop.'

'Why?' I said, lifting my head.

Clare sat forward suddenly.

'Oh . . . !'

'What is it, love?' I was alarmed now.

And Clare's breasts spouted forth, like some comical Rubens painting, milk gushing in great arcs over my chest, my hands, the sheets.

'Oh bollocks!' shouted Clare, hurrying from the bed and ripping fresh breast pads from a packet in the bathroom.

That episode pushed my libido into hiding for a while, until Clare finally stopped breastfeeding Emily, the maternity bra was put out to grass and breast pads became things of folklore. With breasts back in play, I felt reasonably optimistic that full-blown sex might not be far away. But I was deluded. Clare still wasn't feeling up to it. It was much more complicated this time. It wasn't her body coiling up into a protective ball. Nope. There was nothing amiss in that department. It wasn't even the exhaustion. Tiring as things still were, Emily slept from 8 p.m. until about 7 a.m. the following morning. All we had to do was go to bed early, right? Wrong.

Initially, it was a bit hard for me to understand. Quite simply, Clare was feeling sexually a bit numb. She couldn't quite put her finger on it, but she somehow felt different – perhaps more self-conscious – about her body. And after a brief panic, when I thought she'd stopped fancying me, I started to see how bloody obvious this all was. Let's face it: a woman's body undergoes the most astonishing transformations in form and function. It contorts beyond belief during pregnancy. Then it goes through the horror of childbirth, stretching unimaginably and suffering unthinkable pain, before becoming optimised for nourishing offspring. And once the offspring are able to wear Size o clothes, the hormones drain from the system and, supposedly, the whole cycle starts again. So, logically, even as a red-blooded male, I grew to realise that Clare couldn't just zip up her old skin and get on with life as though nothing had changed.

About a year after Emily was born, we started having sex again. Proper sex. Spontaneous, relatively abandoned and carefree, and increasingly frequent. And we were set fair for at least a year, maybe more – it's all such a blur – until we got pregnant again. I know saying *we* is a bit of a cliché, but I'm making the point that it was nobody's fault. We knew what we were doing. And the whole barren cycle started all over again. For Brian it was worse, because Tanya got – sorry, *they* got – pregnant sooner. They had barely had time to get to know each other again. And I know for a fact that it has put them under more stress than us. At least we had a break.

And then there's Donald, whose life with Judy is marvellously unfettered with such complex problems. It's impossible not to feel jealous of him, sometimes. Sure, he is missing out on something unique and special and natural. But it doesn't seem to be doing him any harm.

After Ralph was born, I started to realise I was getting rather desperate. Now, I don't subscribe to the notion – propagated by men, with our propensity for distorted self-image – that we're all sex-mad monsters who literally can't do without it. I've spent much of my life going through months – years on one occasion – without sex, and I lived to tell the tale. It really wasn't a big deal, though I'd never admit as much to anyone. And the funny thing was I don't think I was desperate for sex; it was more that I needed the security and comfort of knowing I *could* have sex if the mood was right. But that wasn't the case so, well, I guess I panicked. Or maybe it was testosterone overload, but I doubt it. Either way, I found myself getting seriously wound up. I started to think my testicles were weighing more.

I've always known I'd never have an affair – touch wood – but even so, odd things happened. I dabbled with porn. Brian lent me a DVD; one of the more sordid transactions in the history of our friendship. It was about some bloke called Ben Dover, and frankly it was more like an X-rated *Carry On* film than anything remotely erotic. I gave it back to Brian, who supposedly gave it back to the friend it belonged to. Yeah, right.

But the subtle yet significant difference between borrowing and buying a porn flick represented the next stage in my slow descent into depravity. The internet is a terrible thing. I found myself typing rude words into Google to see what came up. And each time I clicked my mouse, I felt closer to the devil. I read rude stories, looked at rude pictures, and eventually found myself on an American website selling Japanese bondage DVDs. Not exclusively, but those were the ones that caught my eye.

And I bought one. As I tapped in the numbers on my visa card, I could almost imagine the face of the FBI officer hacking into the porn ring. I could see my plaintive mug attached to my fresh new Interpol record. But I still didn't stop. I plugged in the three-digit security code and . . . click. Done. What a shocking state of affairs.

The DVD arrived two weeks later, delivered in person by the local postman demanding fifteen quid in import tax. Thirty-five pounds' worth of Japanese bondage. Hmm. Money well spent? I knew the answer to that already.

What I didn't know was just how appallingly guilty I'd feel

when the DVD fired up on my Macintosh. There I was, sat at my desk in my solitary little office, wondering if many blokes did this sort of thing or it was just me.

The early collage of scene clips looked . . . interesting. Certainly, the Japanese women were beautiful, with their pale skin and lustrous black hair. But the bondage, at a glance, looked a little weird. As the first scene began to unravel, I realised that I was going to have to scrap this DVD, and quickly. A woman was tied to a chair and three Japanese men were chattering away. Two were wearing suits and one a white coat. I scanned the scene forward, disgusted, until I could see that the woman had been loosed from her bonds and was now having sex with one – no, two – of the men.

And it hit me. A sense of betrayal as shocking as a punch in the chops. I have a wife, whom I love, whom I fancy, who is sexy, and OK so we're having a lean time for a very good reason, but there is surely no excuse for doing this. I was surprised by the force of feeling that swept over me. I ejected the disc, put it back in its box and locked it shut in my top drawer. And I decided I had to tell Clare all about it.

'Darling,' I said, calling her at work. 'I have a confession to make.'

'What's that, love?'

'I bought a porn DVD.'

'You bought one? Couldn't you just borrow one from someone?'

'Er, well I did that and it was rubbish. So I bought one.'

'What's it like?'

'It looks a bit odd. But I didn't really watch it, to tell you the truth. I felt bad.'

'Aw, that's sweet, honey. So . . .' I could hear Clare muttering to someone in the background. She was obviously busy. 'Well look, that's great. Um . . .' Clearly distracted by something now. 'Listen, Rob, I've got to go. But let's watch it together then, OK? Might be fun.'

And she hung up.

Christ, and you think you know someone. I thought she'd be horrified.

So we sat together, with the lights dimmed, and watched a

few sketches from my Japanese bondage flick. Clare seemed to think it was incredibly funny, but I can honestly say it was one of the most uncomfortable experiences of my entire life. I wanted the earth to open its big gob and swallow me whole.

Objectively speaking, it *was* funny. At one point I paused a scene and we both squinted and leaned forward, thinking the disc was faulty. Both the woman's and the man's private parts were fuzzy, to the extent that we couldn't actually see what was happening at the coal-face at all. Bloody fifteen pounds in import tax and the damned disc doesn't work, I thought, and skipped to another scene. A man in overalls was pouring bucket-loads of dead fish over a semi-naked woman tied to a shopping trolley. Skip. A woman tied to a chair was being force-fed marshmallows by a man in a white coat. Skip. Ah, another sex scene.

'More like it?' I said.

Clare shrugged.

A nurse was undoing a man's flies with her teeth. But as the trousers dropped to the floor, a grotesque, amorphous blob appeared, and the woman began bobbing her head against it. It was impossible to make out what was happening, but she seemed to be eating some kind of grey candyfloss.

'It's pixellated,' I said, as reality dawned.

'What's that?'

'There must be some law against showing their bits on film, so they fuzz them out.'

'Oh, that's ridiculous,' said Clare. 'What a waste of money.'

'You're not kidding.'

Clare got up from the sofa.

'I'm going to have a bath,' she said, and I was left to skip through the remaining few scenes in grim solitude. A fairly run-of-the-mill doctor and nurse scene, another with a woman wrapped entirely in bandages looking like something out of *The Mummy* . . .

And I laughed. Hard. I was appalled with myself for buying such filth, but there was no doubting the comic value of seeing all this absurd humping with the bits blurred out, as if it really preserved the actors' respective dignities. It made for quite hilarious viewing. But the joke was over. I took out the disc and stuffed it deep into the swing bin in the kitchen, filing Japanese porn under F-E for 'Failed Experiment.'

I suppose what I'm learning now is that I don't actually need sex quite as much as I thought I did. It's true that blokes think about sex all the time. What's the statistic? Eighteen thousand times a day, or something? That sounds about right. But does that mean we actually want or need sex the whole time? No. We're obsessed by the thought of it.

Ralph has reached a stage now that allows Clare and I to feel our way back to some kind of normality as far as sex is concerned. But I still find myself sitting in my office fantasising. Just last week I got spammed by a website advertising New York escort services. I swear I did nothing to deserve the spam. Nothing at all. But I'm attending a book fair there in ten days or so, so maybe they got my details from somewhere.

I scrolled innocently through quite tasteful images of the women who could be available for my pleasure, and double-clicked on a particularly horny-looking brunette called Carla. Carla's portfolio of pictures was undeniably impressive, and at the bottom of the page there was a tempting little link: *email Carla now*. Well, why not?

Hi Carla, you're cute. Don't suppose you're available the week after next? I think I arrive Tuesday evening.

Of course, I didn't expect a reply, but the act of sending the mail was sufficiently titillating. I was about to log off, when my email blinked.

I'll bet you're cute too. Yes, I could be available. Just let me know when you're in town and what hotel you're staying in.

OK, so my '.co.uk' email address was a bit of a give-away.

I don't get in until 9pm. Don't think I'll be up for a big evening. I'll be jet-lagged, probably.

That's fine. I'll soothe you and pamper you and tuck you in.

My bravado began to wobble.

I've never done this sort of thing before. What exactly do I get for my money?

Honey, if you're serious, I just need you to contact my agent and discuss terms.

Are there things you don't do?

Look, I just wanted to know.

Hi, this is Carla's agent here. She is $500 per hour, she doesn't do anal, you wear a rubber for everything. Just confirm your hotel and contact details and we can talk T's and C's.

I ran a mile, metaphorically speaking. I wasn't serious, for God's sake! It was just a bit of fun! I logged off, shaking slightly with the shock of it all. There's a fine but very distinct line between fantasising about something and actually having the slightest intention of doing it, and that line almost got crossed. Seriously out of control and, frankly, best forgotten.

The BlokeMiles idea has been growing like a fungus in my mind over the last week or so. And it will come as no surprise, given my sexual angst, that my first thought was *BlokeMiles for sex*. I imagined a shopping list of sexual favours, each requiring a pre-defined number of BlokeMiles. Something like this:

ACTIVITY	BLOKEMILES REQUIRED
Blow job	~~100~~ 50 BMs
Blow job with blindfold (and hands tied)	Add another 50 And 50 for the hands bit
Baby oil-based body-to-body massage	Add anther ~~50~~ 20
Early-morning sex, woman on top	100 BMs
Sex with role-play prelude (e.g., nurse / patient, must include outfit)	150 BMs (I'll pay for outfit)
Erotic massage whilst wearing black basque, stockings/suspenders	50 BMs (taking into account a nice new set of undies)
Sex (woman on top) with Japanese wig and eye make-up	To be decided (after watching DVD together)
Let me tie you up and pour a bucket of dead fish on your naked body	Free of charge (such will be your pleasure)
Invite Tanya round for threesome	To be negotiated

And so it would go on. I realised as I was doing it that this was just my silly, one-track mind in action again. I found myself effortlessly sucked into the vortex of a fantasy world, where the beautiful woman can think of no better way to spend her free moments than indulging her man in one-way, erotic sexual rewards.

Silly or not, though, I've decided to show it to Clare, roughly printed out. I produce it, as if by magic, as we get into bed. Presumptuous, I know.

'I thought we gave up mutual masturbation ten years ago in favour of proper sex?' she says, after giving my creation a cursory read.

'What do you mean?' Innocence. Wide-eyed innocence.

'You know, at the beginning, before we had sex. It was always one of us doing something to the other. I hated it. Well, I didn't hate it, but it was so ungratifying because it wasn't mutual.'

'But . . .' I try not to let my face look too boyish, but I can feel the mask of a sulk arriving. 'It would be fun.'

'Fun for you!' She's smiling, which is something.

I wonder if I've had my last ever blow job. It shocks me that the idea of my wife pampering me erotically seems so unequivocally out of the question.

I snuggle up to her, touching my nose against the soft skin of her neck. I run my hands up her body to her breasts, noting belatedly that she has forsaken her pyjamas. Shit, she was already in the mood before I mentioned this rubbish. Typical. But still, I think, I'll give it one more try.

'Anyway, love, the bad news is you owe me a blow job already.'

She turns her head sharply towards me, her nose giving mine a painful biff.

'Oh? And how do you work that one out?'

'Special introductory offer. As the inventor of the concept, I qualified for 150 free BlokeMiles. It was in my starter pack.'

She pauses, but doesn't slap me, which I find a source of some hope. I watch her stern face, and notice the furrow of her brow unfurrow itself, just a little. She quickly reaches over me to my bedside table, and retrieves my BlokeMiles list.

'Hmm,' she says, discarding the paper and smoothly moving her body on top of mine. 'If you think you're tying my hands you can forget it.' She kisses my chest, then again about three inches lower. Woo hoo. Yes. YES. This looks promising. More than promising.

'It'll be worth 150, love,' I gasp. She's almost there now. And so am I.

She stops and looks up at me, her face a picture of evil.

'Don't get any ideas, Robert,' she says. '*I* invented BlokeMiles.'

Chapter Five

I'm running Brian ragged on the squash court. Across the spectrum of all the sports we play together, squash is one where I have a distinct edge. He's fitter and faster than me, but I seem to read the game better than him, so I have to run less. And for the last ten minutes, I've ruled the 'T', just knocking the ball from side to side, sending my mate scrambling madly to retrieve the ball. I try a delicate drop-shot, but it's too high on the wall and Brian's making good ground. In fact, he gets there in plenty of time and has the whole court at his mercy, but only succeeds in scooping the ball straight back to me, giving me an easy volley. Two sets to love.

'Fuck!' he snaps. He's breathing heavily and there's a drop of sweat dangling on the end of his nose. He wipes it with his sleeve. Even his bare arms are glistening.

I repress a slight smirk. It's not a gloat – trust me – but we play so much sport together that there's something rather humorous when one of us gives the other a good pasting. We're both good sports, gracious in defeat and modest in victory, but sometimes there's this irresistible urge to laugh out loud at the other's misfortune. Like on the golf course, when the first bunker shot hits the lip and dribbles back to exactly the same spot. Sometimes when you're watching your partner play, you only see the look of concentration, the fierce swipe and then a puff of sand. It really is funny. And then he makes the mistake of taking the second shot too quickly, and the ball scuds across the green into another bunker. At that point, I can tell you, you really are ready to dissolve into a puddle of hilarity. It's hard to bottle it up.

There are times, too, when a well-timed quip wouldn't go amiss, but on this occasion, I sense I need to give it a few more minutes. Otherwise it could get ugly.

My friendship with Brian has, to a large extent, been cast on squash courts, tennis courts, football and rugby pitches, and even in bars, where we've fought just as fiercely across the table football table. It's sometimes spiky and uncomfortable, but the competition – the winning and the losing – brings us closer, and we talk about things that few male friends ever discuss.

In contrast, whilst Donald probably knows more about sport than either of us, he has never really been much of an active participant. His thing was swimming, and he actually made it onto the Olympic water polo squad when he was twenty. But the fact that he and I don't compete means we have a very different kind of friendship. It's very calm and stress-free.

Brian towels himself down and we start rallying gently. We usually play a best of three, then knock the ball about again, and if there's time we'll throw in another game or two.

'So how's Tanya and the kids?' I say. I've managed to relax my smirk muscles at last.

'Yeah, fine,' replies Brian without really considering his answer.

Whack. Whack. Whack. We're in a nice rhythm now, each one of us hitting a shot up the wall and then another cross-court. The court's really hot so the ball's bouncing nicely off the back wall.

'Actually . . .' He pauses, apparently wondering if he should tell me something. 'Tanya's struggling, to tell you the truth.'

I hit a sharp forehand off the side wall, and Brian doesn't bother stretching for it. He's suddenly a bit leaden-footed and, well, distracted.

'In what way?'

Brian's absent-mindedly bouncing the ball on his racket. 'I just think she's not really enjoying the full-time mum thing.' He pings the ball back at me and we're rallying again. 'She's exhausted the whole time.'

'Well, it is tough, isn't it, with the kids at the stage they're at,' I say, trying to be constructive. Olivia is three and Paul is nearly a year old now.

'Course it is, but . . .' There's an edge of frustration to his voice. 'Oh, I don't know. She seems to be blaming me. I feel like I'm doing something wrong, but I haven't a clue what.'

Brian works for a financial services firm in London. He's done really well for himself, earns a packet and gets involved in all sorts of high-powered projects. But he works his bollocks off, up at the crack of dawn every day, wriggling onto a packed commuter train into Victoria, and doing the same thing every evening. He rarely gets home before 8 p.m. There's always a flip-side.

He lets another ball drop over his shoulder, and this time just leaves it there and leans wearily against the coolness of the wall.

'What am I supposed to do, Rob? I've got a job. It earns us good money. Allows us to live in a nice house in a nice village. I can't just start cutting back my hours. I mean, Jesus, I'm that close to getting a partnership.' He gestures with his finger and thumb to illustrate the likelihood of his impending promotion.

'Why don't you get her a bit more help? You know . . . what's that woman called?'

'Diana?' Brian sighs, and trudges to the back of the court to get the ball. We start another rally. Seriously low-energy stuff now. 'She's already there three days,' he continues. 'I mean, does a full-time mum really need full-time help?'

I don't answer that one straight away, partly because I'm not sure what the answer is.

'I know I'm probably sounding mean,' Brian continues. 'But I'll be honest, Rob: I hate the thought of Tanya being at home while some other woman brings up our children.'

'I'm sure that's not what she wants either,' I say.

'Well, no. She decided not to go back to work so she could be a full-time mother. That's what I don't get. Maybe she's changed her mind or something. Then, fine, she can go back to work and we'll hire a nanny.'

There's a bit more zip in our shots now. I'm just following Brian's lead, and there's anger in some of those backhands.

'Maybe she's depressed, Brian. You know, post-natal depression. It sounds a bit like it.'

Brian's quiet for a minute. 'Yeah. I hadn't thought about that. But Paul's ten months old.'

'Still could be,' I say. 'Delayed reaction.' I'm not bullshitting. I have heard about this exact thing happening.

It's strange how a man who loves a woman and knows her intimately and has spent years with her can just miss something really obvious. And it can happen the other way round, too. It's scary really, how the stress, pressure and tiredness of the first few years of parenthood can just kill off the bits of the brain that feel empathy and compassion for the one you most love.

As we start up our robotic, rhythmic rallying across the court, my mind wanders back to the early days of Brian's relationship with Tanya. They met in our final year of university. She was at a teacher training college no more than a mile from campus, so used to spend a fair amount of time attending gigs at the students' union.

Tanya could light up a room with her beauty. Tall, blonde and incredibly striking, she stood out as a group of students from the college edged into the union bar one night. Of course we spotted them, and naturally our attention homed in on Tanya. So did several hundred other blokes' in a show of perfectly co-ordinated male gawping. But of all of them, something about Tanya had struck Brian to the core. He couldn't take his eyes off her. And much to the amazement of myself and Donald, he downed his pint and headed straight for her.

After university, both of them threw themselves into careers. Brian got his dream job in the city, and Tanya started working in a primary school. She was passionate about children and passionate about education. It was a true labour of love.

But it was when they moved in together a year or so later, I started to see the first signs of a disconnection between the two. They both seemed to resent the other's career. Brian became fixated with money, and felt that since he earned several times Tanya's salary, her career was somehow less important. Tanya would argue, forcefully and convincingly, that teaching was far more fulfilling, challenging and worthwhile than corporate finance, but she couldn't escape the jibes – not only from Brian but from others – that teaching was a doss, the hours were a doddle and the holidays were a huge perk.

When Olivia was born, Tanya gave up her job. I was never sure if it had been her choice, or if she'd felt obliged to, or if Brian had somehow coerced her. I doubt it. Brian has some old-fashioned views, but he's not a bigot. Either way, Tanya put a serene gloss over what she was feeling.

I look over at my friend, who has been quiet for a while now.

'One more game?' I suggest.

Brian nods, and we play on, somewhat half-heartedly and in complete silence. I win 9-4 and it gives me no satisfaction at all.

'Mate,' I say, as we gather our possessions from the front of the court.

'What?'

'I've got a mad idea to share with you. Never know, it might help things.'

We're in the bar, having showered and changed, and we're sipping pints of orange juice and lemonade. No sense in denting the shiny halo of health and fitness.

'BlokeMiles,' says Brian dully.

'Yeah!' At least one of us is excited. 'We get to earn miles by treating our wives – could be anything from a bunch of flowers to taking the kids away for a weekend.'

Brian looks at me suspiciously for a moment, and then his eyes ignite and he smiles broadly. Christ, he's got good teeth.

'And we can use them for boys' nights out!' he says.

'Precisely,' I say in a Machiavellian sort of way, as though he's just walked into my devious trap. 'And for going to Sydney for the World Cup final.'

Brian inhales a little of his fizzy drink up his nose and snorts it all back out noisily.

'You've got to be fucking kidding,' he says, using his towel to mop up the mess. His voice has gone all squeaky in an effort not to cough. 'I can't see us pulling that one off.' He looks up at me and can see I'm serious. Dead serious. 'Rob, there's no way Tanya's going to buy that. Absolutely no chance.'

'She will if you get enough BlokeMiles. She'll be so drunk on your kindness and generosity she'll hardly notice you're gone! It's only for a long weekend.'

'A long weekend in Sydney? Christ, what about the jet-lag?'

'We'll just drink through it.' I'd already thought of that.

Now he's shaking his head slowly, muttering to himself. 'You're off your chump,' he observes.

'Are you in?'

He sighs again. 'I think I'd best concentrate on getting myself out of the dog house with Tanya.'

Shit. I've lost him again. 'Use your BlokeMiles,' I suggest, and my imagination is off again, careering after a daft idea like a greyhound chasing a fake rabbit. 'You see, when you're in a debit situation – you know, when your BlokeMiles balance is negative – you are in the dog house.' I picture a BlokeMiles statement arriving in the post, with a cartoon bloke sulking in a big red kennel stamped over the front sheet. 'It's just like being overdrawn at the bank, so you have to talk to your bank manager – Tanya, in this case – about putting the situation right. Anyway, take a look at this.'

And I pull a piece of paper from my back pocket and unfold it. It's my latest BlokeMiles points list, significantly updated since the early, sexual favours version which, despite being somewhat one-dimensional, did me proud. Brian straightens the paper out in front of him. I can see a grin spreading stealthily across his face. It's like he doesn't want to smile really, but he can't stop himself.

I've got him.

Draft 1 of the BlokeMiles 'Miles for Smiles' list, as I've called it for the time being – cheesy, I know – looks like this.

ACCRUE	SPEND
Bunch of flowers N.B. Timely/not an apology	Round of golf at weekend
Surprise dinner for two N.B. No curry permitted	Overnight golf trip
Night in romantic hotel (baby-sitter organised as appropriate) N.B. Avoid rugby weekends or other major sporting events	Kid-free rugby viewing (e.g., Six Nations)
Romantic evening in (e.g., cook something nice) N.B. No pre-prepared food permitted	Overnight (out of town) piss-up with boys
Massage (scented candles, soft music, etc.) followed by rampant sex, guaranteed multiple orgasms N.B. Use Viagra as appropriate, but do not exceed recommended dose	Boys night out (unlimited booze) with lie-in next morning
Weekend without kids (e.g., Dad takes them away somewhere) N.B. For Judy, weekend without Donald should do the trick	Lap-dancing club

BlokeMiles Ltd accepts no responsibility for any marital strife, subsequent psychological disorders or health problems associated with any of the above. Seek Doctor's advice before taking Viagra, or attempting vigorous massage without previous training.

Brian's chuckling quietly to himself and shaking his head, presumably at my audacity.

'It's a bit loaded in our favour, don't you think?'

'Course it is. What do you expect?'

'Lap dancing. Yeah, right.'

'I know, I know. I got a bit carried away.'

'No, no. It's a good idea.' Brian is feigning seriousness. I think.

'Well, I thought so.'

He's scratching his chin, thinking hard. Maybe he is serious!

'How about we have two lists: the official one, which we share with our wives, and an unofficial one, where we spend our BlokeMiles . . . you know, covertly?'

'You mean, without telling them?' Is he for real?

Brian nods, eyebrows raised, seeking my approval. But I can see his face starting to split into a smile, with the tiny lines around his mouth spreading in ripples across his face. He *was* joking.

'Christ, you had me going for a minute there!'

'Anyway, look, if we decide we really want to go lap-dancing, we'll just do it. We don't need permission, right? I mean, that's not what this is all about, is it?'

'Well . . .' It's a profound question and I'm not sure of the answer. 'It kind of is. We get permission by using our BlokeMiles, which we've earned. It's a goodwill thing.'

'Yeah, but . . .' He's scratching again, up and down the temples this time. His hair, still damp from showering, is sticking out at right angles. 'Are you saying we now have to ask before we can go down the pub? I mean, seriously, we'll be asking if we can take a piss soon!'

'Fair point,' I say, reflecting. 'But, you know, the theory is that we live a guilt-free life, and if I'm honest about it, I still feel guilty sometimes after a couple of pints with you and Donald down the Horseshoes. It's mad, but it's true.'

'Well, it's up to us not to feel guilty,' says Brian, and I know he's dead right. It's just easier said than done sometimes, because there's no specific behaviour from Clare that causes the guilt. It's almost as though it's me that's making me feel guilty. Maybe it's me whose permission I need to seek.

There's a short, urgent silence as the two of us grapple with the greying lines of demarcation between BlokeMiles and non BlokeMiles-related activities.

'OK,' I say, with optimistic finality. 'So, a few pints in the local is deemed normal activity, and therefore shouldn't require BlokeMiles, since it doesn't need anyone's permission.'

'Right,' says Brian.

'Although . . . I guess if we go out three or four times a week, that's different.'

'No. Bugger it. Don't be such a girl's blouse, Rob! As long as the kids are safely tucked up in bed, we can do what we like. Our work is done.'

Brian's body language now looks as painfully defensive as Matthew Hoggard's batting. He's sitting up with his arms folded in front of him, looking at me defiantly. Daring me to disagree.

'Blimey, Brian, you have got problems at home, mate!'

It's meant to be a throwaway line, but as soon as it's in the public domain, I know I've made a mistake. Brian's eyes narrow a fraction.

'Sorry. That was meant to be a joke.'

Shit. I'm such a tosser sometimes.

'Look,' says Brian, irritated now. 'This is a lovely idea for a perfect bloody couple like you and Clare. But me and Tanya . . . well, no, things aren't right at the moment. We're struggling. And yes, I do need some space and some freedom to be able to be myself, and I need to do it without feeling like shit.'

Whoa. I'm speechless. Maybe I should have seen that coming, but I didn't. I'm not quite sure what to say.

Brian drains the remainder of his drink and sighs heavily.

'I don't think she knows she's doing it,' he says. 'But she hangs this guilt thing on me the whole time and I wear it like a fucking uniform.'

The humour in the conversation has fizzled out like the bubbles in a dodgy bottle of Kingfisher, and what's left is flat and unappetising. Brian's zipping up his kit bag, ready to go. I've still got half a pint of orange and lemonade left.

'I get it, too,' I say, draining half my drink and smacking the glass down on the table. 'But I don't think Clare really gives me the guilt. It's self-induced.'

'Well good for you, Rob.' Brian's breathing a little heavily as he speaks. Stress, I suppose. He hitches his bag over his shoulder. 'That's where we differ.'

He slaps me on the arm. 'See you soon,' he says, unsmilingly, and walks out of the club without looking back.

Chapter Six

I'm on a plane to New York and I'm bored out of my skull. It's only a seven-hour flight, which isn't so bad. No longer than breakfast, a round of golf and a couple of reflective pints after taking the money, but nowhere near as enjoyable. I'm beside myself already and only two and a half hours have passed, during which time I've eaten lunch and watched an unspeakably appalling movie. It was supposed to be sci-fi – I'm quite a fan of the genre – but it turned out to be about a bunch of genetically modified sharks plotting to take over the world. I should have ditched it after half an hour, but instead dutifully watched it through to its dizzyingly daft conclusion.

I'm on my way to my first ever New York Book Fair, and I'm there to promote my latest effort at a novel, called *The Last Tiger*, which I have come to loathe to the point that I am barely willing to acknowledge its existence to anyone other than my agent who, unaccountably, seems to think the thing has real commercial potential. Apparently, every author hits a wall of doubt, insecurity and self-loathing at some point in the writing of a novel. I hit mine after five chapters and the wall's still there, tall and unmoving. I'm not sure whether to climb it, knock it down, or simply shrug and walk in the opposite direction. In fact, I'm only pushing on with it because of the encouragement of my agent – bless her heart – but even she doesn't believe in it enough to pay for my flight. Or even subsidise it.

How the mighty fall, I muse, looking around the claustrophobic confines of the economy cabin. I used to be quite a successful technology journalist, back in the days when everyone was slagging off Microsoft and the IT industry was full of intrigue. And, I guess, I was in the right place at the right time. IT ruled the world, businesses spent a fortune on technology, so manufacturers spent heaps on advertising, so journalists like me got to fill pages and pages of fat, bloated magazines, week in, week out, with nonsense about who was doing what to whom. I had a reputation as something of an 'investigative' journalist, sniffing out crappy stories about how London Underground's Oracle system was costing them millions of pounds in downtime. Half the time my sources were extremely unreliable, but it didn't bother me. Looking back on it, I was no better than a tabloid hack. But I got reasonably well paid for it, and it was fun. The best part was the ridiculous juxtaposition of living in a run-down little bachelor pad in Neasden whilst being flown around the world first-class by people like Microsoft, Intel, IBM and their ilk. It was like having a double life.

In fact, now I look back on it, I really did have power back then. I had influence. There was the time I found out that one of the most high-profile technology CEOs – to this day, I'm still not allowed to divulge who – was having an affair with a high-class escort in London. Worse than that, according to my source (an insider this time), this rather unpleasant gentleman had a hooker in every port, and would play around in penthouse suites in almost every city in Europe during his travels.

I researched the story meticulously, zooming in on the man's recent behaviour in London, where he was spotted with a consort hanging off his arm in a hotel bar, and my editor and I prepared a front-cover piece. The article catalogued the CEO's relationship with the escort from its early stages a year or so earlier, and hinted at his parallel affairs elsewhere in the world. I had summoned up my most delicious English irony in highlighting the man's protest-ations of good, wholesome, American family values, and all the pictures of his wife and three children on the company's website. This was explosive stuff.

And then all hell broke loose. Someone, somewhere, found out about the impending story. I was suddenly buried up to my neck in squirming PR people and over-polite corporate lawyers from the US, all – in their own particular ways – begging me to drop the story. The lawyers started out playing hard-ball, but my editor refused to budge. After all, the information had been sourced perfectly legally. And then the PR and marketing people appeared on their hands and knees.

Ultimately, editorial integrity had to lose out to commercial pragmatism. The paper couldn't afford to be without this company's advertising spend, so a compromise was sought. I was flown to Boston and given a world exclusive on a new generation of hand-held computing devices set to revolutionise the industry. I got my front cover, but most thrillingly, I was treated like nobility. First-class travel, the Bostonian Hotel, limousine transport, exquisite food, attentive, not to say beautiful PR people looking after my every requirement . . . it really was the pinnacle.

In the end, there wasn't much I could have done to prevent my steady slide from grace. The main catalyst was the recession, and in particular the spectacular crash of NASDAQ. I had mixed feelings. On a personal level, it was disastrous for my career. But in all honesty, I'd become jaundiced with the overblown egos – Ellison, McNealy, Gates – and had met too many talentless idiots who'd become millionaires by simply being on the right payroll at the right time. I'd begun to find it all rather sickening. So when the tech industry went down in flames, it reminded me of Mr Creosote in Monty Python's Meaning of Life. So greedy, stuffing himself full of baked beans, he eventually exploded.

People forget that the whiff of decay was already in the air well before those planes flew into the World Trade Centre. But the IT industry collapsed with the twin towers, and in the immediate aftermath, everyone halted their big technology projects, the magazines wasted away like famine victims, and experienced journos like me were put out to grass to usher in a new, hungry bunch of fresh young graduates who designed their own web pages and were willing to work for a salary barely sufficient to buy them breakfast at McDonald's.

An entire generation of computer hacks was thrown to the vultures. Today, most of my contemporaries are scratching a living prostituting themselves to PR companies, pretending it's really important to understand the curious workings of a journalist's mind, and pretending even harder to give the impression they still know what's going on in the technology world.

I decided to take a purer approach and try to earn a living doing proper writing. But it's not gone well and I'm beginning to wonder at what point to admit defeat. My first effort was called *The Truth Hurts*; a non-fiction project I attacked with considerable gusto when I first made the career move. I thought someone needed to expose political correctness for all its irrelevance to human nature. You know, sexism, racism . . . we're all sexist and racist, so why fight it? But two things went wrong. First, Donald read the first few chapters and said no one would read it because I wasn't a well-known sociologist or philosopher. That kind of took the wind out of my sails. And second, I wasted too much time thinking and not writing, and now political correctness is considered decidedly 'last century'. My book missed its window.

I have to say I feel little nostalgia for the old days, other than wishing I could still travel in First, or even Club class. Yes, I was successful and quite well known in my field, but only because I was in the right place at the right time. And it was all bullshit, really; the fake glamour of IT and the pretend seriousness of the life of the journalist. Yes, I enjoyed the trappings, and to some extent the power, but at least now I'm in the real world, scrapping it out for an honest living.

I'd be lying if I said I didn't miss anything. I do miss some things. Essential things for stoking the ego. Things like success, and a sense of achievement. Recognition. The male ego is like the male private part. It's either proud and erect, and slightly overrates itself, or it's flaccid and rather pathetic. Right now, mine is the latter. I'm just plodding along, waiting for some kind of lucky break, but all the while sensing that life is passing in front of my eyes, like the scenery 40,000 feet below me. It looks as though it's hardly moving, but reality suggests something else.

New York has always been a fairly comfortable cultural fit

for an Englishman, and from the moment I step into the cab I feel at home. My taxi driver is Indian; a turbaned Sikh called Gurdeep, and his singsong retroflex conversation is soothing and reassuring.

When I check in at my hotel, the conspicuous lack of any unnecessary courtesy is equally reminiscent of my native land. I'm happy with my choice. Much as I pine for the five-star luxury of my past life, I feel it's only right to maintain 'certain' standards, so – in an entirely hollow literary gesture to myself – I've opted for a rather chic-sounding, 'boutique' hotel called the Algonquin, where Dorothy Parker's Vicious Circle used to meet.

The room's nice, although much smaller than I expected. The bed takes up most of the space, and there's a huge TV occupying the rest. So much for high culture. I go through my old ritual, unpacking a few essentials – things that need to be hung up, lining up all my bathroom utensils on the white marble – and leaving the rest in the suitcase. Then I flop on the bed and browse the 'hotel amenities' list. It's something I've always done, even though there's never anything of interest. Except the telly but, it seems, you have to switch the telly on and browse the on-screen menus to see what's on offer.

Naturally, I go straight to the porn. Well, why on earth not? I'm away from home, I've got sex on the brain, and no one ever need know. If the worst happened and Clare decided to peruse my bill, I could simply say I watched *The Two Towers*. No worries.

It's always important to know if the porn on offer is the real McCoy or soft rubbish where erect penises are strictly forbidden. But this stuff looks good. There's about ten movies and they are fifteen dollars a pop. Tempting. Very tempting. I click on a movie called *Barely Legal* 14. Usually, they let you watch a minute or two before you have to commit to purchase. I press 'select' and – dammit – the movie starts. I am a stupid git.

But ho hum, what can you do? I settle down as the first scene unfolds, taking up an unimpressed posture on the bed with my hands behind my head. And within minutes I'm asleep, whilst supposedly eighteen-year-old nymphets are cavorting enthusiastically – not to say, athletically – on the screen in front of me.

An hour later, there's a knock on the door and I jolt awake, disoriented. I jump off the bed and go straight to the door and open it, still trying to blink some life back into my eyes. A small, pretty, dark-haired woman with olive skin is standing in the doorway, smiling brightly at me. She looks vaguely familiar.

'Can I help you?' I say, still rubbing my eyes and trying to focus clearly.

'You must be Robert,' she says in a marginally foreign accent, difficult to place.

'Rob, actually.' I'm struggling to catch up with the situation here. 'Er ... how did you know that? Who are you?'

'I'm Carla.'

'Carla?'

'Carla.'

From behind me, there is an orgasmic shriek, followed by the animal bellowing of at least two men close to climax themselves. Oh shit. The movie's still running. How bloody embarrassing.

I'm about to ask Carla what she wants, but she's put her hands on my shoulders and is nudging me back inside the room with her pelvis.

'You naughty boy,' she says, as we both witness a spectacularly rude eruption on the big screen. 'I guess you'll be ready for me, then.' The foreign accent has gone. She's a New Yorker.

Carla pushes me into a sitting position on the edge of the bed, and starts kissing me. Or rather she's chewing rather painfully on my lower lip.

'No, no, no. No!' I try unsuccessfully to keep the panic out of my voice. There's a grim reality dawning on me now, slow but unavoidable, like middle-age spread. This has something to do with that stupid website I was looking at a few weeks ago. Carla. Yes, Carla. Spanish – about as Spanish as George

W. I look at her again. It's definitely the girl in the pictures, though – and I hate to say this – she's actually a lot cuter in real life. Not a terribly helpful observation, really.

'Carla. I . . . um . . . there must be some mistake, I'm afraid.'

'No, Robert, no mistake.' She opens her handbag and shows me a print-out of an email exchange between me and her agent. I scan to the bottom line, which says, in somewhat small print – Treat This Message As Confirmation of Your Appointment.

'No. No. No.' I'm shaking my head spastically. 'I was just messing around.'

'Well, I'm not messing around.' She's yanks my T-shirt over my shoulders and is now pawing at her breasts with my hands, which she has in a vice-like grip. She's breathing heavily and, frankly, it's all incredibly unsexy.

'I can't,' I say. What the hell am I supposed to say? 'Really, I can't.'

Carla can sense my panic, so she decides to throw caution to the wind and grabs my crotch. Little does she know that what she is looking for has long since disappeared deep inside my body. I have scarpered up the chain of evolution – or is it down – and become a whale. The slight thickness of my voice could be due to the fact that my private package is wedged in my oesophagus somewhere, quaking in its metaphorical boots.

She's not done yet, though. She drops to her knees, unzips me and rather insensitively pulls out what little she can find of my genitalia. For an escort – or whatever crap bloody euphemism you want to use – a penis in this state isn't good for business. I'm quite clearly incapable of raising a smile, let alone something that could cost me $500 an hour.

Carla stands up, finally looking defeated and, it must be said, incredibly cross as well.

'So what kinda gig you on, buster?' she says, lapsing into her raw vernacular now the Spanish act has been booed from the stage.

'I'm really sorry,' I say, lamely. There's a huge amount of relief flowing through my veins. Not enough to facilitate an erection, mind, which is probably a good thing. 'I had no idea I had actually booked you. I was just messing about. I'm married.'

'They're all married.'

'Well, I'm happily married.'

'They're all happily married.'

'I'd never do anything like this.'

'None of 'em will.'

'And . . . it's way too much. Five hundred bloody dollars an hour? I've just rented a movie for fifteen!'

I don't know why I said that. I guess the apologetic approach wasn't getting me anywhere. But this works. She gives me a look of sheer, unadulterated hatred, suddenly not looking pretty at all, but rather scary, grabs her handbag and struts from the room, slamming the door so hard behind her that a framed print of Dorothy Parker falls from the wall. Dorothy's now looking up at me with a look of disdain, so I quickly re-hang her, muttering an apology.

'Jesus H. Christ,' I whisper to myself and put a hand to my chest to feel the beat of my heart slowly returning to normal. 'What a bloody nightmare.'

'Yes, yes, YEEEEEEES,' whoops the young blonde on the telly as she's humped by a well-muscled guy with a ridiculous mullet. Suddenly all this seems beyond filthy. It is tasteless, inhuman, degrading, and I want nothing at all to do with it. I march to the telly, my relieved chap still dangling inertly from my jeans, and switch it off.

Chapter Seven

'So how did those meetings go on Thursday?' Clare is perched on the edge of the bed, watching me unpack.

'Um, yeah, they were all right, actually.'

On the outside, I'm trying to work out which pairs of socks need to be thrown in the laundry basket and which ones I didn't get round to wearing. I have a horrible feeling I only wore one pair, but I can't let Clare know that. On the inside, I'm in complete turmoil. Do I tell Clare about the escort, Carla? Except of course there's no way this woman should be permitted a name. Hell no. She is a faceless whore.

'Er, Rob?'

'What? Sorry?'

I have a pair of socks in each hand – one clean, one soiled, but I can't work out which without having a sniff. I can feel Clare's eyes on me. I probably look a bit of a sight, actually. I look beyond my wife to the mirrored door of the wardrobe, and sure enough my hair is all over the place and my clothes are crumpled. I probably smell a bit fruity too. Must have a shower.

'The meetings with those editorial types. Scouts, or whatever you said they were.'

I can hear Clare's voice . . .

'ABOUT YOUR BOOK.'

'Oh, that,' I say, dismissively. But then I force my mind to focus. 'They went well. Actually, very well. One of them said he really liked it. My agent thinks he might make an offer.'

And it's true. This scout chap from a major publisher – I

can't remember which – was almost drooling with enthusiasm for my daft novel. I put it down to American positivity and took it with a pinch of salt, but then my agent called as I was boarding the plane – I'd forgotten to switch my phone off – saying there was an offer on the way. I suppose it hasn't quite sunk in yet.

I sniff the two pairs of socks in turn, but they both smell musty, so I lob them across the room into the basket. Swish. Some talent, I am.

'Rob, that's brilliant!' squeaks Clare enthusiastically, and she jumps up and gives me a squeeze.

'Yeah. Class shot, wasn't it?'

'Not that, you idiot! The book deal. So when will you know?'

I had a bit of an incident with an escort. Nothing happened. No, I just can't find a good way of saying it. There is no good way of saying it. Too much explaining to do. Sure, nothing happened, but that won't help much. Well, it might eventually, but her initial reaction is likely to be . . . extreme.

'Rob. When will you know? God, what's wrong with you? Why aren't you excited about this? This is huge for you.'

'Oh, sorry. I'm just a bit jet-lagged. Need a good night's sleep.'

'Are you sure you should be going out for a pint, then?' A raised eyebrow suggests she's not entirely convinced.

'I'm just going for one. Be nice to catch up with the lads. And I want to check Donald's OK. He left me a message, sounded a bit strange.' And I'm not lying. Donald called me at the airport before I flew out of Heathrow. He'd forgotten I was going and seemed disappointed. There was something in his voice. Something I hadn't heard before.

'You don't look fit to go to the pub. In fact, you look terrible. Rob, you're shaking.'

I look down at my hands, and it's true; they are trembling. *Clare. There's something I need to share with you.* No, I just can't do it. And not only that, there's no point. Nothing happened. No damage done. In fact, my conscience can feel quite satisfied by the restraint shown in extreme circumstances. Telling Clare might offload some of the guilt, but the potential price is too high. We'd get through it, of course we would, but it would be painful. Just not worth it.

Decision made, I can feel myself start to calm down. I sit next to Clare on the bed and pull her close.

'I missed you,' I say. And I mean it.

The Four Horseshoes is one of about three pubs we tend to frequent. It's about as close to a traditional pub as you can get these days, in the sense that you can still drink and not eat, but only if you don't mind cowering in a smoky corner directly outside the toilets. I'm first to arrive, as usual. I'm one of these people who simply can't avoid being on time, even when I try to be late. I absolutely detest getting to the pub first. You feel like such a lemon. So tonight, I actually forced myself to leave quarter of an hour later, hoping that one or other of my mates would be sitting at the bar hesitantly nursing a first pint when I walk in. No such luck. So it's me, sitting at a table on my own, trying not to drink the cool lager too fast because then I'd be a beer ahead of the others and it would sort of muck up the rounds.

The pub's a bit dead, but it is only just after seven. There's a few spotty youths playing pool and reckoning themselves rather cool but, looking around, there really isn't anyone to be cool to. No women other than the girl behind the bar, who is shaped like a moose and has a nose to match. Ho hum. Someone's got some Elton John on the jukebox. I'm not a fan but it's decent enough background music.

Brian and Donald walk in together. It's always a bit unsettling when that happens. Have they been chatting about me? Did they meet for a drink somewhere else before coming here? Have I done anything wrong? Or did they just arrive at the same time?

I jump up and get to the bar first. I don't know why, but I always love getting the first round in. People think it's a really generous trait, but the truth is I like getting it out of the way so I can just relax for a while and know I can stay safely seated, chatting away unhindered. I hate having to worry about when exactly it's my round. Anyway, their two pints of Stella are on the way before we've even shaken hands.

73

We settle at our table, slinging our jackets behind chairs and noisily dragging the seating around the wooden floor until we've got just the right feng shui for a few pints and a blokey chat. I am absolutely dying to spill the beans on my New York experience, but blokes never go straight into the juicy stuff. It's a pretty smart tactic, actually, because by sidestepping the deep issues at the beginning of the evening, the potential is created to avoid them altogether.

So we talk about rugby.

'Do you think they picked the right squad?' I ask. It's an open question. Kind of a starter for ten.

'Yeah,' says Brian. 'There weren't really any surprises, were there?'

'Balshaw wasn't a dead cert. Nor Luger.' Brian and I are warming things up, giving Donald a little longer to consider his position.

'Actually, I really think they should have taken Shaw,' Donald says. 'He's been playing so well, it's criminal.'

'Maybe he upset someone,' says Brian.

'Maybe. No, seriously, he must have done something wrong.' Donald is clearly quite a Simon Shaw fan.

'So who should they have dropped from the squad to make way for him?' I ask. It's time to see if Donald has a deep knowledge of the subject. He usually does.

'Like for like. Kay or Grewcock. I'd drop Kay, personally.'

A silence ensues, punctuated only by the sound of pork scratchings being masticated. Neither Brian nor I know enough about second-row forwards to challenge Donald's prognosis. And, after all, who cares? The selection's made now. We've just got to go and win the World Cup, and picking Shaw or not is unlikely to change that.

'How's everything at home with you two?' I ask. I'm quite keen to get the trivia out of the way so I can tell my story.

They both nod.

'Yeah, fine,' says Brian.

'Good,' says Donald.

There's a pause.

I'm watching Donald carefully. I'd been meaning to give

him a ring earlier to see what that phone call was all about. It's a little awkward now.

Donald's staring at his pint and avoiding my gaze. But then he raises his eyebrows and our eyes meet, partially interrupted by the thick rim of Donald's glasses. He smiles nervously – no more than a flicker – and returns his attention to the beer.

'Judy OK?' I know I can't push it, but maybe it's nothing much and Donald will talk.

'She's fine,' says Donald, but there's something jumpy in his reaction to the question. Like he seems nervous. 'Yeah. Fine, thanks.'

Brian is watching Donald, too. But neither of us can force our friend to open up. If he doesn't want to talk, so be it.

'Tanya's got tonsillitis,' says Brian. 'Picked it up from Paul, I think.'

'Oh shit,' I offer.

'Got them on antibiotics?' asks Donald, apparently pleased the attention has been diverted to Brian.

'Yeah. Our GP tried to tell Tanya it wasn't a good idea for Paul, and I think she had a fit. So she got the drugs.'

'And how is she? Tanya?' I ask.

'Pretty miserable,' says Brian, and sighs. 'Pretty fucking miserable.'

'Well, the drugs should sort her out in a few days,' says Donald, trying to be upbeat.

'Yeah, but that will only fix the tonsillitis,' says Brian, and his words hang in the air like poisonous gas. 'Anyway, how was your trip, Rob?'

There's a palpable sense of relief around the table that Brian has opened a path for a more comfortable conversation. Plus I have a story to tell.

'It was . . . um . . . good,' I say, unable to stop a smirk from appearing.

'What happened?' says Brian, sensing there's something worthwhile coming.

'Well, work-wise it was fine. You know, nothing much to report. But I did have a rather strange experience.'

I pause for dramatic effect, checking that my audience is paying attention. It is.

'So a few weeks back, I was on the web, right – '

'Not looking at porn, by any chance, were you?' asks Brian.

'No, not really. Well, sort of. Anyway, I found myself on an escort site, and I just did a search on escorts in New York. You know, just for a laugh.'

'Just for a laugh?' chuckles Donald, shaking his head.

Brian's eyes open wide as dinner plates. His mouth drops open.

'You shagged a hooker?'

'No I bloody didn't,' I say firmly, quickly wanting to squash that one before it goes too far. 'And she wasn't a hooker. She was an escort.'

'Come on now,' says Donald. He's not going to let me off the hook easily, and why should he? 'An escort? You mean you were shopping at the top end of the market.'

'She was an escort,' I say, immediately knowing I've dug a rather large hole for myself, not to mention providing the large paving stone that fits perfectly over the top.

I can see Brian trying to control his mirth, and readying himself for some kind of quip.

'Anyway!' I hold my hands up and look at both of my friends, one after the other, making it clear that I need some airtime and would they shut up.

'Do go on,' says Donald.

I sigh before continuing. 'Right, so anyway, I sent off an email enquiry just to see how much it cost . . .'

As I'm speaking, I know this doesn't sound good. And that's because it isn't good, and articulating it out loud is making it sound worse. Bollocks.

'Just out of interest, you know.'

Brian has one eyebrow raised and his arms are folded. He is sitting in judgement. Donald is hiding behind his pint glass, but the lines around his eyes are creased with amusement.

'Look. I don't really know what I was doing, but I can tell you I had absolutely no intention of taking a whore while I was in New York. I guess I was just curious.'

It is the truth, but now I realise that it really doesn't sound at all convincing. Of course, my friends will let it go, but that's not to say I'll have won them over. And perhaps it doesn't matter. But Jesus, I'd have stood no chance with Clare. I make a mental note to implore them not to tell their wives.

'So I get to New York, check into my hotel, and this supposedly Spanish bird – the one I was enquiring about – turns up.'

'No!' yelps Brian. The judgemental stance is replaced by a rabid eagerness to hear the rest of the story. He puts his pint down and sits forward.

'What, she comes up to your room?' Donald is chuckling from somewhere down in his belly, and shaking his head in disbelief.

'Yes. Wakes me up from a kip and pushes her way into the room. Course I've gone to sleep with a porn movie playing.' I'm starting to get into the flow at last, and my audience is suddenly hooked.

'Hang on, let me get this straight,' interrupts Brian. 'You settled down in front of a porn flick and fell asleep?'

'Yep.'

'And then this tart shows up and you let her in!'

'Yep. Well, I didn't have much choice. I opened the door and she more or less pushed me back in with her groin, shoved me onto the bed, and started ripping my clothes off.'

'No formalities?' enquires Donald, calmly, like some kind of prosecuting lawyer. 'Didn't want to check who you were?'

'Well, yes. She did do that, because I asked her who the hell she was. And she had a copy of the email enquiry with some crappy small print saying I'd signed a contract.'

'You mean you'd made a commitment?'

'Yep. That's what it said.'

'Oh, that's complete bollocks,' says Brian.

'Not necessarily,' says Donald. 'It all depends on –'

'Anyway!' I jump in. This story is just never going to get told. 'She forces me onto the bed, pins me with one hand while taking her kit off with the other . . .'

I pause for effect, wondering if they still want to interject their piffling nonsense. But I've got them. Both. On the edges of their respective bloody seats. Ha.

'And?' says Brian.

'Come on!' says Donald.

I pause. I'm at a mental fork in the road: the truth or 'the truth'.

'She reaches into her handbag and pulls out this enormous dildo. Huge pink thing. And I'm, like, what the hell are you planning to do with that?'

'NO!'

'Yes.'

Donald's mouth is hanging open spastically.

'So I'm thinking she wants me to use Pink Betty on her, and I try to take it off her, but then she gives me this evil look and says, 'Uh-uh sweetheart, this is for you.''

'NO!'

'Yes!'

'You're kidding!'

'Yes!'

'What? You are kidding?'

'Yeah, course I bloody am.'

They seem disappointed.

'So what did happen,' says Donald, straight-faced.

'I told her I couldn't.'

'Seriously?' says Brian.

'Look, I might be a bit sex-starved at the moment, but I wouldn't shag an escort, for God's sake!'

I feel a little put out that my best friends in the universe seem rather let down by my whiter than white behaviour. Would they had rather I'd betrayed my wife and kids?

'Why not?' says Brian, suddenly looking a little sullen. 'At least it's anonymous. You'd never have seen her again.'

I'm not quite sure how to take that, and neither is Donald. There's an awkward hiatus.

'What did you say to her?' says Donald, kick-starting the mood again.

'I said I was sorry, it was all a big mistake ... and I'm married!'

'Bet that went down well,' says Brian.

'Like a bucket of cold sick. She gave my nob one final yank, and stormed out.'

'What, so it didn't cost you anything?' says Donald.

It never ceases to amaze me the different angles three close friends can take on a subject. Donald, it seems, has been more concerned about my financial wellbeing than anything else. And Brian thinks I should have got my leg over.

'Why didn't you just shag her and be done with it?' he says, proving my thesis. 'I mean, Christ, there you are, in a hotel room in New York, miles from home, with a beautiful woman clutching your dick. How the hell did you stop yourself?'

'Well there wasn't a great deal for her to clutch, to be honest. Au contraire. My chap had done a complete runner. I was terrified.'

Brian slaps his hands on the table and hoots with laughter. Donald is in some distress, he's laughing so hard. I've told it as it was, and it is unbelievably, painfully funny. And both of them can relate to it, because the truth is so vulnerable and comforting and real.

So my story's out at last. It didn't go as smoothly as I'd hoped, but it ended up in a good place. Donald gathers up our three empty pint pots and heads to the bar – OK, so it'll be two pints rather than the one I promised Clare – but no big deal. Brian is still catching his breath. I'm left basking in my relative glory. It is a good story. Funny, touching in a way, innocent, sort of, and it has a happy ending. I watch Brian's face and notice that his features are darkening again.

'What's up?' I say.

'Sorry about my reaction just then,' he says, eyes downcast. 'I was just imagining what I'd have done in the same situation. I'm not sure I'd have been so honourable.'

'Sure you would,' I tell him. 'Truth is, you don't know how you're going to react, but I think you'd be surprised.'

Brian sighs heavily and shakes his head. 'I don't feel particularly in control at the moment.' He looks up at me. 'Honestly. I don't.'

'Look, you've got to hang in there, mate. Things will sort themselves out.'

But Brian's not listening. 'There's this girl at work who's got the hots for me. And she's fucking gorgeous.'

'Suzi?' I know I have to act shocked and surprised, but Brian probably doesn't realise how much he has mentioned that name in passing over the last few months. It's almost as though the more he feels troubled by things at home, the more he talks about this girl who works for him.

Brian's looking at me again, perhaps wondering how I know, and then probably realising it's been bloody obvious.

'Yeah, Suzi.'

'Has anything happened?'

'God, no. And it won't. I mean she bloody works for me, doesn't she? Can you imagine? What a bloody nightmare.'

Donald's back at the table, distributing beer. I wonder if Brian is going to carry on. He's staring straight ahead, and doesn't seem to have noticed Donald's return.

'And anyway,' he says. 'I don't want to screw everything up at home. I still love Tanya. And I've got the kids. We're having a tough time, but I don't want to throw everything away. I could lose everything, couldn't I? Jesus, I'd never forgive myself.'

Brian stares hard at his new pint, then picks it up, takes a breath and downs half of it. Then he lets out a soft, contained belch and gently places the glass back on the table. Donald and I keep quiet.

For the next few minutes, the three of us sit in silence. Brian finishes the rest of his beer. Donald follows suit, and I realise I'm way behind. Drinking Stella at pace has nasty repercussions, but needs must, and I tip back the glass and glug down the rest of my pint. It's Brian's round, though I figure it's probably a little unfair to expect him to be that on the ball, given his state of mind.

Brian's got one of those expressive faces. When he's up, he looks like a puppy waiting for someone to hurl his favourite frisbee. And when he's down, he looks so unbelievably melancholic, you fear he's going to burst into tears at any moment. And yet I've never seen him cry. Probably never will.

Time to go to the bar. I quickly stand and gather up the

glasses. I'm painfully aware I told Clare it would be just the one drink, but she knows me well enough. As expected, Brian is far too wrapped up in his own little world to know it's his round. Never mind. He'll be allowed to get away with it just this once.

While I'm waiting at the bar, my heart goes out to my friend. Tanya is absolutely lovely, but she's a little – what's the phrase? – highly strung. Gets very worked up about things, and has clearly been suffering from some kind of depression. I know that blokes can often hide behind their work and shirk their parental responsibilities – and maybe Brian's been guilty of that from time to time – but the truth is the guy has a pretty high-powered job and he can't be half-arsed about it. Employers like his expect 110 per cent the whole time. None of the blokes there give a toss about their families. All they care about is money. Brian's not like that, but it's an environment he has to survive in, and it's not easy.

I'm not sure where Donald's at – he seems OK now – but given that Brian and I have bared our souls, I'm wondering if it might be Donald's turn to let rip.

I tip-toe back to the table, the three inviting Stellas squeezed delicately together in my two hands.

'I just told Donald about BlokeMiles,' says Brian.

I stand for a moment, frozen. 'You did?'

'Yep.'

'And?' I sit down and the guys grab their beers thirstily.

'I love it,' says Donald. 'I was a bit worried it was sort of a family management technique. You know, a way of divvying up the childcare responsibilities. But then I thought bugger that, it still applies to me and Judy. We still have the whole thing of being a couple, with our shared life, but trying to be individuals too. So . . . cheers.'

'Cheers.'

'Cheers.'

We sup our fresh pints. A timeless moment.

It hadn't really occurred to me that Donald might feel excluded by BlokeMiles. But he's right. It isn't about kids. It's about the whole dynamic and yes, Brian and I will certainly use our accrued miles to enjoy some child-free time. But at the end of the day, it doesn't really matter whether you've got ten kids or four wives. Me time is me time. It's possible that Donald might not be quite as desperate for it as me and Brian, but that's the only difference.

'What I'm wondering is how involved our wives need to be,' Donald continues. 'Do we just establish the rules ourselves and start accruing points? Or miles, or whatever they are?'

'Don't be daft,' I say. Being the architect of this idea, I can speak with some authority about these issues. 'The whole point of BlokeMiles is to get buy-in from your other half, so she is happy to reap the benefits but understands that you also get to spend your miles. Both sides agree the ground rules so, basically, Cold Tongue Pie becomes a thing of the past.'

'What about the Rugby World Cup? Do we tell them about that?' asks Donald.

Believe it or not, I'd kind of forgotten that idea. I look over at Brian.

'C'mon, you're not copping out now, are you?' he scoffs. 'It's a bloody great idea. I've started looking into flights.'

'And?'

'Still plenty on the Asian airlines.'

'So,' continues Donald, his line of thinking unshakeable as ever. 'Do we tell our wives about the Sydney idea?'

'I don't know,' I say. And I don't. But I could imagine Clare thinking that the whole thing – the whole BlokeMiles idea – has been twisted so we can have a blokes' jolly in Australia. Or simply not allowing me to go. I mean, if you ask, then you have to accept that 'no' is a possible outcome. So don't ask, right?

'No way.' Brian is a little more certain than me. 'Obviously, we don't just bugger off without telling them, but we keep it back until the last minute.'

'But anyway,' I say. 'The first step is, we need to introduce our wives to the idea of BlokeMiles. Sell it to them.'

Donald nods in agreement. 'Let's have a big old Sunday lunch. We haven't got the whole crew together for a while. It would be nice. We'll host.'

'Top idea,' says Brian enthusiastically. 'We'll ply 'em with wine and then drop the idea in.'

'Seriously, guys,' I say, feeling a little exasperated that my brainchild is being misunderstood. 'They will love it! What do we have to be worried about? It will be just as good for them as it is for us, right?'

'Right.'

'Yep.'

And we proceed to get out our Palm Pilots and Pocket PCs and identify potential dates, being careful to avoid England's opening World Cup match against Georgia, which is coming up fast. The fact that it's a morning kick-off makes no difference. The date is sacred. The conversation dips in quality terms, Brian buys his first round of the night, and the evening begins to blur round the edges. I am still vaguely aware that the only person who's not been in the confessional is Donald. Still, you can't force these things. My friend's booming laugh would indicate that he's happy enough now, but occasionally, just occasionally, I have noticed his eyes flitting across the pub as though he's hiding from someone.

Something's definitely up.

Chapter Eight

As the Rugby World Cup hostilities begin in earnest for our England team, it has been deemed prudent to move all women and children as far from the danger as possible. So the lads are round my place again and the ladies are all meeting for coffee over at Brian and Tanya's, offspring in tow.

But there's more. The kids are being dumped – sorry, dropped – back here at lunchtime, and the men are to take over. We'll give 'em lunch, put the smallest ones to bed and lark around with the others, while our wives head off to a nearby spa hotel for an afternoon of massage, facial, pedicure, manicure, arsicure, and whatever else they get up to at those places. Cucumbers in the eyes, courgettes in the ears, that sort of thing. We each bought our spouse a voucher for the day, and boy do we feel smug about it.

Then, this evening, we're all congregating over at Donald and Judy's place for dinner, with babysitters having been arranged as appropriate. We've got it all sorted. The day is a micro-parody of the BlokeMiles concept, and we will introduce it formally over dinner, while our women are still glowing from their afternoon of pampering. They'll be chilled and full of the goodness of life, and we'll be stoked by England's magnificent opening salvo, knowing that if BlokeMiles lives up to its undoubted potential, we'll be in Sydney to watch England triumph in six weeks' time. It looks like a win win.

The atmosphere in my front room is electric. The tournament

may have started last weekend when Australia beat Argentina comfortably, but for us it's all about today. England. Our England. The team that can, and maybe even should, win the whole thing and bring a major trophy back to our shores for the first time since Sir Alf's boys of 1966. As Englishmen, our instinct is to brush it all under the table, and scoff at those who are over-romanticising just how big a deal an English win would be. But to hell with that. To be alive and able to witness a triumph of this magnitude would be something else. And Donald, Brian and myself are jittery with excitement.

But our Englishness does manifest itself in the way our belief starts to wobble, even before a match against Georgia. 'Christ, I hope we don't screw this up,' says Donald. He has misguidedly squeezed his bulk into a skin-tight Nike rugby shirt, despite the grief he got last time he wore it, not to mention the fact that it looks hideously uncomfortable.

'Come on,' snorts Brian. 'We're playing bloody Georgia, for God's sake. How many rugby players are there in Georgia? I reckon we'll win by a hundred points.'

'Don't say crap like that!' snaps Donald. His face is red. 'All this jingoistic bravado, it really . . . pisses me off!'

Brian and I are speechless. Donald. Quiet, level-headed, calm, by far the least volatile of the three of us. Brian decides not to respond. Donald sips his Guinness and focuses on the game that's about to begin. The moment passes.

With Brian and Donald enjoying their draught Guinness, my resolve to avoid alcohol for the day – never particularly stiff at the best of times – wobbles and then collapses completely. I skip out to the kitchen to get myself one, not bothering to mention live pause.

The game gets off to a blistering start, with England keeping the ball, phase after phase, not letting the Georgians get a sniff of it. And then we get a penalty, and Wilkinson makes it look oh so easy. Three-nil and the nerves begin to settle. But then they equalise about five minutes later. Who's taking the kick? Does it matter? I scan the newspaper, which lists the players on both teams.

'Mal-khaz Ur-ruk-ash-vili,' I state, separating the syllables to make the pronunciation easier.

'Oh, him,' says Brian.

Malkhazwhatshisname slots the kick and the crowd goes wild. Everyone loves an underdog. Everyone hates the English. Thousands in the stadium and in front of TV sets around the world have spontaneously transmuted into avid supporters of East European rugby.

'Shit!' mutters Donald.

There's not much conversation in my front room at this juncture. Perhaps we were a little uptight to begin with, but Donald's mood has made matters considerably worse. He is biting the fingernails of his non-drinking hand, and does seem genuinely concerned that England might lose. But soon the game begins to settle into a more reassuring pattern. Tindall scores a busting try after about fifteen minutes, then Dawson ducks over, Wilkinson is kicking everything, and England are safe. Now it's just a matter of how many.

'You all right now?' I say in Donald's direction.

'Yeah. Sorry about that. Don't know what happened then.' Donald smiles weakly and wipes the sweat off his upper lip with his finger.

The mood is considerably more relaxed by the time we've sunk our third Guinness, and I remind myself to stay sober. It's going to be a long day. On the scoreboard, England are meting out a total thrashing, but on the pitch it looks like a worthy contest. The Georgians just won't stop tackling. Sure, England are scoring a hatful of tries – Back, Dallaglio, Greenwood, Cohen . . . but it looks as though they are in a game.

By the final whistle, I'd imagine Woodward and his men would be well satisfied. Twelve tries, but a tough workout. More importantly, the three fellows at Cherry Tree House are more than happy. The tournament is underway, England look sharp, and our blood has been sweetened by a few glasses of the black stuff.

'So . . .' I say, letting the word sink in so I have Brian and Donald's undivided attention. 'Are we gonna win it?'

'I don't think you can tell much from a game like that,' Donald says.

'No,' adds Brian, carefully. 'I reckon we'll have a better idea after the South Africa game. If we win that, we're pretty much into the semis.'

'Against France.'

'Yep.'

But I'm not buying it. 'Come on, you two frigging fence sitters. Are we going to win the tournament?'

I know I've asked an uncomfortable question. It is simply not very English to say we will win the World Cup. It's the sort of thing an Aussie would have no problem with, but not a Pom. It's one thing being cocksure about beating a new East European Republic, but to believe you can win the World Cup . . . the words sound hollow. It almost feels as though you are willing your team to lose by being too bullish about their prospects.

'We're certainly capable,' says Brian.

'To hell with capable. Will we win it?'

'No,' says Donald.

'No?'

'Oh, sorry. Wasn't that one of the available answers?' Again, there's an uncharacteristic needle in his voice, and he stares at us both, as though challenging us.

'Who are we going to lose to, then?'

'I think we'll lose to France. We'll underestimate them because we're too focused on the southern hemisphere teams. And they'll beat us.'

I scratch my chin to make it clear I'm giving Donald's hypothesis due consideration. He may have a point.

'Brian?' I say.

'We'll win.' Bullish as ever. 'We've beaten all the top teams, we haven't lost for ages – apart from that game in Marseille – and . . . well, this team wins even when it plays crap. So yeah. Why not?'

'I agree,' I say, uncomfortably aware that I'm in danger of isolating Donald. 'I can't see any reason why we'll lose to anyone. If we play the All Blacks in the final, that could go either way, but I think we'll still win.'

'Are we placing bets, then?' says Brian defiantly.

'No,' says Donald.

'Bollocks to that,' I say.

Women and children turn up promptly just before midday, and the scene that greets them leaves them open-mouthed. Is it admiration or shock? Who cares? The effect is what we were looking for, and it looks as though we've scored.

Brian, Donald and I are lined up in the kitchen like the staff at one of Jamie Oliver's restaurants, all wearing aprons, slaving over the kids' lunch. A colourful variety of small plastic plates are in front of us – Thomas the Tank Engine, Bob the Builder, The Fimbles, Spiderman, Scooby-Doo and, I hate to admit it, Barney. Sausages and oven chips are already in place for the older children, and Brian is dolloping a spoonful of baked beans on each plate. Donald now turns and puts the finishing touches to the kitchen table, where paper napkins and plastic cutlery denote place settings. His big head, dominated by those Marx Brothers glasses, disappears into the fridge for a moment, and he re-emerges with an armful of kiddie fruit juice bottles. He puts one next to each place setting. All we're missing is balloons. Shit, that was my job. Ho hum. I don't think Tanya, Clare or Judy is about to give me CTP treatment about the lack of balloons.

'Well look at this!' says Tanya, her hand over her smiling mouth. Her green eyes are open wide. Christ, you'd think we were wearing stockings and suspenders! Thank God that idea got thrown out.

Tanya really is a strikingly beautiful woman. Tall, blonde and graceful, with long, model's legs. She's wearing black, loose trousers that kind of flow when she walks, and a similarly long, smock-like cream blouse. It all adds to the illusion that she's not so much walking as gliding.

I examine her face to search for signs of the stresses and strains she is undoubtedly feeling at home, but there's nothing. She just looks perfect.

'Bloody hell, you guys have been busy!' says Clare. My little treasure looks tiny next to Tanya, and even tinier when Donald's wife Judy steps alongside and checks out the scene.

Judy is a big girl, but not fat. She has a wee, balding, freckly Scottish father and a Samoan mother, and it's hard to discern any Celt in her DNA at all. She's heavy-boned, with powerful thighs and broad, swimmer's shoulders, and huge hips I wish Clare could have borrowed for a few days around childbirth time. If Judy ever does have children, they will enter the world through double doors. Facially, she's a knock-out. Dark hair – not quite black, but almost – deep brown eyes and olive skin. Her face is so open you feel you could just walk straight on in and make yourself at home.

I've always been a big Judy fan. She's an incredibly strong woman, not only physically but emotionally too. She's been a rock for Clare on more than one occasion, and always seems to be there to provide a supportive word at just the right moment. She's also forthright in her opinions, unafraid to argue the toss with anyone. If the world needed an advocate for not having children and not feeling guilty about it, Judy would be duly elected. She's not stroppy, exactly, but she likes a good argument, and there's no question I've had to work hard to earn her approval on occasion. She doesn't give it away.

'Boys,' says Judy now in her big, husky voice, 'it's so nice of you to forfeit your rugby match so you could prepare lunch for the children.'

'Forfeit their rugby? Fat chance,' scoffs Clare good-naturedly. 'So, come on. Who won then?'

I glance over at Brian, who has put his head in his hands. Donald is chuckling. It doesn't matter how much sport we watch, or how much we drone on and on about it, we will simply *never* be able to get our wives to give the remotest shit about it, much as they might pretend.

I consider a scornful put-down but decide against it.

'Er . . . England did, darling. Quite handsomely.'

'Who were they playing?' says Tanya innocently.

'Georgia,' I say.

'The country, not the state,' says Brian. It's meant to be a joke, but Brian's got the timing all wrong.

Tanya's reaction is instant. Forget the light-hearted quip, it's as though Brian just plunged a dagger through her heart.

Her eyes fill up with tears, her chin trembles and she quickly walks from the room. The others exchange awkward glances. Brian looks shell-shocked.

Half an hour later, equilibrium at least temporarily restored, the girls bustle excitedly out to Judy's Saab to head off to the hotel for their luxury afternoon, stopping to kiss their respective kids, telling them to be good, giggling like schoolgirls, saying their goodbyes to the men, who are now trying to corral the kids to sit down and eat the lunch we've so lovingly prepared. There's something in their smiles, in the little lines around their eyes, that betrays just a touch of disbelief that they are off to have their bodies rubbed with aromatic oils in sensuous surroundings, whilst we pass the afternoon surrounded by screeching youngsters. And there's just a smidge of childish enthusiasm in their body language. Enough to make me think that maybe, just maybe, women aren't so different from men. They get excited about things too.

As the Jeep transports its happy cargo away, disembodied hands wiggling at us through tinted windows, we address our first challenge of the afternoon. Getting the toddlers around the table to eat their lunch. Ralph is already taking his afternoon nap, which makes life marginally easier, and Brian plans to put Paul down as soon as the others have eaten.

Paul already looks wired to me. He's currently crawling round the kitchen, hauling himself up on things and gratuitously dragging anything he can find off every shelf within his reach. The floor is already strewn with baby food jars, kitchen roll, plastic knives and forks and recipe books, and now he's heading for the pedal bin. I hesitate, fatally, unsure if Brian is on the case. He is, but he's got to dance nimbly round the table and across the room and, fit and fast as he is, Paul is a knee-stride too quick. He's pulled himself up on the bin and – oh God, no! – he's trying to drag it over. Wallop! Paul has fallen backwards and the bin has gone with him. Pop goes the back of his head against the tiled floor – nothing to panic about, but it's going to smart – and then, in a kind of ghastly slow motion, the bin flips open as it's careering towards Paul's small, prone body. It's only plastic, so it doesn't hurt him, but the contents fly everywhere. This morning's discarded breakfast – porridge, mushed-up Weetabix, banana skin, the expended coffee muck from the cafetière – empty cans of Guinness that still manage to summon some nasty, frothy dregs, bits of potato peel from last night's dinner. Paul starts howling from the shock of his fall and the knock to his head, probably not fully aware that he is partially buried under a heap of fresh family detritus. It is an ugly scene, and Brian and I descend quickly to fix it, grateful that our wives need never know this small débâcle has ever taken place.

Donald, meanwhile, has wisely maintained his distance and concentrated on keeping the older children anchored to the kitchen table. It proves an easier task than he expected, since they are all transfixed by Paul's predicament, kneeling on their chairs and gawking enthusiastically.

'What happened to Paul?' asks Emily.

'He fell over, poor little chap,' says Donald.

'Why?'

'Well, he tried to pull himself up on the bin, and it fell over.'

'Why?'

'I don't know. It just did.'

'But why?'

'I don't know, Emily. It just happened, OK?' Donald says, with a shrug.

'Paul's silly, isn't he?' Emily just won't give up.

'No, he's not. Don't be mean, Emily,' I say, feeling the need to step in and protect little Paul from my daughter's abuse. 'You were a baby once, you know.'

'But I didn't fall over,' she says.

'Oh, yes you did!'

'No I didn't.'

OK, I'm not going to win this one. Best shut up.

Brian's got Paul cleaned up now, and his sobbing has subsided. He still looks pretty wretched, though, with globs of snot oozing from both nostrils, tears still glistening at the sides of his eyes, his face the colour of a cricket ball. Poor thing. I'm on my knees wiping the kitchen floor, and the status quo is threatening to return.

'Come on, you lot,' says Donald, kindly but firmly, and the toddlers obediently turn away from the accident and start prodding their sausages suspiciously.

I find kids utterly fascinating. I notice that Olivia, Paul's sister, has shown absolutely no interest in her brother's plight. In fact, she's already munched her way through her chips, and made good progress on a sausage. Strange how dispassionate they can be about each other.

The rest of the day, thankfully, proceeds without any major dramas, and it doesn't seem long before the Jeep reappears and three very chilled-looking women emerge, wreathed in smiles and, in Clare and Tanya's case, apparently more than happy to reassume control of their respective offspring. All this is done with good grace and plenty of gratitude, and Donald, Brian and I try to look as cool and in control as possible, as though the afternoon has been an absolute stroll in the park.

'Oh, Rob!' cries Clare shrilly. 'The foot massage. *Oh*, the foot massage!' And she groans pseudo-sexually, as I try to grasp how someone rubbing one's gnarled, callous-ridden feet could be so utterly heavenly.

Each of our wives seems to have taken an entirely different route to nirvana. Clare has had wall-to-wall treatments, including a last-minute manicure that made them all late. She has literally scrambled from appointment to appointment, and she's breathless with it all.

'Aw, it was *wonder*ful,' she exclaims again, kissing me on the cheek. I'm thinking BlokeMiles but I'll wager she's not at this precise moment.

Judy has done a fair bit, too, but preferred to spend a good chunk of time in the pool, exercising those powerful shoulders. She's swum forty lengths, done a water aerobics class and then just gone to sleep in one of the loungers by the pool.

'God, I can't remember the last time I just fell asleep like that,' she marvels. 'With nothing to think about . . . except dinner tonight, obviously. But I've done most of it, so I could relax.'

'Glad you enjoyed it, love,' says Donald.

Tanya has done the least of all. A half-hour sunbed and then she's just crashed in a quiet area designated for 'reading'. She's read half a dozen magazines, done two crosswords, and dozed. And she looks a million bucks.

There's a significant moment happening between Tanya and Brian, which the rest of us instinctively back away from. They are in an embrace, talking quietly and gazing meaningfully into each other's eyes. I tune in briefly.

'I'm sorry.'

'No, I'm sorry.'

They both look close to tears. I want to look away but can't, so I pretend to be concentrating on something on the other side of the room. I'm pretty certain they aren't aware of anyone else right now.

Tanya says something I can't make out. She's lowered her head onto Brian's shoulder.

'Babe. You just needed some time to relax.'

Tanya lifts her head again and looks her husband in the eyes.

'Yes. I did. Thank you, Brian.'

And they kiss. About as long a kiss as is acceptable in someone else's kitchen.

Donald and Judy live in a lovely Victorian cottage on the edge of Guildford. They are both warm, generous individuals and there is always something accordingly cosy, welcoming and convivial about the social activities they host. The perfect backdrop for the inception of BlokeMiles.

Judy is a mean cook, too, and we've just spent the last hour and a half savouring three wonderful courses and supping good wine. The mood has been harmonious, effortless, and without tension, although the longer the evening goes on, the more I sense that something odd is afoot. I have no idea what. Anyway, it's time for my party piece. I give Donald the nod, and the two of us sneak out to the kitchen to pour the champagne that Donald has chilling in the freezer.

'Good man,' I say, as Donald hands me the bottle and arranges the glasses on a tray. I start pouring, making a pig's ear of it in my impatience, filling each glass with nothing but froth.

'Er . . . Rob.'

Something in Donald's voice makes me stop pouring. It's the same tone he adopted on the phone before I flew to New York.

'What is it, mate?'

Donald is leaning against the kitchen counter, nervously biting the fingernails of his left hand. His eyes are glazed, fixed on nothing in particular, but then they latch onto me. There's something vacant in his expression, quite unlike anything I have seen in this familiar face before. The warm, kind, gentle features I'm used to look strangely haunted.

'I'm not sure about this. This . . . BlokeMiles thing. I'm not sure I can go along with it.'

'Why on earth not?' I say. 'It's just a bit of harmless fun.'

'Going to Sydney's not harmless. It's just . . . I'm not . . . I just don't think it's the right time for me.'

'What's up, Donald?' I've shifted gears, from flippant to deeply concerned.

'Nothing really. I've . . . no, nothing. It's fine.'

'Something wrong at home? You and Judy?'

'No. Really, no. We're fine. She's lovely. No, it's just me. I've . . .' He sighs. 'I'll get over it.'

I wait. Donald has stopped nibbling his fingers now and rubs his eyes as though he's just been woken from hibernation. Something seems to snap, and now he's all businesslike bustle, as though the conversation we've just had never took place.

'Come on, chap. Time for your little speech. It had better be good!'

Donald takes the champagne bottle from my grasp, tops up the glasses and picks up the tray.

'Shall we?' he says.

'Oh my!' Judy exclaims. 'What's the occasion?'

'Are you trying to get us completely trolleyed?' says Clare, slightly slurring her words. She's small, you see. Can't take too much alcohol.

'We have an idea we want to share with you,' says Donald earnestly, handing out the glasses. His hands are shaking slightly.

I clear my throat nervously, wondering where the nerves have come from after such a relaxed evening. 'I hope we all agree that today has been a super day,' I begin, hoping for an immediate response, as one would at a wedding speech.

'Wonderful,' says Tanya softly.

'Absolutely,' says Clare, her eyes twinkling.

'My best day for ages,' says Judy, and we all chink glasses happily.

The ladies probably think that's it. We just wanted to share champagne to celebrate the day. Judy looks as though she's about to clear away more debris from the table. I'd better push on.

'We got to watch our rugby which, as you ladies know – all joking aside – is important to us blokes. So thank you for that. And part of the deal was that we'd take the children for the afternoon and you could spend your afternoon being expensively pampered.'

'Was it that expensive?' asks Clare, looking a little concerned.

Aarrgh. 'No, no. That wasn't my point at all. I just meant that it was a nice treat for you, right?'

They all three nod.

I take a deep breath. Here goes. 'Well, we'd like to . . . sort of . . . institutionalise what we did today.'

I look around the table. Tanya and Judy are looking blankly at me. I can see a slow dawn spreading across Clare's features, until her left eyebrow pops up above the right one and stays there. There's a slight smirk at the edge of her mouth.

'The best thing about today was the balance. We did stuff we wanted to do as blokes, and you did stuff you wanted to do as girls. We all got to indulge ourselves, and you can tell by the atmosphere this evening that, well, there's kind of an equilibrium.'

Still blank faces. Shit.

'Anyway, we want to introduce you to the idea of BlokeMiles.'

Oh, Christ. The cat's out of the bag. I suppose it's like the unveiling of any big idea. You know you're either going to get booed off the stage or wildly applauded. Suddenly, the whole thing sounds utterly stupid to me. Is this deeply flawed? Are we insulting our wives? Have we missed the point altogether? I feel panic welling up inside.

'Well, go on!' says Tanya, and I can see her face is still open, interested. I haven't alienated her. Judy still looks a little confused, and Clare's body language is coiled up, her arms folded. She's just pissed off that I'm pretending it's my idea, not hers.

'We men can be selfish buggers at times, as you know. So we want to change that, by doing more for you.'

'Hallelujah,' says Judy sarcastically. 'Where's the catch?'

'We earn points – that's what BlokeMiles are – which we can redeem against blokey things.' Silence. 'With your permission, of course.'

More silence. I've said my piece now. Throw me to the lions if you will.

'So let me get this straight,' says Judy animatedly. 'You guys want to carry on doing guy things – like you do anyway – but you want to have to earn the right by treating us in some way. Right?'

'Right,' I say, not wanting to pick her up on minor inaccuracies.

'Not exactly,' says Brian. I feared this would happen. He's been awfully quiet. 'I mean, we're not going to ask permission to go down the pub for a couple of pints.'

'No,' I jump in quickly. 'But if we wanted to get totally shit-faced and not have to get up with the kids the next morning—'

'Or if we wanted to stay the night in a country pub and have a round of golf the next day,' adds Brian.

'Then we'd need to earn enough BlokeMiles,' I offer, feeling somehow that we might have shot our bolt.

I glance at Clare and flash her a despairing smile that

probably looks more like a grimace. She picks up the cue. God, I love her.

'I think what you're trying to say is that if there's things you guys are dying to do together, that's OK, but you are going to be more open with us about them, and you'll only do them if you're giving us the same kind of opportunity.'

'Exactly,' says Brian.

'Quid pro quo,' I say.

There's another silence, as brains chew over what's been said. Then Tanya speaks up.

'I think it sounds quite a good idea. Do you negotiate these points . . . miles . . . BlokeMiles, or whatever they're called, as a group?'

It's a good question and, handily, it's something I'd been considering in the bath only this morning.

'Good question,' I say. 'Sometimes yes, but more often, I think, not. We might be negotiating for the same thing, but how we earn our BlokeMiles is down to each individual couple.'

'OK,' says Tanya, slowly. 'So, for instance, I could propose that Brian comes home from work at 6 p.m. for a week. Just as an example.'

Oops. There's a painful pause. We are suddenly peering off the edge of a sheer cliff to the rocks and swirling surf below.

'Sure,' says Brian. His voice is soft and compliant, and we're all yanked back from the precipice by some greater being than us. God. Brian. Whatever. Brian smiles at Tanya and she smiles sheepishly back, perhaps just a little ashamed that she put him on the spot like that.

'It's probably not a great example, though,' he says, and once again we're hanging on his every word. 'Because I'd far rather be at home at 6 p.m. every day. I don't need the extra incentive.'

'Why don't you, then? Ever.'

The cliff is back, and there's a strong offshore wind pushing us closer and closer to the edge. This is one of those terrifying privately public moments when, despite there being six people in the room, there is a harsh spotlight on just two. And they are oblivious to the rest of us.

'It's difficult, Tanya.' Brian hasn't taken the bait. His voice is pleading, but not defensive. 'I want to, but it's not just a case of packing my bag and high-tailing it out of there. People watch these things. I can't allow it to count against me. Against us.'

Tanya nods and sips her champagne, keeping her eyes down.

'My point is, this is something I want to do. I will work on it. But I don't expect to be earning BlokeMiles for it, OK?' Brian makes a grand gesture of inclusion to the group. He looks like Jesus at the Last Supper.

Tanya nods again, and smiles weakly in Brian's direction.

I wonder if Brian is going too far here, because I know him and I know the company he works for, and it will require a Herculean effort. Imagine the subtle jibes and sneers as he packs his bag and leaves at 5 p.m. God forbid.

'Well, I'm happy,' says Judy, and starts clearing the rest of the side plates from the table. 'Seems a sound idea.'

I look at my watch and notice it's almost midnight. Wow. Where's the evening gone? But . . . where's Donald? His chair is empty. I didn't notice him leave, but he's clearly missed the last part of the conversation.

'Where's Donald?' I ask.

Judy shrugs.

'No idea,' says Brian.

A shiver runs down my spine. Donald's behaviour has been off-colour all night, but he won't come clean. Something serious. I walk through into the kitchen, and shudder at the cold air flowing in through the open back door. I can see him out there, leaning on the back gate and staring out into the darkness.

'Donald? You all right?' I approach with caution and, as I draw near, I can see his shoulders shaking. He's surely not crying. What, Donald?

Now I can see his face, although he turns it a little away from me. He *is* crying. Holy crap. I put an arm on his shoulder and talk with genuine concern in my voice. It's just more than a whisper.

'What's up, big man?'

He's controlling himself, breathing in artificially deep gasps, until his shoulders are level again. It takes a minute or two before he can talk.

'I've lost my job,' he croaks.

'What?'

'I've lost my job.'

I'm bewildered. 'When? Why?'

'A month ago. They made me redundant.'

'A *month* ago?'

He nods. I'm speechless and my mind is racing. That means the last few times we've been in the pub, talking about work, women, sport . . . he's sat there, bottling up the fact that he's been laid off. He's been at the same estate agent for ten years or more, and has run the Guildford branch for the last five. Redundant?

'Why didn't you tell us, Donald?' I say, gently. My voice is tender enough, but I'm having to work hard to suppress my anger. I mean, surely, that's what friends are for, right? To help out in a crisis? For the first time in a while, there's a little speech bubbling up through that little fault line in my brain. I suppress it quickly.

'Rob, I haven't even told Judy,' he says, and now he really has lost me.

'What?' This is too much for me to take in. I was all ready to lend my support, but what I'm hearing makes no sense. 'What have you . . . how have you . . . I mean . . .'

'I've been pretending to go to work every day. Sitting in parks, sitting in pubs, sitting in the library. For a month. I just couldn't tell her.' Donald's voice is a flat monotone now, empty of feeling. He's spent.

Oh, God. I need Brian out here. Suddenly I feel an overwhelming sense of responsibility. This is one of my closest friends. There's desperation in Donald's voice, like he's got himself in such a deep hole he doesn't know how to get out. He is dangerously low, and I'm fearful as to what he might do next. It's almost an out-of-body experience. I can see myself standing next to my friend. What am I supposed to do?

'Donald,' I say, slowly. 'You've got to get yourself

together, OK?' I have no idea if this is the right approach, but it's all I have. It's from the heart and its authenticity is raw and scary. 'We are your best mates. We go through thick and thin together. We always have. Shit happens to all of us, and we have to cope, and friends are there to help. Now, I'm actually pretty pissed off that you haven't shared this with me, or Brian, but forget that. Now you've told me, I'm grateful, because we're going to talk it through, talk about what help you need, talk about how you tell Judy now, and then help you get back on your feet. But you've *got* to tell Judy. Soon. Now. You've got to.'

Whoa. That was a speech . . . and yet, for once, I said it aloud. Donald's trying to keep his emotions in check, but he looks at me directly for the first time since I stepped out into the cold.

'Thank you,' he says, and I feel a gentle flicker of hope that maybe I've at least partially hauled my friend out of the pit.

I can hear someone approaching the back door. It's Brian.

'Guys? What the hell are you doing out here?'

'Just coming in!' I shout. 'Fancied a bit of fresh air. Donald was feeling squiffy.'

I can see Brian's black silhouette hesitate in the doorway, before he mumbles something and goes back inside.

'OK,' I say. 'How shall we handle this?'

Donald looks composed now. He takes a deep breath.

'I'll take it from here,' he says. 'It's out now. I can't tell you how different I feel. Wow.' More deep breaths, and then he shudders, as though feeling the cold for the first time. 'I'll tell Judy tonight.'

I smile and nod. Then I point my eyebrows enquiringly in the direction of the back door.

Donald lets out one more puff of breath into the cold air.

'I was feeling squiffy, right?' he says.

Chapter Nine

What a difference a week makes. Brian's BlokeMiles drive has started with a bang. He's been home before 6 p.m. every night this week and didn't get fired. And he seemed a transformed man when we spoke on the phone last night. He was blissfully happy, almost as though he had discovered a period of the day he didn't know existed. And he clearly felt it was doing his relationship with Tanya the world of good.

Donald, well . . . Donald has had more important things to tackle, such as telling his wife he's lost his job, adding in the small detail that this happened a month ago and he's been living a lie ever since. I didn't envy him, but I was pretty sure that Judy's reaction would be to floor him with a left hook, pick him up by the scruff of the neck and then give him a huge smacker on the lips. She's a strong woman. Then again, so is Clare and, in her own way, so is Tanya. So much stronger than us men. I am under no illusion. The stereotype is that we're supposed to be the rocks: the anchors to which our families are attached. But the reality is, I think, that it's the women who play that role. We're strong in our own way, but we're also flaky as hell.

And me? Well, my opening BlokeMiles gambit has been to suggest Clare head down to Poole to see her parents, and I'll take the kids. It's been a while since she's seen them, so she jumped at the offer. We agreed it was worth 300 BlokeMiles, which is going to give my account a nice kick-start. But right now, on Saturday morning, while Clare's upstairs packing her weekend bag, I am regretting it in a very substantial way. I forgot about the rugby.

England are playing South Africa, and it's the first time for about four years that Brian, Donald and myself have failed to watch an important international together. It doesn't feel right at all. And how ironic is that? We come up with this brilliant idea for wallowing happily in a sea of blokey indulgences, and what happens? We end up spending the first weekend of the new regime under the bloody thumb! Donald's redecorating his and Judy's bedroom and painting the study pink. That last small detail does make me wonder if Judy isn't starting to get broody. And Brian? I don't honestly know. He just seems to want to immerse himself in his family right now, which is fair enough, I suppose.

But bugger me, it feels extremely weird to be watching – or rather *trying* to watch – the game all on my own. The situation is very tense at the start of the second half. It's six-six and I'm suffering. England were appalling in the first half and would have been out of it if the Springbok stand-off had slotted his kicks. What if they can't get their game going soon? It's unthinkable. New Zealand in the quarter-finals. Our BlokeMiles-funded trip to Sydney could be null and void. A beautiful shrub of an idea, brutally axed to earth before it's even had a chance to flower.

What makes things worse is that Ralph is in a filthy mood, and has been since he screeched me awake at just after 6 a.m. There's a little monitor base unit that sits in a remote corner in his room, on its lowest setting, and the receiver sits outside our bedroom with the volume turned right down, under a pile of luxuriant towels. But Ralph still managed to send eight million volts of baby anger slicing through my slumber the moment he woke, and it's been uphill ever since.

I've got Emily set up in the kitchen with her colouring-in books, and she's OK provided I pop my head in every ten minutes to admire her handiwork. But Ralph! What a nightmare. I don't know if it's his teeth or something, but he is utterly miserable. He wants to be picked up, but then he screams and attempts to gouge my eyes out. And when I put him down, the only thing he's even vaguely interested in is trashing the remote control. I can't win.

My instinct is to hand him to Clare. It's a deeply ingrained behaviour so I'm having to force myself not to. I think, quite honestly, that Clare has an equally strong compulsion to take control of Ralph at times like this – you know, to give him a bit of motherly TLC – and of course I take advantage. Well, why not? But since this is all about BlokeMiles, and my willingness to go the extra mile so Clare can have some space to herself, I have to be a touch more stoic than usual.

Problem is, I'm just getting irritated, and the tension of the rugby ain't helping. Wilkinson has popped a couple of penalties over to give us a bit of a cushion, but now the Springboks are looking really threatening. We just seem to keep kicking the ball away and . . . shit, they are going to score a try. SHIT! A huge South African second-row forward is bearing down on England's line with only Jason Robinson to beat. Robinson looks like a midget trying to stop a charging buffalo, but he somehow manages to bundle the giant into touch.

I sit down again, only then realising that I'd actually stood up, and notice Ralph is bawling in that inconsiderate, selfish way very small children do. I pick him up and hold him tight, which he doesn't seem to like, and the Springboks are looking menacing again. They've ripped us open. Three man overlap. It's all over, but . . . oh, man . . . the full-back, for some inexplicable reason, has chipped it instead of passing, and the attack has fizzled out.

Ralph's really crying now. I think I squeezed him a touch too hard.

'Everything OK in here?' says Clare, poking her head round the corner and trying not to look concerned. She's got her jacket on, ready to go.

I stroke Ralph's head to try to stop the howling, but it just gets louder still. If only there were a mute button on the back of his neck, or live pause, or something.

'Er, fine. Fine. Absolutely fine,' I say, sounding breathless with stress.

Emily appears in the doorway and looks up at Clare.

'Daddy won't help me with my colouring, Mummy.'

'Course he will, darling. He's just watching the rugby for a minute.'

'He always watches rugby for a minute.'

Clare flashes me a look. We're both trying hard not to have a confrontation here, in the spirit of BlokeMiles. I wish she'd just leave, so I can stumble my way through to the end of the game and then start clearing up the mess. I'm buggered if I'm going to miss this. It's too tight, and it's too important.

'Mummy, will you come and sit with me?' says Emily in her most pathetic, squeaky, persuasive voice, bottom lip bloated and extended towards the floor.

'I can't, darling. I'm off now. Going to see Grandma and Grandpa.'

'Can I come?'

'No, you're staying with Daddy. He's going to look after you for the weekend.'

I smile enthusiastically at Emily, simultaneously keeping half an eye on the action. I feel utterly compromised, but I am absolutely, unequivocally unable to rip myself from the sofa. Especially since . . . oh my gosh . . . England have scored a try! Thank the Lord. Sort of lucky, really. Charged down kick and some smart play from Greenwood, and suddenly the match feels a good deal safer.

I wrench myself from the couch, Ralph in one arm, and lead Emily into the kitchen. Of course, I still plan to watch the rest of the game, but I consider it prudent to at least allow Clare to depart under the comfortable illusion that her husband is not a singularly selfish bastard who can't haul himself away from sport to indulge his own kith and kin.

'Bye, sweetie,' I say, kissing my wife softly on the lips. 'Have a great time and give them my love.'

'Will do. Hope it goes well. Call me if you need me.'

'I won't,' I say, wishing I meant it. Of course I'll need her. But I won't call. Can't call.

She says her goodbyes to the kids and she's gone.

Now, I must get back to the game.

England have won. Our dream of travelling to Sydney to see the lads in the final, with our VIP Gold BlokeMiles passes, is still intact. They didn't play well but they did the business, quite comfortably in the end. The path is now clear to the semi-finals – or at least it should be – where the French, most probably, lie in wait. They are good but should hold no demons. The final beckons. Oh yes.

But it's all gone a bit flat for the boys. I don't know what's happening with Brian. I just came off the phone to him and he sounded on particularly poor form. I worry for him. He seemed to really enjoy last week, making the effort to get home to see the kids. Tanya responded positively and Brian was clearly surprised how much he relished his time at home. But I'd question whether or not it's a sustainable strategy. Soon, the pressure will build at work. Not so much the volume of stuff he has to get done, but the whispers behind his back, the perception that he's not pulling his weight. That awful crap in office environments where it's all about appearances and performance doesn't come into it. That was the nice thing about being a journalist, really. You had to submit your copy on time, but nobody really gave a shit about where you were, what you wore, or how you behaved, provided you met your deadlines. So I have a hunch that Brian may be kidding himself ever so slightly.

While Brian's being a reluctant father, Donald's being a novice decorator, and I'm stuck at home with the kids wondering what to do next. Clare has gone, my friends are preoccupied, so I think it's time to be positive. Get busy. Start collecting BlokeMiles.

Part Two

BRIAN

Chapter Ten

It's all going according to plan – not that Brian McIver actually has a plan – until he finds himself fumbling with the clasp of her bra. There's some distant muscle-memory twitching from the days when Brian would take Tanya's clothes off, but it doesn't appear to be up-to-date. Just push towards the centre and pull apart. Something like that. But the bloody thing won't shift, and she's not helping him. In fact, she seems to be finding his embarrassment mildly amusing.

Brian is anything but amused. Up to this point, he's been relying on instinct. He's shut down his conscious mind – always so cluttered with rationale and guilt and reasons not to do things – and is following his biology. He fancies this woman. He's a red-blooded male. Let it flow. But suddenly, in an instant, the spontaneity has been shattered. What does she want him to do? Ask her to undo it for him? Ask how it works? His brain is whirring again, and that's just what he was trying to avoid.

Brian forces the door to his conscience shut again. It takes a monumental effort. There is a legion of negative thoughts, each laced with self-doubt or even self-hatred, trying to get out and ruin the moment. He's got to keep them at bay, at least for now. Just this once. Get it over with and deal with the consequences afterwards. It's too late for all that now.

He pulls back and looks at Suzi Seymour. In the half-light of the hotel room, her skin has a translucent quality. Her dark bob is shimmering and her huge brown eyes are searching Brian for signs. He wonders if she can hear the demons hammering on the door inside his head.

Slowly, deliberately, Suzi reaches out and takes one of Brian's hands. She sits forward slightly on the edge of the bed and guides him to the front of her bra. *The front.* No wonder he was struggling. Brian reaches out with his other hand now, and the bra comes away. Suzi wriggles her shoulders out of the straps and waits for Brian to make the next move.

He drops the underwear on the floor and surveys the naked flesh he has uncovered. Suzi's breasts are much smaller than he expected. Smaller than Tanya's. Not as full, not as sexy. *Not as nice.* He tries to shove the thought – the comparison, for goodness' sake – from his mind, but the floodgates are opening.

Suzi kisses him aggressively, her tongue forcing its way into his mouth, and immediately she can tell that something has changed. She pulls back quickly and looks at him unblinkingly. In that one instant, he communicates everything. His doubt. His hesitation. His guilt.

They are at the Gore Hotel in Kensington in a tiny, overpriced room. Brian knows he's drunk too much and he suspects Suzi has too. He has the familiar thud of a headache coming on. And as the two of them stare into each other's faces, he knows that he is not going to make love to this woman. He's surprised by just how quickly his desire has evaporated, leaving him feeling empty, passionless. He was ready to give in to it only moments ago, but now, with an ice-cool certainty, he can see that he has made a colossal mistake.

The clarity is reassuring, but it doesn't help his short-term predicament.

'Brian?' Suzi says his name slowly, as though she's addressing a small boy thinking about doing something naughty.

Brian is unable to think of anything to say that doesn't sound clichéd. He shakes his head.

'What is it? Don't you fancy me?' she says.

It's a daft notion. How could she think that? But still, he can't think of a meaningful word to utter.

'You don't fancy me!' she cries, close to tears.

'Yes I do.'

'No you don't.'

'Yes I do.'

'Then why don't you want to sleep with me, then?' Now her words are coming through sobs. Her face is red and blotchy. Suddenly her naked body – and Brian's – look comical, and he suppresses an awful urge to laugh.

'It's not that I don't want to, it's just that . . . I can't.'

'Why not? Oh, please don't tell me it's because you're married,' Suzi snorts angrily. 'I could have told you that. What happened, did you just remember?'

She sniffs away the last of her tears.

'And anyway,' she says, an edge to her voice now. 'Maybe you should have thought about that before you brought me back to your hotel. Maybe you should have thought about that over the last God-knows-how-many-months you've been flirting with me and touching me and giving me the come-on.'

Brian has to concede he has behaved indefensibly. He has no retort to her accusations. He has been a complete shit. A bastard. In some ways, he's pleased that he doesn't want to make love to this woman, but he is equally appalled at how it must look to her. He knows she must think he is the type who just plays games, getting his kicks from the hunt and then discarding his prey.

Suzi pulls her clothes on, breathing heavily but calmly. She picks up her handbag and turns to look at Brian, who is standing naked at the foot of the bed. She looks him up and down – and then down again – and he realises he must look fairly ridiculous.

'Well. It doesn't look as though it would have been worth my while anyway.' Suzi yanks the door open violently. She's halfway out when she stops and walks slowly back in and stands in the doorway. 'Don't think this is the last of it,' she says softly, and then she's gone.

The moment he is alone, Brian has an overwhelming urge to shower, to cleanse himself, to wash off the guilt, to flush away the whole experience. He turns the water on full power, hot, and stands under the jet. Relief, along with the scalding stream, washes over him. His stomach flutters nervously. It's over. It's done. This slow-burning, soul-destroying affair that's been building and threatening to derail his life, has come and gone. He's still in one piece, his honour – and his wife's – still intact.

Brian knows that to all intents and purposes he's been unfaithful, but the truth is it could have been so much worse. He had to get it out of his system, and when the crunch came, something stopped him from going too far. In some ways, sex is just a transient physical act. It has a start, a middle and an end, and when it's finished it's finished. But it's also symbolic. If he'd had sex with Suzi, he'd have polluted his marriage. It would have been like contracting a virus with no cure. It probably would have killed them. Now there's hope. Real hope.

He knew this would happen eventually. It was a matter of time. Perhaps she had a hold on him, maybe the opposite, but his will to resist had been slowly draining away. His denial was stubborn, but futile. He can almost hear his words to Rob and Donald in the pub last week. *Nothing will happen. Can you imagine? What a nightmare.* He's lied to himself. He's lied to his closest friends.

Brian lifts his head so the searing water is cascading over his hair and face, willing it to wash his conscience clean.

What about Suzi? Brian could feel her pain just then. Her humiliation. But what was motivating her, anyway? She knew he was married. Did she want to replace Tanya in his life? No, that's unlikely. Suzi just seemed to be enjoying the ride – the thrill – in the same way Brian was. Before she started working for him, Brian was disinterestedly aware that she had a reputation for being something of a man-eater. A predatory type, with an almost masculine appetite for the hunt and kill. But Brian had never felt like Suzi's prey. Nor the reverse, he didn't think. They had just had a chemistry, that's all. He liked her. Still does. *She's a good kid.*

Brian steps from the shower into the steaming bathroom and pulls down a fluffy white towel. He wonders what will be left of his relationship with Suzi now.

He wraps the towel round his torso and lies back on the bed. It seems odd, being there alone. The truth is, if he hadn't had a hunch that tonight was the night for him and Suzi to get together, he'd have drunk mineral water and driven home. Home is where he needs to be right now. Pissed or not – he feels a damned sight more sober than he did half an hour ago – he needs to be in *his* bed, next to *his* wife, with *his* children in *his* house.

He jumps from the bed and begins to dress. It's 1 a.m., but if it had been 5 a.m. he'd have done the same thing. His home is calling him.

Brian slides into his silver BMW estate and starts the engine. He loves his car and the security it provides him, especially when he steps off the hideous, crowded train out of Victoria. It's only four months old, with all the extras, but it's unmistakably a family car. A far cry from the two-seater boy racers of his youth.

As he pulls out onto the deserted main road, every fibre in his being, every instinct, now tells him that this is time for him to concentrate on Tanya. On his family. Until this morning's outburst, Brian had felt a distinct thawing between him and Tanya. From the moment his wife returned from the spa, seemingly chilled and content, life had been a good deal more upbeat.

But this morning had been grim. She knew he had a company bash later, but he didn't tell her he was planning to stay in town until he was on the verge of leaving the house.

'Have fun with that tart of yours, then, won't you?' she'd screamed at him.

Of course, it was as though Tanya had plunged a needle into Brian's heart. How did she know? *Did* she know? He was cornered, and he came out fighting.

'What are you fucking on about?'

'You know perfectly well what I'm on about. That tart who works for you. You used to bang on about her all the bloody time, and then suddenly you didn't talk about her at all. But you changed. You went all bloody shifty on me. I know, Brian. I'm not stupid.'

'You just *want* me to have an affair, don't you? You hate my work. You resent me being there, working the hours I work. So . . . great, me having an affair just about completes your evil little picture of my working life, doesn't it?'

And Brian had stormed out, slamming the front door theatrically behind him. That was the act, at least. In reality, he was fleeing, racing away from the truth.

Tanya's brief, bitter summation of her husband's dalliance with Suzi had been right. She'd sensed the moment when Brian had started being unfaithful in his mind, even though nothing had happened. She hadn't said anything at the time, or accused him of anything, but a frost started to form between them. She knew there was something wrong, and deep down Brian knew she knew. But it was all unspoken, and the tension became increasingly hard to bear.

The truth was he had already overstepped the mark with this woman, and the guilt was accumulating like bad cholesterol. He was trying to fight it through sheer force of denial, but it was no good. Tanya had him rumbled. She knew his defences were down. That some foreign body had found its way into the delicate chemistry of their marriage.

His first reaction had been anger. It was as though he had to fight his way out of trouble. He felt that overt shows of outrage were the only way of throwing Tanya off the scent. He would punch walls, doors, scream and shout with almost comical fury, all the while, most probably, simply strengthening his wife's conviction that he was up to something.

The daft thing was, he didn't even want to have an affair – with Suzi or anyone else – but he felt like a stupid dog on a leash, being yanked along, choked every time he stopped to think.

At one point he tried with all his will to kill the whole thing off. He spent the best part of three weeks doing everything in his power to be at home at one or other end of the day, having breakfast with the kids or bathing them and putting them to bed. Tanya seemed to calm down initially, but then she started to freak out all over again. And Brian found himself running away and burying himself in his work once more. He knew it was only a superficial remedy, and he hated himself for it. What kind of man was he, to feel more comfortable in a stuffy office on his own than with his wife and kids?

Brian's out beyond the speed cameras now, onto the A3. He feels as though he's just walked unhurt from a bomb blast, and now he has to get back to his life. His real life. He is under no illusions that there is plenty to sort out. Maybe Rob's right, and Tanya has post-natal depression. He needs to talk to her about it, but how? Is now the time? Either way, Tanya needs him right now, and it's time to be there for her.

With a renewed sense of perspective, determined now to grasp the nettles that surround him, Brian turns up the Red Hot Chilli Peppers, and steps on the gas. It's nearly 2 a.m. and he's heading for home.

He's nearly there when the awful, annoying Nokia ring tone that he's been meaning to change cuts brutally into the music. Christ. It's 2.30 a.m. Who would be ringing at that time? Surely not Tanya, checking up on him? Maybe one of the kids is sick? Without taking his tired eyes off the road, he presses the phone button on the BMW's multi-function steering wheel.

'Hello?'

There's a slight pause, but it's enough to tell Brian this isn't Tanya.

'Oh, we're in the car are we, Brian? Decided to run home to wifey, have we? Or is wifey there right now? Do you want to put her on?' It's Suzi, and she's spitting out the words in a rage. She sounds hysterical.

'Suzi,' says Brian. It's about all he can think of.

'Hello, Mrs McIver, it's Suzi here. Have you heard of me? No? Well, that's because your husband is a spineless little . . . shit. He's just taken all my clothes off and touched me intimately. And I touched him too. Everywhere. Oh, sure, he didn't fuck me. Didn't have the guts. But he will. Oh yes, he will. He thinks he's being faithful to you, but that's a laugh, isn't it? He virtually sleeps with me every day. Everyone in the office knows. I'm surprised you don't know, Mrs McIver. Oh, do you mind if I call you Tanya? No, I'm surprised he hasn't told you about me, Tanya. After all, he's very unhappy at home. Or hasn't he told you that, either?'

Every time Suzi says Tanya's name, it's like a sharp skewer through Brian's heart. There's been an unspoken rule that her name doesn't get mentioned. Now Suzi's stepped into his and Tanya's life, like an occupying force.

Brian's hands are white-knuckled on the wheel. He's at the house now, but can't bring himself to pull into the drive while Suzi's disembodied voice is hissing at him. He says nothing, hoping the storm will blow over.

'Of course she's not there. But what are you going to tell her when you get home? Are you going to tell her about me? About us? Because if you don't, I fucking will. You think you can just forget about tonight? Pretend it didn't happen? Pretend the months of come-on didn't happen either? Pretend there was no chemistry? Have you really just been fucking me around all this time? Playing with me like I'm some kind of boy gadget?'

Suzi's voice is a shriek, but her anger is blending with tears now.

'I'm sorry,' says Brian softly, trying to keep the tremor out of his voice. He's been round the block once and now he's pulled into the driveway. Why the hell did he do that? If he keeps the engine running, Tanya might wake up. And he'll have to make up some story – who the hell would he be talking to at nearly 3 a.m. if it wasn't Tanya? And if he switches it off, she could still be woken by the banshee threatening to destroy their lives. He leaves the engine running. Tanya is a heavy sleeper, and maybe this will end soon.

Suzi has fallen silent. He can just about hear her irregular breathing. Maybe the storm has blown itself out.

'You know what I nearly did just now?' Suzi's voice has turned calm, but cold as a north wind. 'I nearly called your wife. Tanya.' She savours the word, swilling it round in her mouth like a good cabernet sauvignon. 'I nearly called her to tell her what happened.'

Brian feels a cold sweat break out on the back of his neck.

Maybe he's just been in the eye of the hurricane, and the worst is about to come crashing over him.

'I'll bet she knows nothing about me; am I right?'

Brian doesn't answer. He daren't.

'Am I right?' she asks again.

'Yes. No. I haven't told her about you.'

'That figures. You don't have the balls.'

He can hardly breathe.

At the other end of the line, Suzi sighs. 'Don't worry. I am not going to call your wife. Not yet, anyway.'

'Thank you,' he says, daring to let out a breath, desperately hoping upon hope that this conversation will end now.

'I might pop round though, if that's all right,' she says, and hangs up.

Brian takes his hands from the wheel, and the blood creeps its warmth back into the white fingers. He turns his palms towards his face and tries to hold still. He's shaking like a leaf.

Chapter Eleven

Brian's initial take on BlokeMiles was that it was a devious ruse to help the lads get out more. He certainly didn't foresee its potential as some sort of marriage counselling aid.

It's Friday now, about 4 p.m., and he's considering heading home. He's left at 5.30 p.m. every day this week; today he's leaving even earlier and sod the consequences. It's odd. Each day, he gets a nervous flutter in his stomach as he's walking past his colleagues' offices, knowing it'll be noted. But the more he's done it, the more he's developed a sense of *fuck you*. What are they going to do, fire him?

It's been a liberating experience, made easier by Suzi not being around. She's been off sick, or at least that's the information in the public domain. But it's clearly too much of a coincidence. Brian is wondering if she might quit, and make both their lives a damned sight easier. Time will tell, and for the moment, he's grateful for her absence.

There have been moments this week where Brian has felt like a prisoner released after six weeks in the hole, emerging blinking, eyes adjusting to the sunlight, marvelling at the world. It's not just been about Tanya, either. He's been utterly thrilled by his children, Olivia and Paul. Unpalatable as it may be, he has never felt that way before – never *allowed* himself to feel that way. He's been trapped in a numbing, robotic work-mania mindset, where nothing else seems to exist. For how long? Well, years probably, his whole picture of the world rendered off-centre. He has sat at his desk, deeming it absolutely out of the question that he might leave before seven. He's just got too much to do. He is certain the world will explode if he doesn't work the long hours and make the sacrifice.

A few layers beneath the surface, where Brian starts to see things as they really are, he's been dreading going home. He's been frightened of scenes with Tanya, and he's felt inadequate as a father, which has provoked him to flee from it. Did Tanya make him feel like that? No, that's an unfair accusation. But she hasn't helped him, either. And he's not helped himself.

The contrast this week has been mindblowing. He walks in and either his wife kisses him on the lips, or his baby boy zips across the hall to greet him with his sturdy little hands slap-slap-slapping on the wooden floorboards, grinning from ear to ear, or little Olivia hears the door open and runs out shouting, 'Daddy, Daddy, Daddy,' wanting to show him something she's painted at nursery. It makes him feel incredibly . . . at home. Where he belongs.

The flower stall at Victoria Station, on this particular Friday, seems to have been placed in Brian's path for a reason.

'Twelve nice red roses, please, mate,' he says to the vendor, who looks as though he ought really to be slumped against a wall outside the station slugging from a can of Tennants Extra.

He man nods and starts gathering the flowers, while Brian quickly dials Rob's number.

'Hello, Rob Pearson,' he says in his customary self-important tone. He's not been able to shake it since his days as a hack.

'Rob.'

'Hello, Brian,' he says. 'All right?'

'Yep. Great, actually. I'm at Victoria.'

'Jesus wept! Did they fire you?'

'No. Wish they would,' Brian says, not meaning it at all. 'Just getting a bit of work-life balance.'

'Good for you!'

'Now, listen. Friday evening BlokeMiles opportunity. Bunch of red roses.'

'Bloody smart idea. You might even get lucky.'

'No, I mean, we all should.'

'Where am I going to get a bunch of red roses at five o'clock on a Friday afternoon?'

'I'll get them for you and drop them round.' Brian catches the vendor's eye and mouths to him. 'Another bunch please.'

'Brilliant. I owe you one. Do you think you could . . .'

'What?'

'. . . grab a bottle of champers as well?'

'Champers? You smooth bastard.'

'Well, Clare's got this huge pitch on at the moment and she's seriously stressed about it.'

'OK. Two of those, then.'

The vendor hands over the second bunch of roses and Brian now realises that these, plus champagne, plus his PC in its silly little leather case, is going to be quite an awkward cargo. But still, he's only got to lug it to the car at the other end.

'Who's going to call Donald?' he says.

'I will.'

That suits Brian. He senses that there's something going on between Donald and Rob that he doesn't know about. It was just the way they were hanging out after dinner that night. Slightly secretive. But that's fine; it doesn't worry him. Much.

'OK, I'll drop the stuff off in forty minutes or so.'

'Cool. See you then.'

Brian likes the idea of the triumvirate working together on their BlokeMiles strategies. He doesn't think any of them is particularly romantic by nature, so they need to create some peer pressure – a bit of competition – to stir things up a little. And he's quite chuffed that he beat the others to the punch on this occasion.

At Guildford Station, Brian ruefully accepts that he actually could have saved his aching bones and bought the champagne and flowers here. In fact, the flower stall looks a good deal classier. But never mind. He makes it to the car in one piece, slings his PC in the boot and carefully arranges the flowers and champagne so the former don't get squished and the latter doesn't roll around and explode.

He's listening to the Chillis again – hasn't removed the disc since that night after the Suzi thing – as he pulls into Rob and Clare's drive. Clare's at home, which surprises him. She usually works late on a Friday so she can duck the traffic, but her little red Mini Cooper is parked in front of the garage. Hmm. That makes keeping delivery of the goods under the radar a little tricky. Hopefully Rob will have thought of something.

Brian decides to leave the booty in the boot until he's sure the coast is clear, which is just as well, as Clare answers the front door. She's still wearing her work clothes, a shortish grey skirt with a white blouse that's looking a little crumpled. She looks tiny in her stockinged feet.

'Oh, hi Brian,' she says, sounding distracted. Brian's not convinced she looks particularly pleased to see him, but he could be imagining things. 'Rob! Brian's here!' she yells in the direction of the back of the house. And then, almost as an afterthought: 'Come in.'

She holds the door open while he walks in, but doesn't look at him. Then she shuts it and marches quickly up the stairs, her little bottom twitching powerfully. Brian tries not to notice, but reassures himself with the fact that he is not being sexual. Clare is a pocket rocket, she really is. Cute, but scary at the same time.

He feels a bit of a lemon, standing on his own at the bottom of the stairs. It's not the normal welcome in the Pearson household. By this stage, Brian is more often than not sitting at the kitchen table with a cold beer in his hand. This is his second home. He wonders if he should just stroll through to the kitchen. Or wander down the garden to Rob's office. But he hasn't really been invited in properly, so he just stands and waits.

Even Emily seems subdued. Brian notices her leaning against the wall in the doorway to the dining room, watching him, thumb in mouth and her favourite teddy bear – or is it a dog, he's never sure – tucked under her arm.

'Hello Emily,' he says in that over-enthusiastic half whisper adults use with other people's kids. 'How are you?' A ridiculous question.

She doesn't answer, but rather sucks another centimetre of

her thumb into her mouth, and lowers her head a little, a shy gesture that treats Brian to a touch more of the whites of her eyes.

He crouches down to her level. 'Is that Wilf?' he says, pleased to be able to remember the name of her cuddly companion.

She nods. We're getting somewhere, thinks Brian. Slowly.

'Can I see him?' He holds his hands out.

She shakes her head and recoils into the doorway, half round the corner now.

Christ, this is hard work.

'Hey Brian,' says Rob, emerging through the kitchen.

The two men shake hands.

'Everything OK?' Brian says quietly, his eyes momentarily looking up the stairs.

'Er, yeah, fine,' says Rob, but his face says something else. He ushers Brian back through into the kitchen. Brian looks over his shoulder but Emily has disappeared.

'Where's the little fella?' he asks.

'Upstairs with Clare. Might be having a snooze, actually.'

Brian sits down on a pine chair at the head of the kitchen table and Rob gets two beers from the fridge without asking if his friend wants one. Of course, Brian's thirsty, but Rob would normally offer. His mind is clearly elsewhere. Brian takes a closer look, and the truth is that Rob looks all over the place. He's his usual scruffy self. Tatty old Levi jeans with a huge hole in the left knee that seems to be getting bigger each time he wears them. Then there's an ancient Microsoft T-shirt, which has the word 'Chicago' and some kind of colourful jigsaw logo on the back. That means it actually pre-dates Windows 95, because Chicago was the codename for the product when it was being developed. And it's showing its age. Rob's brown hair doesn't look as though it's been brushed or combed for a week or two, and his skin has a slightly unhealthy pallor, as though he's been cooped up inside and hasn't seen the sun for a while. Which, Brian figures, is about right.

Today, whilst Rob's appearance is true to form, his mood isn't. He sighs heavily.

'We've had a bit of a barney,' he says, and Brian notices that his normally bright eyes are looking dull and careworn.

'I must admit,' Brian says carefully, 'I thought something was up.'

There's a snuffling noise and Emily reappears, like a ghostly apparition Brian keeps inadvertently summoning. She's in another doorway, this time between the kitchen and the lounge. Rob and Clare's house is a rambling old cottage, and they knocked some walls down when they moved in to give it an open-plan feel. It certainly makes it easier for Emily to spy on guests.

'Ah, it's no big deal,' says Rob, swigging his beer. He smiles knowingly, but his eyes still look haunted. 'Clare didn't win her big pitch. Found out today and she's pretty upset about it.'

'Shit,' says Brian. That explains it. Sort of. 'You didn't say the actual pitch was today.'

'No,' he says. 'I didn't know it was. Well . . . I forgot. Thought it was next week.'

'Oops.'

'Yeah. And she's pissed off because I hadn't got the kids' dinner ready, and she's been working her tits off, blah blah blah.' He looks at Brian wearily. 'I think it's fair to say I'm in the dog house.'

'CTP?' Rhetorical question.

'CTP.'

'So the champagne . . .'

'Not really appropriate, I don't think.'

Hmm. All in all, flowers and champagne on an evening when Clare is in a whole world of pain might not go down well. Unless she thinks he's just gone out to get them to cheer her up.

'What about if you say you called me while I was on my way home and asked me to pick the stuff up, you know, to cheer her up?' Brian says.

'How would you have got them so quickly?'

'There's a flower stall at Guildford station. And an offy.'

Rob's eyes regain some of their sparkle.

'OK, you're on.'

'Not sure it's enough to get you out of the dog house, though.'

'Sure it is. She never keeps me in the dog house for long. I reckon if I hang in there for a while, she'll cool down and let me out free of charge.'

'Rob, your optimism never ceases to amaze me.'

It truly is a remarkable thing. Brian sometimes wonders if perhaps Rob and Clare really do have this incredibly forgiving relationship, where their fights never last more than a few minutes and they just have a shag and make up. That's the impression Rob gives, sometimes, but frankly Brian doesn't buy it. They seem like a pretty normal couple to him. They fight, they sulk, they hold each other to ransom, but eventually they get tired of the stress and agree to differ. The best Tanya and Brian ever do is concede the argument was stupid in the first place. They rarely reach any kind of resolution. And sometimes quite hurtful things are said, by both of them, and Brian is left with the sensation that layer upon layer of scar tissue is building up in the aftermath of each spat. One day they will lose all feeling.

'Well,' says Rob, draining his beer and looking considerably more cheerful than he was a few minutes ago. 'We live in hope. At the very least, I'll get myself back in credit.'

Brian glances at his Tag Heuer watch. He bought it for himself last year to celebrate a nice fat bonus at the end of the firm's fiscal year. Donald and Brian have only just stopped taking the piss out of him. About what? Brian has never quite understood – it's just a bloody nice piece of kit.

So much for leaving work early. He'll be lucky to get home for 6.30 at this rate. Still, it's a big improvement on his previous form. He'll have time to play with the kids, do their baths, read Olivia a story and put them to bed. And while he's doing that, Tanya can pour herself a stiff drink and put her feet up. Surely that has to count for something?

He's swinging the car round the country lanes between Rob's house and his and Tanya's, and the phone rings, interrupting his enjoyment of 'Californication'. It's the same song he was listening to at 2 a.m. on the A3. And it's the same caller.

Brian's heart leaps in his chest. His vision blurs. He's short of breath. He abruptly pulls the car off the road and snaps on the handbrake. Surely this can't be happening? Suzi had disappeared for a week. Stupidly, Brian had pushed her out of his memory, enjoying the clear air. But this had to happen. She wasn't finished with him, oh no.

'On your way home, Brian?' says Suzi breezily, not waiting for him to speak. 'Well, you'll be glad to know your wife . . . Tanya . . . is at home.'

Oh, fuck. Brian wipes his brow, which is pouring with sweat. His heart is pounding dangerously. His chest actually hurts. Is this what a heart attack feels like? he wonders. His mind is racing, too, like the Red Queen, faster and faster but getting nowhere at all.

'And you'll be even more pleased to know that I rang the office today and spoke to Branighan.'

Branighan. Director of Operations. Hatchet man.

'What did you say?' says Brian breathlessly. Did she tell him about the two of them? What is she trying to do?

'Oh . . . nothing for you to worry about, sweetheart.' Her voice is still light and cheerful, but the viciousness is simmering just below the surface. 'I shall look forward to seeing you back at work on Monday then. Oh, and give Tanya my regards, won't you? Toodle-oo.'

Brian slumps in his seat and covers his eyes with his hands. He is living a nightmare. A horrifying, self-inflicted nightmare, and he has no idea when or how it will end. What will she do? What does she want from him? Does she want him to sleep with her? Surely not. Does she want him to quit? Does she want him to divorce Tanya? It could be any of those things. Or none.

He puts a hand on his chest and can still feel the thumping of his heart through his ribcage, slower now, but heavy. He contemplates his next move. He has to go home now, and confront Tanya.

He puts the car in gear, and pulls slowly into the traffic.

Olivia and Paul are getting in the bath as Brian comes up the stairs, so he wordlessly takes over from Tanya. They kiss quietly on the lips, almost in passing, like two relay runners passing a baton. Swiftly, his entire being is absorbed into the cosy, frantic, intense world of his family. He tries hard to forget entirely about the conversation he's just had. Maybe she was bluffing.

He knows it's a temporary reprieve. Soon the fear begins to build, like an alien army amassing before the final great invasion. He finds himself working slavishly, getting Paul out of the bath, giving him his milk and settling him off to sleep before zipping back to intercept Olivia before she gets out on her own steam and starts dripping bathwater around the house.

He's got her room ready, and her glass of milk, and he doesn't even think about seeing if she'd rather her mother read her a story. Just sits down, opens up *Winnie The Pooh*, and starts reading. Olivia is happily going along with it. Despite all the parental back and forth about whom the children would prefer to undertake which task, they basically don't care a jot.

And then, without stopping to take a breath, he's ushering her through the lounge to kiss her mother goodnight, supervising the brushing of teeth, putting up with the ritual end-of-day-last-ditch-attempt-to-put-off-bed-time conversation.

'Daddy.'

'Yes, love?'

'What did you do today?'

'I went to work. In London. Like I always do.'

'Did you . . . did you . . . did you write some stories?'

'Well, not really. I wrote a few letters, though. And sent some emails.'

'Why?'

'OK, Olivia, I'm not getting into this now. It's gone half past seven and it's past your bedtime and you have to go to sleep now. All right?'

He bends down at this point and administers a kiss, but the

fact that she doesn't present her pouted lips – leaving him to peck an apathetic cheek – suggests she's not quite ready.

'Daddy.'

Sigh. 'Yes?'

'What's an email?'

'It's . . . look, I'm not talking about that now, OK? It's just a stupid thing I do at work.'

'Who do you send them to?'

'It doesn't matter.'

'Why?'

'Because it doesn't.'

'But why?'

'Because I say so. Now . . . GOODNIGHT!'

He crouches again, and this time she knows the game is up, so she turns and presents her beautiful, soft, innocent face and Brian kisses his daughter's perfect little mouth.

'Sweet dreams,' he whispers, slipping out of the room and pushing the door to behind him.

'OK, Daddy,' he hears her say as she rolls over to face the wall.

Brian stands outside his daughter's bedroom and takes a deep breath, trying to steady himself before heading downstairs. He's certain Tanya has been holding something back. Heaven only knows what. And then suddenly, quite by surprise, Brian loses control. Tears are welling in his eyes, and he leans weakly against the wall. He has just put Olivia to bed. Soft, loving, vulnerable. His family is precious to him and he is plagued now by a terrible fear of losing everything. Everything he has worked for.

He quietly pushes the door open to Olivia's room and pads to her bedside. Miraculously, she's already asleep, oblivious to her father's torment. He stands there for a moment, admiring her, loving her, until he's calm enough to face the music downstairs.

Tanya is sitting with her feet up – exactly as prescribed – sipping what looks like a gin and tonic. She smiles at Brian.

'Hey, you won't believe what happened this evening. We've got one of those phone perverts. Keeps ringing and doing heavy breathing down the phone.'

'You're kidding, really?' says Brian. He instantly knows this is Suzi, calling but either deciding to say nothing or not being able to. Or maybe she's trying to intimidate, in which case it didn't work. Tanya seems amused.

'No, I'm serious. First two times I hung up, and the third time I told him to fuck off and get a life!' She laughs heartily.

'Well, if it rings again, I'll get it.'

'You'll sort him out, will you?'

'Bloody right I will.'

Brian is flooded with relief, though he knows this saga has some way to run yet. At least he can forget about it for the moment. Maybe even for the weekend.

'Anyway, what got into you tonight, honey?' Tanya says, guiding Brian to sit very close to her on the sofa, switching off *EastEnders* at the same time.

'What do you mean?' he says.

'You know,' she says. 'Doing all the kids' stuff, preparing their milk, making their beds, reading their stories. Are you on some kind of mission?'

As she's talking, Brian realises that Suzi is still stalking him. Her angry, red face is popping up in front of him at every turn, her bitter voice slicing into him, and the threat of her confronting his wife with what he's done seems frighteningly, horribly real. He is truly petrified. He cannot relax.

'No. Just enjoying being home early on a Friday evening. You know . . .' He strokes Tanya's neck as his brain frantically catches up. 'Enjoying my family.'

'Aw.' She nuzzles into his shoulder and looks up at him with watery eyes. 'That's nice. And I thought you were just trying to earn some BlokeMiles.'

Chapter Twelve

Brian wakes after a night of tormented, shallow sleep, punctuated by the conviction that Suzi was about to ring the doorbell. He looks at his haggard face in the bathroom mirror. His eyes are red-rimmed, his stubble uneven and his dark hair looks lank and in need of a wash. His sense of not feeling at all together is dramatically heightened when he realises he's completely forgotten that England are playing South Africa a little later on this morning. It's a game he's been thinking about for months. How could it slip his mind?

Normally he'd be straight on the blower to Rob or Donald, or even more normally, they'd have it all planned in advance. Who's hosting, who's buying the beer, who's organising food, and let's just cross-check the validity of BlokeMiles passes because we can't have wives and children diluting our enjoyment of the occasion. But this morning's a shambles. And worse yet, Brian can't shake the awful, nagging feeling that he needs to keep plugging away, being a good father, showing willing, or perhaps being on guard in case a deranged woman pounds on the front door. He cannot believe the call he's about to make.

'Rob, it's me.'

'Brian me ol' mucker.'

'What are you doing for the rugby this morning?'

'I wondered when you'd ask.'

'Aw, come on,' Brian jumps in, defensive. 'You didn't mention it yesterday when I was round your place.'

'I know. Do you know what? I completely forgot about it.'

'Me too. And I've been reading the frigging papers all week.'

'Me too.'

'Anyway . . . I think I'm just going to have to hang out here. I don't even know if I'm going to watch it.'

'What? Why? What's up?'

'Nothing,' Brian says. Too difficult to explain. 'I just . . . well, I might watch some of it. I'll have to see.'

'I'm bloody watching it,' Rob grumbles. 'On my fucking own.'

'On your own? Is Clare out? Hope she's taking the kids.'

'She's not. She's going to see her parents. Leaving the kids here.'

'Bit odd, isn't it?'

Rob doesn't answer straight away, and Brian wonders if he's said something he shouldn't have.

'Erm, not really. She hasn't seen them for a while. I wanted to score some points.'

'Jesus, serious points I hope. Watching rugby with the kids!'

'I know. Nightmare.'

'Well, yeah.'

Another silence.

'Christ, Brian, when was the last time we didn't watch an England game together?' Rob asks.

'I don't know. Honestly. I can't remember.'

'And do you know what Donald's doing?'

'No,' says Brian. He'd just been wondering the same thing.

'He's painting their bloody bedroom.'

'Oh shit. He's not, is he?'

''Fraid so. But I guess he'll still be able to watch the game. Lucky fucker.'

'Rob, what's going on? I thought BlokeMiles was this brilliant concept that was going to give us *more* opportunities to hang out together, not less.'

'Well . . .' Brian can sense Rob building up to one of his little speeches. 'It is pretty ironic, isn't it? You know, we come up with this idea and the net effect is we miss our first England game for years.'

'Yeah, and not just any bloody game.'

'Right. But the thing is, the idea was always that we'd earn enough points to bugger off to Sydney for the final. We can't forget that.' He sighs. 'But you're right. This was a fuck-up.'

'You're not kidding. Anyway, enjoy the game. Give us a bell after?'

'Sure. See ya.'

Brian hangs up, feeling distinctly unsatisfied by the conversation he's just had.

Tanya sweeps down the stairs into the hallway, in some kind of rush.

'I'm off out to see Judy, OK love?' She kisses Brian on the cheek before he can even compute what she's said.

'Er, sure.'

It's not exactly what Brian's thinking, but his brain's labouring to form an opinion. She's seeing Judy? Why didn't she tell me last night? Didn't I tell her there was a big game on? Isn't she taking the kids with her, or Emily at least? Obviously not.

'When will you be back?' he asks. There's something pathetic in his tone, or maybe his face betrays a lack of enthusiasm for his predicament.

'Oh, after lunch some time. Bye.' And off she goes. Whoosh. Bang. Gone. Done deal.

The game's on, but Brian's not watching it. He has descended into the blackest of dark moods. He's managed to get Paul off to sleep and Olivia's playing quite happily on her own, organising about a dozen or so dolls of different shapes and sizes. His daughter has a strange ritual where she sits them all on the sofa in a line, then painstakingly reorganises them. Then one of them turns psycho and knocks the others off and the whole thing starts again. It's quite reassuring to see that girls have a violent streak too.

No, Brian can't blame his children for his state of mind, but he's fuming nonetheless. He feels trapped. The game's on the TV and he's semi-consciously aware that it's been a struggle, but England are beginning to pull away. He can't concentrate on it, because the children are in his charge and he knows for a fact that the moment he relaxes and tries to enjoy the game, he'll be called to the scene of a poo, an accident or just a bored child wanting some attention.

As he sits on the sofa, arms crossed, lips in a childish pout and brow deeply furrowed, Brian's thoughts are sucked further into the dark vortex of his morose mood. Does he really like having children? Does he regret it? He knows he shouldn't listen to these things when he's feeling down, but it's not the first time his subconscious has spoken up in this way. It's the same sensation as hating all 1,045 CDs in his music collection, when he knows he has to get out of the house and do something constructive to shock himself out of his slough, but can't be bothered. It's not something he would ever say to anyone, but that's when he wonders if having kids has killed his life, and that other people feel the same but won't admit it.

He's listened to Donald – and Judy for that matter – talk with absolute lucidity about their decision not to have children, and for God's sake it makes perfect sense. They say they just don't feel the need. They want to enjoy their life together as it is. Grow old together. And they don't need children. Need. Why do people talk about need? Did Brian feel a need? No. Truth is, he didn't.

And he had a great life before. Before children. Before marriage. Up to that point, he could do what he wanted. Work hard. Play hard. Go on nice vacations. Eat out. Lie in. Read the papers. Listen to stupidly loud music. Have sex. Relaxed, unhurried, erotic sex. In the living room. In the kitchen. Wherever. They were carefree times for him and Tanya. They were a happy, good-looking couple who had it all going for them. And they were stupidly, crazily in love. Set fair.

Brian knew that things wouldn't remain that way for ever. That his sparkling relationship with this beautiful woman would weather with the passing of time, acquiring a strong, matt finish as opposed to its youthful gloss. And the changes after they were married were subtle rather than striking. They still did many of the same things together, but more because they could rather than because they particularly wanted to.

And the sex, perhaps naturally, became just a little mechanical and less spontaneous. Again, Brian knew it was perfectly normal, but he still couldn't quite buy it. Couldn't quite understand how sex could be so much a part of a relationship one minute, and feel like a necessary evil the next?

Then Tanya got pregnant. Brian didn't know what to think. He was shocked, scared and happy all at the same time. Relieved, too, because everyone lives in fear of IVF these days. He knew it would change everything fundamentally, but had no idea how.

Tanya made an early decision to give up work when the baby was born. It was her call, and Brian supported it. He would have been comfortable with her returning to work, too – they could easily cover the cost of a nanny – but he had to admit, the idea of his wife being at home bringing up his kids, rather than a total stranger, was reassuring. Tanya seemed content, too, with the thought of being a full-time mother. That is, until Olivia came into the world.

Brian and Tanya were no better or worse prepared for children than any other couple. Tanya read books, Brian tried not to think too hard about what lay ahead, and by the time Olivia was born they were as ready as could be. But they struggled from the moment Tanya was wheeled away for an emergency Caesarean. She had been in labour for eight hours, was still some way off being fully dilated, and the baby had started to show signs of the distress.

Only later did it become clear just how deeply the operation – and its symbolism of her failure to give birth to Olivia naturally – affected Tanya. She was almost sick with disappointment, and was certain that she had given her new daughter a terrible start to her life. Brian did his utmost to convince his wife otherwise, but her theory started to look plausible when Olivia refused to breastfeed, compounding Tanya's feeling of incompetence. And when she did start to latch on, slowly and agonisingly, Tanya picked up mastitis. It was awful for Brian, watching his wife suffering, emotionally and physically. And Olivia? She suffered almost every known baby ailment. Colic, reflux, chicken pox . . . and a meningitis scare to boot.

Brian and Tanya simply tried to hang on. Brian's paternity leave – the statutory minimum, of course – came and went, and suddenly the deeply contrasting hues of their two lives began to create a distance between them. From Brian's perspective, he was doing what he had to do: earning a living. From Tanya's, she was a prisoner in her own home, alone. Even hiring a home help – Diana – for three mornings a week failed to lift Tanya's gloom.

Eventually, Olivia emerged from the mayhem of early babyhood to become a healthy, gorgeous toddler, and life settled into some kind of rhythm. But Brian and Tanya now seemed to be living separate lives. Neither seemed able to do anything to close the gap.

Paul, like Olivia, was born through Caesarean section, this time because the medics wanted to play safe and Tanya's blood pressure was deemed problematic. Again, she was distraught. This time, perhaps even more than before, she had wanted to deliver her child naturally. At least Paul was a more robust baby than Olivia, which meant that parenting seemed less stressful second time round, albeit twice as draining.

Brian is unsure whether or not the kids have changed him, but he is sure they have changed Tanya, and they have changed the relationship between Tanya and him. And that's a euphemism. They have drawn the charge from their batteries – slowly and surely.

Brian's eyes are filling with tears. He has a nervous flutter in his stomach. He's scared. He knows something's wrong, but he's not really sure what. At least, he's not sure where to start. He knows he and his wife are both unhappy. The last week has just coated their anxiety with a veneer of tranquillity. It's not built to last. He knows he can't sustain leaving work early every day, so how is Tanya going to react when he starts staying later again? Not for fun, but simply so he can do his job properly and keep his career prospects moving in the right direction. The truth is, all he's doing is postponing something. Something he doesn't understand.

The rugby is now blurred by Brian's tears. Oh Christ, what's going on? *What is going on?*

'Daddy, are you OK?' says Olivia, in her best cutesy little girl voice.

She's in the doorway, looking unfeasibly beautiful, with her exaggeratedly straight, dark fringe setting off her big, doleful brown eyes. Brian wonders if she's been watching him. The thought makes him feel uncomfortable, and vaguely embarrassed.

His daughter drops a dishevelled doll on the floor and comes briskly over to him, offering herself to his embrace and holding him tight. Brian can feel his love for her mingling with hers for him. He is astounded. Olivia is reassuring him, flooding him with her warmth and support. It's an utterly mindblowing moment, and Brian is now significantly choked up, trying to stop his breath from catching. He doesn't want his little girl to know he's crying.

But he guesses she knows. She's put her silky soft cheek next to his, and he's pretty sure a tear or two has found its way out of his closed eyes. Her hands are clasped tightly behind his neck, and she's not letting go.

'I love you, Daddy,' she says softly.

'I love you too,' says Brian, trying hard to regain control.

The phone rings moments after the final whistle has blown on England's hard-fought victory. Brian takes a deep breath and disengages from his daughter.

He picks up the cordless phone and answers while he walks round the sofa and sits back down next to Olivia.

'Well, we won,' he says. 'But that's about all that can be said for it.'

There's a silence on the other end of the line.

'Rob?'

Still nothing.

'That you?'

He can hear an intake of breath, and a woman's voice starts humming gently. It's a child-like hum, tuneful but tuneless at the same time. Distracted.

'Suzi?' Brian's heart starts its familiar acceleration.

There's a momentary pause, and then the humming starts up again. It's her. Brian waits to see if she plans to say anything, but the sinister sound doesn't stop.

He hangs up. Slowly. He's not sure if it's a mistake, and perhaps his mildly defiant act will send her into a fury, but what was he supposed to do?

The phone rings again and his heart jumps. Is this make-believe or real life? Is this really happening? He slows his mind down and leaves the phone to its shrill music.

'Livvy, you go in the playroom for a minute, OK? I'll be in in a sec.'

His daughter obediently slips off the sofa and shuffles out of the room.

A glint of anger shines through Brian's fear. How dare she! He's going to have to warn her off, in no uncertain terms.

He grabs the phone and thumps the green button with his thumb.

'Look,' he says in a harsh whisper. But he is drowned out.

'Eng-er-land, Eng-er-land, Eng-er-land! Eng-er-land, Eng-er-land, Eng-er-land!'

It's Donald.

Brian is shaking his head, running a hand through his dark hair.

'Donald,' he says, weakly.

'Did you watch it, then?'

'Yeah. No. Sort of.'

For once, Brian doesn't feel like confiding in his friend. It's too complicated. It's too awful.

'So what's happening at your gaff? Are the ladies there?'

'Ladies?'

'Yeah. Tanya said she was hooking up with Judy this morning.'

'Erm, she might have been, I suppose, but Judy didn't mention it. She's gone to the gym, I think. Maybe they were meeting for a coffee.'

'Yeah. Or lunch. Or something. So . . . I guess you're not up for some company?'

'You've got the kids, have you?'

''Fraid so.'

'Well, you could come over but I've got to get this room finished, or I'm toast.'

'Fair enough. Don't worry.'

Bloody hell. Brian suppresses a flutter of panic as he hangs up. *What the hell am I going to do?*

What he can do is take a deep breath, get the kids ready, suitably garbed, bags packed with snacks and emergency nappies, load them into the car, and head out. Like when he plucks a random CD from his over-sized collection, usually one he hasn't listened to for a while, Hüsker Dü or something, and puts it on. Then he sits back and waits. Either he'll marvel at it and wonder why the music has lain dormant for so long, or he'll switch it off, cursing the fact that he has more than a thousand CDs of total bollocks music. Except this time he's betting his mood on his kids.

There's a little boutique zoo only twenty minutes away that usually does the trick. Olivia loves it – or at least she did last time Brian took her there – and Paul's usually good-natured enough as long as they don't stay still for too long. It's not an inspired choice, but a fairly safe one. As they drive, Brian can tell that his children can see straight through the fake enthusiasm.

'Daddy,' says Olivia slowly, suspiciously.

'Yes?' Brian glances in the rear-view mirror. She's gazing out of the window, her slightly curled bottom lip suggesting she's not in a particularly radiant mood.

'Why do we have to go to the zoo again?'

'What? Oh, come on, you love the zoo!'

'But we go all the time. It's boring.'

'It's not boring, Olivia. It's fun. You always enjoy it. And Paul loves it. And anyway, we don't go all the time.'

'We went last week.'

'What, with Mummy?'

'Yes.'

Oh bollocks. Bollocks. Their eyes meet in the mirror and she gives him her best doleful, put-upon, you're-a-lousy-father look. The zoo is a nice, easy, low-maintenance option, mainly because it's so familiar. The kids love the routine of it, or at least Brian thought they did. Olivia doesn't get bored watching *Mary Poppins* over and over and over, so why would she have tired of the local zoo? Well bugger it, he thinks. We're going anyway. He reckons she'll perk up when they get there.

Paul, who's been suspiciously quiet up to now, decides to kick Brian between the shoulder blades through the back of his seat.

'Don't kick the seats, Paul!' he yells. He's genuinely annoyed. This is a new car and it's already got muddy footprints all over the black leather. But what's the point of shouting at a baby? He doesn't get it, does he? Paul does it again. Whack. Whack. Brian has to crane his neck to see his son's face in the mirror, largely obscured by the neck rest. He looks defiantly back. Challenging. *Your move, bucko*, his face says. Brian decides to ignore him.

'Anyway, Livvy,' he says. 'I bet you didn't see the otters last time.'

'Yes we did. It was feeding time.'

'And the penguins? Were they out?'

'Yep.'

'Bet they weren't doing anything, though.'

'Yes they were. They were all in the water.'

Jesus. Brian has never seen the penguins so much as dip their toes in their little pool, and you can't blame them. It looks filthy and freezing, although it's unlikely they mind the freezing bit. They are usually either shacked up in their dingy little huts or just waddling around the water's edge, as though they'd really quite like to have a swim but can't summon the enthusiasm. It doesn't look a great life, to be honest. Poor bastards. Plucked from the clear waters off New Zealand and dumped in a tiny, under-funded zoo in England's commuter belt.

And it's not just the penguins. Today, the entire zoo seems to be sombre. The otters are nowhere to be seen, the little ocelot is hiding and most of the goats are off their food, too. Olivia apathetically tosses the entire contents of the nibble bag over the fence and watches as the big billy with the barbed horns scoffs the lot. Then she lobs the bag in and he eats that, too. Brian has to restrain her from throwing Paul's gloves in as well.

Another half an hour, Brian reasons, and they can get back

in the car and go for lunch. He's thinking McDonald's, because there's a Lion King theme to the Happy Meals at the moment. But first they've got to get to lunchtime. They've completed one circuit already.

'How about an ice-cream to cheer you up?' Brian asks, stopping outside the hut.

Olivia's expression remains unchanged, staring into the distance. But then he spots her shifting from foot to foot, and it's a clear sign that something's going on in her head. That, or she's about to wet her knickers. She looks up at him, and a little light comes on in her eyes, a flicker of a smile, and she nods. It's a brisk, positive nod, and thank Christ Brian's finally had a good idea.

'OK, wait here with Paul. I'll be back in a min.'

The girl behind the counter really does confirm Brian's impression that they are on the set of *Night of the Living Dead*. She doesn't look at him. Doesn't even speak. Just grunts. And now she's grunting about not having any pound coins and having to get some from the shop. She ambles out through the back and leaves him standing there with an ice-cream in each hand. He takes some small consolation in the knowledge that they can't possibly melt, because the café is sub-zero.

Brian surveys the animal displays on the walls, and it occurs to him for the first time that the place really is a dump. It's so convenient having a zoo just round the corner, and they are always talking about its charm. But it's a complete anachronism. The animals live in horrible, dirty little displays, and the educational stuff is dog-eared, covered in dust and probably dates back to the seventies.

He does a double take when he gets outside. The kids aren't there. He steps back inside the door and quickly looks around, but they're not in the shop, either. Is this where he left them? Course it is. He takes a deep breath. Olivia must have pushed Paul round the corner. The otters are just round there, so she probably wanted to see if they'd emerged.

Brian's there in twenty paces, and there are two families peering over the wall. He peers in amongst the adult limbs for Olivia's red-tighted legs, but they're not there. And for the first time he feels a little flutter in his chest, and can sense a swirling, demonic surge of awful thoughts trying to force their way into his conscience. He pushes them back and tries to think clearly, logically and realistically. They've just gone the other way, that's all. The image of some dark figure holding hands with his daughter flickers briefly across his eyes.

They're not at the penguins, even though half a dozen of the poor things are tentatively dipping their toes in the water. They're not at the owls, and already Brian has covered about as much ground as Olivia could have managed pushing Paul in a pram that's almost as tall as she is.

The battle in Brian's mind is starting to rage now, with cool pragmatism under intense pressure from the murky horror of his imagination. He's walking faster. His breathing is getting jerky. He can feel his heart thumping. All the while he has this vague feeling that this isn't really happening, and in a minute everything will be all right, as though he's accidentally fast-forwarded a scene in a video.

He's walked the perimeter now and there's no sign of them. But there are four or five paths that criss-cross the zoo and they could be on one of them. Well, they *must* be on one of them, so he's off, almost jogging now. His imagination is toying with him. The budgies, looking ridiculously blue, yellow and green in the muddy light of the day, seem as anxious as he is, hopping from perch to perch, twittering agitatedly. The two macaws eye him sympathetically and nudge closer to each other, as though seeking their own solidarity in the face of Brian's isolation. The kookaburras are respectfully silent, the big peacock retracts its extravagant plumage; even the lemurs stop playing and watch him with wide eyes. One path left and he can hear his breathing rasping, like the girl in the *Blair Witch Project*.

Oh, Christ. He's just traversed the last path and is back outside the otter enclosure. It's deserted now. His chest is heaving and he strangles a sob. What the fuck has happened? My kids. Oh my God, my kids. My little, beautiful, innocent children. My responsibility. My babies. Me. My family. Gone. Taken away. Abducted. Murdered. What am I going to do? Oh, Christ. He has a sudden urge to talk to someone. He needs help. He must act fast.

Brian's brain is working again, now he has come to terms with the fact that this isn't just a bad dream and something awful has happened. He marches round the corner, past the tea hut. He can see the kindly lady who has worked at the zoo for as long as anyone can remember, issuing tickets to some new arrivals from her little kiosk window. Then she ducks back into the shop. Brian pushes open the door, breathing hard, trying to control his emotions.

'Ah, there you are, sir,' she says, matter-of-factly.

And there they are. His children: Paul fast asleep and Olivia leafing intently through a book about badgers. She looks up at him.

'You were a long time,' she says flatly, and reaches out for her ice-cream.

They're still there, the two Mr Whippys, much to Brian's surprise, but most of the actual ice-cream has dribbled over his hands and up his sleeves.

It's impossible, and probably inappropriate, to explain an experience like that to a small child, let alone a baby. So Brian doesn't bother, though they seem to sense that something bad has happened to him and they need to give him a little time to himself. They're in McDonald's now, and Brian is robotically shovelling a jar of sweet-and-sour something into Paul's obliging mouth with one hand, and chomping on a Big Mac with the other. Olivia is nibbling on her chips but is far more interested in the little plastic Zazu that came with her Happy Meal. The chicken nuggets are rapidly going cold, as usual.

Brian can feel himself morphing from one emotion to the next. Relief has long since been replaced by an overwhelming numbness. He's been listless and tired more or less since they left the zoo, but now his skin's beginning to prickle, a sure sign he's starting to get angry. Angry with what? Angry with whom? The kids? He looks at Paul and his little mouth pops open, ready for another mouthful. A picture of innocence. Olivia, with a glob of ketchup on her chin, flying Zazu in drunken circles around her tray. She senses his stare and smiles, the warmth permeating his heart and brightening his world in an instant.

Tanya. Where the hell was Tanya? Where the hell *is* Tanya? Suddenly, Brian is hit by a chilling wave of fear. She's with Judy, but Donald didn't seem to know anything about it. Normally, these things are discussed beforehand. So where is she? Did she lie? Why would she do that? Brian realises this is the first time for a long, long while that he does not know exactly where Tanya is. Usually she's at home with the kids, and it's all about where Brian is going, so now the boot is on the other foot.

Is she leaving me? Brian's hands are trembling as he wipes food from Paul's mouth and confiscates Olivia's chips as a means of forcing her to eat her nuggets. This is all irrational, emotional garbage, of course. He's fully aware of that, and maybe it's the shock of thinking he'd lost his kids that's provoking him to think he might be losing his wife.

He takes a deep breath and his two small children suddenly come into focus. Never before has fatherly responsibility felt so heavy. They are his offspring, but for much of their life he's felt that they belonged to Tanya and he was just a privileged minder. Now he knows beyond doubt that he has to change all that. He has to remove the distance and take on the challenge of fatherhood instead of skirting around it. If Tanya and he . . . if she ever did leave him, he'd need his kids to know who he is.

And there's a third entity to complicate matters yet further. A ghostly spectre, haunting his every step, and yet Suzi is no ghost. She is real. Flesh and blood, and spite and vitriol, and she'll be in the office on Monday, lying in wait for him, plotting his downfall. Brian's marriage is vulnerable, and Suzi makes him want to protect it with his life. He can't allow this woman to infiltrate his family. He must keep her out.

And then the vision fades to grey, or rather the gaudy yellow and red of Ronald McDonald's plastic empire. Olivia has a mouthful of nugget and has worked out how to make Zazu talk, and Brian is the frazzled dad once again, looking forward to loading his children back into the haven of his car so he can get them home, hoping upon hope that they both fall asleep on the way. And maybe his wife will be there. Or maybe she won't.

Chapter Thirteen

The moment Brian switches off the ignition, Tanya emerges from the house. She's obviously been waiting for them. She gives him a coy smile as he steps out onto the driveway, and then peers in through the BMW's tinted glass. As Brian had hoped, both kids are fast asleep, wiped out by the morning's exploits. Tanya opens Paul's door and gently prises him from his seat without waking him, and carries him up to his cot. Brian does the same with Olivia, who lifts her head briefly to check her bearings before settling back into her blissful slumber.

Brian's in the kitchen boiling the kettle when Tanya comes in.

'So, how was *your* morning?' she says.

'OK. How was yours?'

'Only OK?'

'Yeah. How was your morning?'

'What happened?'

He sighs. 'Oh, nothing. I just lost the kids at the zoo, that's all.'

'You lost them?' Her voice is sympathetic, not angry.

'I thought I'd lost them. Had a right panic. But they were just in the shop. Bloody stupid really, but I was shit scared.'

'I'm not surprised.'

Tanya comes up behind him as he's stirring his tea. She ruffles the hair on the back of her husband's neck.

'You poor thing.'

'Did you want tea?' asks Brian. He doesn't really want her sympathy right now. He's not sure why. He just doesn't.

'No thanks.'

Brian sits at the kitchen table and sips his tea. He's looking at Tanya and can feel the fear tugging at his heart again. Things have definitely changed. She looks the same. Really very beautiful. But they are so apart it's untrue, and now he's realised it, the gulf seems wider than ever. The connection they once had has gone missing. Will it ever come back?

'How was the rugby? I heard on the radio we won.'

The rugby? What rugby? Oh, that rugby. Jesus Christ, the Rugby World Cup has almost faded from view. The South Africa game seems like weeks ago already.

'I didn't see much of it, to be honest,' he says, keeping his tone resigned but not morose.

'Oh Brian,' Tanya says, with a tremor in her voice. 'I am so sorry.'

He looks up and Tanya's eyes are wide and full of tears. Her hand comes up to her mouth to try to hide the emotion. She stands and walks the few steps between them, kneels at Brian's feet and rests her head on his chest. She is crying now, and the words 'Sorry, sorry,' punctuate her sobs.

Brian puts his hand on the back of Tanya's neck and strokes her hair gently with his fingertips. 'I don't under-stand,' he says softly. 'What are you sorry about?'

She shakes her head without moving it from his chest.

Brian's mind is trying to unknot what's going on in front of him. Images of Suzi's face keep popping into his head. Her face. Her body, naked, willing.

'I think it's me that should be sorry, isn't it?' he says. He has no intention of telling Tanya about Suzi, or having a major confrontation at this time, but the words just had to come out.

Tanya lifts her head and looks straight into Brian's eyes. 'You tell me, Brian. Is it?' She sniffs and wipes the tears from her cheeks. 'I'm not sure it matters who's sorry. I'm not sure being sorry can help any more, can it?'

Brian shakes his head slowly, the unbearable pressure of sadness bearing down on him. A collage of memories flits across his mind. The passion of their early courtship, the joy

of their wedding day. The pride he felt going anywhere –
doing anything – with this wonderful woman. And now this.

'I don't know, Tanya. I really don't know.'

The stand-off between them continues through the day. Brian
feels awkward, as though he knows something Tanya
doesn't. But she's not exactly herself, either. She seems to be
holding back as well, and perhaps because that creates some
kind of artificial parity, they both seem content to just leave
things be, talking more politely than they normally do and
being just a tiny bit too considerate. They simply seem intent
on surviving, neither willing to revisit the discomfort of the
conversation they had earlier.

The kids are down, and just as Brian is beginning to
wonder if they can get through a whole evening playing this
game, Rob rings.

'You up for a pint? Donald just called me and I'm gasping.'

'I thought you were on your own.'

That's what Brian says, but it's not what he thinks. What
he's thinking *is why the fuck are Donald and Rob so fucking
close at the moment and what is it they are talking about
behind my back that they can't share with me?* It's a short,
sharp, brain wobble and then it's over. He's glad he didn't
say it.

'I am, but I just need to get out of the house. I've got
Donna babysitting for a couple of hours. She's on pain of
death not to tell Clare.'

'Good thinking. Listen, I . . .' Decision time. Decision
made. 'Fuck it. What time?'

'Bout eight?'

'See you then.'

Tanya's fixing herself a gin and tonic.

'Want a drink?' she says.

'No thanks. I'm going to have a pint with the lads.'

'OK. Have fun.'

'Thanks.'

It's all very wooden, but it's mercifully free of aggro.
Bugger it. And why not? Brian tells himself he has nothing to

feel guilty about, especially since he has spent the whole day with the kids.

Rob and Donald are already there when he arrives, hunched at the bar and taking their first tentative swigs of lager. He brushes aside a swift wallop of jealousy. Rob is his best mate ... *Christ, we never grow up, do we?* Olivia is at nursery age, and she's already been heartbroken once by a girl called Lucy who apparently ditched her. But when Brian asked what happened, she just said, 'Lucy's got another friend now.' And he tried to explain that you can have more than one friend at once. Here he is, thirty-eight years old, and he's jealous because the bloke he considers his best mate in the world is also good friends with someone else. Who just so happens to be his friend too. *Shut up Brian, for God's sake.*

Brian can see a pint with his name on it just sat there waiting for him, and it looks mighty inviting. They shake hands, exchange pleasantries, and then immerse themselves in their drinks for what feels like a few minutes but is probably only a few seconds. Now they're quorate, there's no need to sip, and Donald all but drains his drink in one go. Wordlessly, they shuffle away from the bar and sit around a table far enough from the fruit machine to hear themselves talk.

'Christ, I needed that,' says Donald, and by the time they've all sat down, his pint's finished. Brian makes to get up, but Donald waves him back down. 'Don't worry, I'll wait for you two to catch up.'

'Bad day?' Brian asks. He's not that bothered about hearing how bad Donald's day was, truth be told. He's still wallowing up to his ears in his own débâcle. But they are mates, so they have to indulge each other to a degree.

'Been painting all day. Not my strong point, so it took bloody ages. And I've got a killer back-ache. But as far as bad days go, I've had worse, believe me.'

There's something in Donald's pointed enunciation that makes Brian sit up and take notice.

'What do you mean?'

Donald gives Rob a sideways glance. I was right, Brian thinks. There is something I don't know.

Donald sighs, and addresses Brian. 'I lost my job,' he says.

'Oh, shit!' Brian's reaction is spontaneous and genuine. 'But hang on a minute, you've been there for ages, haven't you?'

'More than five years, yep.'

'So . . . how?'

'They closed my branch down, and one of the partners took over the consolidated business. End of story.'

'Christ, Donald, I'm so sorry.'

Brian is trying to put Donald's news in perspective. He's lost his job. How bloody awful. How would you cope with that? Brian imagines himself in the same predicament. Much as he likes to vilify his firm, he'd be distraught if he was let go. It would almost be like the end of the world. Everything he's worked for. His pride. His self-esteem. Doesn't bear thinking about.

'Thanks, but there's more.'

There's clearly something conspiratorial going on between Donald and Rob. They exchange another furtive look now, but Brian knows this is all about Donald coming clean with him. Bringing him into the loop on his pain.

'Tell me,' says Brian.

'It happened about six weeks ago now. And I didn't tell anyone.'

'I don't blame you,' says Brian. 'I would have—'

'I didn't tell Judy.'

It takes a moment for this to sink in.

'You didn't tell Judy? What the fuck did you do?'

Donald sighs heavily. The pain of his experience – of talking about it – makes him look old and tired.

'I faked going to work. I left every morning and said I was off. And just killed time at the library. Or walked.'

'Jesus.'

There's a collective silence. Donald stares into his beer, and it's clear to Brian that even if there is more to this story, now isn't the time. He's said his piece now, and it hurts. Brian catches Rob's eye and Rob purses his lips knowingly. He looks relieved now that Donald has brought Brian into the picture.

'So, as you can imagine, I'm not about to whinge about a day painting a bedroom.' Donald smiles weakly.

'You watched the rugby, though, right?' asks Rob, ever the expert in getting the conversation back to Bloke Talk.

'Yeah, thankfully. Wasn't bad. Good result. Keeps our little dream alive, doesn't it?'

'It looks that way,' says Rob. 'But anyway, consider yourself bloody lucky that you got to watch the game.'

'Yeah, well, sorry about that, guys. Sorry I'm so exceptionally fortunate not to have kids of my own.' The sarcasm is so heavy it almost crystallises in the air.

It's a shock. Rob and Brian have always had full licence to moan about the burdens of fatherhood, in the knowledge that Donald has consciously chosen a different path. His comment seems to have no context.

'Anyway,' Donald sighs. 'We're through to the semis now.'

'Well, we've got to beat Wales in the quarters,' Brian offers tentatively.

'We're in the semis, Brian,' says Rob, grinning.

Brian feels ganged up on again, but they're right, of course. With the best will in the world, England are not going to lose to Wales. He doesn't like tempting fate, and he considers it poor form to treat teams with too little respect, but England are too strong. And what's more, they can still win when they play like arseholes. So, yes, they're in the semis.

'Fair enough,' he mumbles.

'Spoken like a gentleman,' says Donald. He's got a slightly smug look about him. And they are about to find out why.

'Now,' he says theatrically, pausing to ensure he's got their undivided attention. Even beer has to take a back seat for a minute. 'I've got something to show you two chaps.'

Donald pulls out an envelope from his back pocket and brandishes it at Rob and Brian. He's grinning from ear to ear. Jesus, Donald looks so childishly excited, Brian can't hide his own growing enthusiasm. What the fuck's in there?

'Come on, you bastard,' he says. Donald's dragging this out something rotten.

Rob makes to snatch the envelope from Donald's grasp.

'No you don't,' Donald says, shaking his head and still

smiling like a madman. And then even he can't hold back any longer.

'OK,' he says, briskly now. Businesslike. 'I think you'll be pleased.'

And he rips open the envelope and pulls out three tickets. He spreads them across the table, and Rob and Brian lean forward to read the print.

RUGBY WORLD CUP FINAL
Saturday 22 November
TELSTRA STADIUM – SYDNEY

An awed silence descends.

'Same again?' says Donald, trying unsuccessfully to keep a straight face. And he pushes his chair back noisily, grabs his empty pint jar and heads to the bar.

Rob and Brian are still staring at the tickets as though they are the winning numbers in the lottery rollover. Brian has a million things going through his head. Can he really go? Did he ever think this was for real? Can he get time off work? Is this what his marriage needs right now?

Rob sighs loudly, animatedly drains the rest of his pint and slams the glass on the table.

'Well, Brian me ol' mucker,' he says. 'Looks like we'd better start racking up the BlokeMiles.'

He sits back in his chair and grins at Brian who, for some reason, although he knows this is fabulously exciting, can't quite let himself go.

'So is this what you two have been planning on the quiet?' he says. It all makes sense now.

'You what?' says Rob.

'Well, you know, all these little huddles I keep seeing you two in. Is this what you've been working on?'

'What?!' Rob sounds a little exasperated. 'You mean these?' He gestures towards the tickets. Brian nods. 'I had absolutely no idea. I mean, this was one hundred per cent Donald. I had nothing to do with it. I'm as gobsmacked as you.'

Brian nods again, feeling a bit stupid, hating himself.

'Jesus, Brian, what's the matter with you? Don't you want to go? Are you gonna wimp out?'

'Sorry,' he says meekly. 'It's great. Amazing. One of us had to do something like this or the whole thing would have been a load of bollocks. All fart and no shit.'

'Exactly,' says Rob.

Brian can feel his friend's eyes boring into him.

'Something wrong, mate?' says Rob. And it's not all that perceptive really. They're on a boys' night out of sorts, they've got tickets to the World Cup final spread on the table in front of them, and Brian is not quivering with excitement.

'I know this sounds pathetic,' he starts, trying not to sound pathetic and failing miserably. 'But what is it you and Donald have been talking about? You know . . . without me?'

'Aw, are you feeling a bit left out?' says Rob sarcastically, but smiling. 'Christ . . . look, he confided in me that evening. About this business of him losing his job and not telling anyone about it. He was in a bad way, he needed to talk, and I just happened to be there. He'd have told you if you'd gone out there instead of me.'

Brian puts his head in his hands. Why is it, when things aren't going well, when you're not feeling on top form, you find yourself on a slippery slope where everything you do just makes the slope even greasier, propelling you ever faster downhill?

'Is he OK?' he says.

'Yeah,' says Rob softly. 'I think so.'

And Donald returns with the drinks, noticing immediately that the mood at the table is somewhat sombre. He looks like a stand-up comic who's just told the achingly funniest joke he has in his repertoire and nobody's laughed. The enthusiasm has frozen on his face.

'What's up, chaps?' he says.

'Nothing, mate,' Brian says boldly. He feels a sense of responsibility now to lighten the mood. 'This . . . these . . . are awesome. Fucking brilliant. Rob and I are just a bit worried about the BlokeMiles situation.'

'But it's nothing we can't fix, right?' says Rob, his eyes flashing in Brian's direction.

'Bloody right.'

'Good,' says Donald, shuffling into his seat and looking relieved.

'Cheers, fella,' says Brian. And they raise their glasses – chink chink chink – and the beer goes some way towards washing Brian's self-loathing away.

Three pints of lager is usually sufficient to create a wave of warm camaraderie. These are three good mates anyway, but there's no question that booze – in sensible quantities – adds a certain feel-good factor. It also completely removes any obligation to talk, and now, with their fourth and final pints sitting in front of them, largely untouched, they are sat back in their respective chairs contemplating their own private little worlds.

Brian's thinking about Sydney, and for the first time he's beginning to feel a flutter of excitement. He's put the complications to one side – at least temporarily – like how on earth he is going to earn enough BlokeMiles to feel comfortable telling Tanya he's flying to Australia for a long weekend? How is he going to reconcile that with the knowledge that the two of them have a God Almighty struggle ahead of them to try to save their marriage? Instead, he's indulging himself and thinking about Sydney harbour, the opera house, the bridge, the beaches, the bars, the rugby, being away from home, away from responsibility, away from work, with his mates . . . it's awesome, and there is no way he is going to blow this chance. One way or the other, he will be there.

Donald is looking at him. Brian can feel his eyes on him before he looks up from his pint glass. Donald makes to talk, but then stops.

'What's up?' Brian says.

'Oh, nothing.'

Brian takes a slurp of his beer. He's feeling so mellow, he's not going to force the issue. If it's important, he'll say it anyway.

'Does Tanya know another Judy, Brian?' Donald's face is sombre. He's peering over the top of his big old glasses, as he does when he's slightly pissed.

'Why?'

Donald wriggles uncomfortably in his seat. Then he sips at his pint and looks Brian squarely in the eyes. He's still waiting for an answer to his question.

'Not as far as I know, no. Why?'

'I'm sure it's just a misunderstanding or something, but Tanya didn't see Judy today. She actually went out to the gym, and had lunch there on her own. Told me just before I came out this evening. I'd assumed she'd met Tanya for lunch, as you said.'

Brian's mind is working slowly. He's sure Tanya said she was seeing Judy. Or maybe he misheard her. No, that's what she said. Maybe she does know another Judy. Or maybe . . .

'Maybe that was the original plan, and something came up and they cancelled?' says Rob, trying to be helpful as usual.

'Yeah. I'm sure it's nothing,' says Donald.

The bell rings behind the bar.

Chapter Fourteen

Brian may not yet have become part of the institution that is Winston Forster – and perhaps he never will – but he is senior, successful, widely recognised as hungry, tenacious, and on a fast track to even greater things. Not surprisingly, then, he normally has quite a strut as he strides through the revolving doors, acknowledging the greetings of the security guard. He enjoys the familiarity of the ritual – riding the glass lift to the twenty-fifth floor, stepping out, turning sharp right and pacing past Amanda on reception, giving her a dazzling smile and doffing a cap that he's not actually wearing. Then he turns left and right again, and walks past the dealers, saying hello to some, until he reaches his office.

Normally he'd hang up his coat, walk up to Suzi's desk, bend down to her level and say, 'Any chance of a coffee?' in a quiet, suggestive voice. 'I'll see what I can do, Mr McIver, sir', she would answer, and the tone of their day would be established.

But today is different. There is no strut in Brian McIver's step. He has been dreading this moment. The moment he turns the corner and Suzi is sitting at her desk. What damage will she have wreaked? Or will she be waiting until she can hurt him in person? What does she want from him? Why doesn't she resign?

Suzi is wearing a new suit, and she's still got the jacket on. It's dark grey and it makes her look like senior management, not an executive assistant. In place of her usual low-cut blouse is a severe white shirt, buttoned to her neck. He hesitates by her desk – he figures he'll make his own coffee today – and their eyes meet. She smiles, but her eyes narrow dangerously.

'Good morning, Brian,' she says sweetly. 'I trust you had a pleasant weekend?'

'Er, fine, thank you.'

'Can I get you anything?'

'No. No thanks.'

Brian hurries into his office and shuts the door. He now realises he's going to have to take her on. He can't live in fear of Suzi's next move. He will have to try to regain some semblance of control.

He sits at his desk, sinking into the dark-brown leather chair, and sighs heavily. The thick oak door to his office gives him a sense of security. At least he can think straight here. He takes in his surroundings. It's an old-fashioned office, with dark wood furniture. The bright, if rather clichéd pictures on his desk of his wife and children lend the room its only cheer.

Was Suzi attracted by what she saw as power? Brian scoffs at the idea of his power at Winston Forster. If he truly had it – and he's never stopped working on it – he'd be a partner and have one of the ludicrously spacious corner offices, at least three times the size of the one he currently occupies. It's a conservative business, and you're supposed to wear your rank like a uniform. Brian used to hate it when he joined fourteen years ago, but in the end he got swept up. If you can't beat them, join them. It's not really ambition that's driven him – that's too premeditated for Brian. No. It's more about competitiveness. He's always thoroughly enjoyed winning and hated losing, whether it's football or tiddly-winks. And the crusty old farts and bloated, ruddy-faced public schoolboys who ponce around thinking they are God's gift to the universe provide more than enough fodder to stoke Brian's desire to prove himself. To beat them.

So what about Suzi? It started with mild flirtation on email, which Brian considered a natural continuation of the easy friendliness they had with each other. But there was more, and he didn't notice until it had developed another few stages. Suddenly she was loitering too long in his office, touching him – on the arm, on the back – just little, subtle things. And he let her, because he liked it.

Perhaps she could sense he wasn't happy at home. Not that he'd ever discussed his marriage with this woman, but one invariably gives away more than one intends. For some time now, Brian's been first into the office and last to leave. What does that say about his personal life?

There had been opportunities for misbehaviour before that night, but Brian had always felt sure of his own defences. Besides, he has never had any desire to screw up his marriage. Despite everything, he loves Tanya. They may have messed things up in a big way, but Brian finds the idea of hurting her abhorrent.

The moment he had sat down at the dinner table and Suzi had put herself opposite him, he'd felt different. Vulnerable. He'd known they would find themselves in the situation they ended up in, and he no longer had the will to stop it. He had no idea what would come of it – probably either they would fall in love, or they'd feel cheap and dirty, and the guilt would flush the infidelity from their systems.

In the event, or rather non-event, it was a relief. It provided some kind of affirmation of his deep-seated moral code, and his love for his wife and family. For Suzi, it was the ultimate humiliation. Instead of goodness, she sees callousness. She has been cast aside.

Brian would never have predicted the viciousness of her reaction. She seemed so sweet-natured and considerate before. Now, he has to admit, Suzi is a monster of his own creation. A monster he will have to deal with.

It has befallen Brian to score the plane tickets Down Under. There once was a time – only a few weeks ago, in fact – when he'd have said he didn't have time. And he'd never have considered wasting his valuable working hours rummaging around on the internet for a good deal. But how things have changed. After years of addiction to the allure of power and wealth, Brian is feeling something that can only be described as apathy. He simply can't be arsed.

The situation isn't helped by the creeping sensation that the firm's senior partners already know all about Brian's mishap with Suzi. Or if they don't, they will soon. She will talk to Branighan. He can imagine them sniggering behind his back. The old boy, public-school clique with the funny handshakes and the sherry bottles, laughing at the misfortune of the pleb in the small office. The place feels tainted now.

So to hell with it. Brian may as well organise his personal affairs on their ticket. His tickets on theirs, so to speak. And the thought of jetting to the other side of the world and leaving Suzi and her bitterness behind has more than a little appeal.

Expedia.com has come up with a good price on Malaysia Airlines via Kuala Lumpur and, at this late stage, there doesn't appear to be a great deal of choice. It's a no brainer. Brian scrolls through the menus, putting in names of travellers, do they want insurance, yes, class of travel – *what do you think?* And then the system asks for his credit card details and the whole thing suddenly seems incredibly scary. One mouse click and they're going. No turning back. No refund. Non-transferable. Indelibly stamped on the calendars of their lives.

His finger hovers over the mouse button but he's got the yips. He just can't do it, at least not without putting his head in his hands and blowing hard with the mental exertion. It feels as though he's signing divorce papers, even though all he's doing is booking a long weekend with the boys that just so happens to be on the other side of the world. It feels like a betrayal. And yet it doesn't. Despite everything – despite the huge shift in outlook on his marriage – he still feels guilt, and knows deep down that he has nowhere near earned the right to do this. His BlokeMiles account could probably justify a day trip to Brighton but that's about it.

It's the old head versus heart thing. His head tells him he shouldn't worry. It's only a weekend, and it won't kill Tanya to look after the kids without him for a few days. And anyway, she'll probably just take them down to her mother's. Plus she left him in the lurch the other day. But his heart won't let him off the hook. When he was working his proverbials off, he somehow felt he had an excuse not to be around very much. But this . . . well, this is different. He doesn't have an excuse. He can't seem to justify it.

The 'pay now' tab on Brian's screen is throbbing expectantly.

He picks up the phone and calls Rob.

'Well, have you done the deed?' Rob says, without so much as a salutation.

'What deed?' Brian's thrown for a second. 'Hey, how did you know that was me?'

'I'm fucking psychic, that's how. So?'

'No. Seriously.'

'I've had Caller ID put on my office phone. It's superb,' Rob chuckles. 'Well?'

'I'm just about to,' Brian says sheepishly. 'But I'm having trouble, you know, justifying it.'

He waits for Rob's scorn to come crashing down on him, but to his surprise it doesn't.

'Yeah, I've been feeling the same,' says Rob. 'But bollocks to that. We're going now, right? Donald's got the tickets, you're going to book the flights, and we'll somehow make it work out fine. Go on. Book the damned seats and we'll worry about it afterwards. It's the only way.'

So Brian does exactly that. Tucks the receiver between his chin and right shoulder blade, hovers the mouse so it's slap bang in the middle of the 'pay now' tab and wham. *Click.* Such an inconsequential noise for such a major event.

'Done,' he says. And it feels good.

'Good man!'

'So now what?'

'Now we have to make our wives worship us. Piece of piss, right?'

'Absolute doddle.'

Brian wishes he meant it.

Chapter Fifteen

It's Saturday 8 November, and a convoy of precious cargo is edging its way through traffic in Reading. Rob is leading the way, with Donald navigating in the front seat, and Brian can't help wondering if he's taken a rather dodgy route, but never mind. They've been inching along for a good quarter of an hour now, and the kids are getting restless, despite the fact that their little stomachs are now full of chicken nuggets and chips. Brian can see Ralph's little arms flailing in the car in front, indicating that Rob's wee ones are going as bananas as his. They were hoping to get close to the venue and stop at a pub, but it's already nearly two o'clock.

They are on their way to a camping and fireworks extravaganza in Oxfordshire. It's not an event that has Brian salivating with enthusiasm. In fact, his first reaction on hearing the idea from Rob was that it sounded utterly daft: camping in a freezing tent on a frozen field, with lots of people dressed as ghouls even though Halloween's been and gone, and then keeping warm by an enormous bonfire as fireworks light up the sky. That last bit appealed, but the camping ... in normal circumstances, Brian would rather hack off his own genitals with a blunt instrument. Still, they're into the home stretch now. One final push for BlokeMiles Gold status and carte blanche to zip over to Sydney in a fortnight's time.

Donald decided to come too, seemingly unfazed by being surrounded by screaming children for the evening. Judy is on some graphic design course for the weekend, so he was at a loose end. Fair play to him.

Tomorrow, England play Wales in the quarter-final, having squeezed past Samoa and then thrashed Uruguay by 100 points a week later. The prevailing view is that an England win is a foregone conclusion, and whilst Brian still feels reasonably confident, he's less and less willing to stick his neck out now the business end of the tournament is nigh. It's a quite conscious strategy to try to protect against the crushing disappointment of an unexpected loss. Or any loss for that matter.

Either way, an England-Wales quarter-final is a huge game, and most likely, Brian will be listening to it on the radio on the way home. It's less than ideal, and he's trying hard not to be just a touch disillusioned with what Bloke-Miles has done for him. It was invented as a way of helping the lads enjoy the Rugby World Cup, and yet in the end it's turning into a huge, all-or-nothing gamble on England getting to the final. And winning it, because if they travel all the way to Australia to watch England lose, and have to suffer the insufferable gloating of the locals, it will hardly constitute a worthwhile sacrifice.

The convoy finally crosses the Thames and explodes happily into the open countryside. Then they turn off the main road and zigzag down an interminably long country lane before emerging into a huge field, where fluorescent-jacketed youths are ushering cars neatly into their parking slots and showing them where to erect their tents. It all seems very well organised, and there are already excited children charging about and screeching like macaws at a salt lick.

There's a large clearing in the middle of the whole set-up, with a huge bonfire ready and waiting. Brian can feel his spirits lifting. He loves fireworks.

Three tents are erected, despite the well-meaning distraction of toddlers filching the pegs and standing on bits of canvas, and the men set about unloading sleeping bags and other assorted paraphernalia. Brian staggers under the weight of an enormous cool-box full of lager. Provision of beer was his responsibility and, naturally, he was fearful of under-catering.

He notices Rob carrying his own, smaller cool-box, and remembers he was supposed to bring food. Not for the group, but for his own family. Shit. He surveys the scene and notices, not far away, a couple of fast-food vans. On top of McDonald's, the thought of more junk doesn't exactly set the juices flowing, but his choices are limited. To hell with it, it's just gonna be a fast-food day. Tanya doesn't need to know.

By 5.30 the kids are dressed to kill, quite literally. Emily is wearing a particularly fetching witch outfit, complete with pointy hat and broomstick, which she holds alongside her more like a pitchfork than a broom because she has terrible trouble getting it between her legs, what with all the billowing fabric. Thankfully, it's made of plastic, because she enjoys the little pop it makes when she clobbers Paul and Ralph over their heads with it.

Olivia is rather less glamorously attired, wearing a large, droopy white sheet with holes cut in it for her eyes. But she's happily 'wooooo-woooo-woooo-ing' away, trying unsuccessfully to scare the little ones. Tanya would probably be looking around at the other kids on show, berating herself for not having made enough effort. For Brian, if the kids are happy, he's happy. And he thinks she makes a very appealing ghost.

'Daddy, I'm hungry,' says Emily, looking up at Rob with imploring eyes.

'Yeah, OK love, we'll have our tea now, shall we?'

Brian's feeling decidedly silly, and not a little embarrassed.

'Er, I forgot food, so we're going to go and grab a hot dog,' he says.

'YAAAAAAAAAAAAAAY!!!' whoops Olivia. Tanya may not approve of fast food, but Olivia clearly does. Off they go: Brian, his wee boy on his shoulders and a small ghost rustling along at his heels.

The two vans are just the sort you get at dodgy fairgrounds, with fat, scowling blokes with huge, dirty hands, occasionally deigning to flip over a greasy burger or scrape some burnt onions off the grill. One van seems to have burgers and nothing else, and the other . . . burgers. Great choice.

'Do you sell hot dogs?' Brian yells up at the bloke in the first van.

'Nah mate,' he says in a deep bass voice, his arms crossed. He sees Brian start towards the other van. 'Vey don't neeva,' he growls.

Brian is stumped. He really doesn't fancy a burger, but it seems there isn't much choice. He orders two burgers and chips, one with cheese, and reckons he'll feed Paul a few mouthfuls of each and all will be fine. He hands the first one – with a piece of anaemic-looking cheese dangling from it – to Olivia, and waits for the thug to piece together the second.

'Onions?' he mumbles, without looking up.

'Yes please,' says Brian without thinking, and certainly without considering Paul's fragile little stomach.

Brian pays up, and they start to walk slowly back to the tents, Olivia already gnawing frantically on her burger, unaware of the globs of fat dribbling down her chin. They sit down cross-legged with the others, who are happily tucking into an assortment of fresh sandwiches.

'Pull up a chair,' says Rob, handing Brian a beer.

'Cheers,' Brian says, and peels the gooey paper from his burger.

For the first time, he notices just how unspeakably unappetising the thing looks. The meat is grey and tough, and the onions smell so heavily of grease that, just for a second, he thinks he might retch. He takes a small bite and discovers, if it were possible, that the taste is worse than the look. Suddenly he's not sure he can eat this, and he certainly can't bring himself to pollute poor Paul's little tummy with it. How about the chips? He pulls apart the top of the bag and sees fat, shapeless, whiteish shapes mushed up together like maggots in a rotting corpse.

'Bit dodgy?' says Donald, obviously spotting Brian's clenched jaw.

'I can't eat that,' says Brian, withdrawing his hand from the bag of chips as though he's just inadvertently touched a used condom, and not his at that.

'Tuck in,' says Rob through a mouthful of roast chicken sandwich. 'I can't guarantee you won't get food poisoning, though – this is last week's chicken.'

'I don't care. It'll taste a damned sight better than this shite.'

'Language,' says Donald.

'Sorry.'

'Daddy, what's shite?' says Emily.

'Shit, sorry,' says Brian. 'Oh!'

They all laugh, and Brian gives Paul a corner of sandwich, which he starts to inhale hungrily. And then he notices Olivia. The poor nipper's eaten her whole burger, cheese included, plus a few of those slimy chips, and she's looking at her father with a slightly startled expression.

'Daddy, I don't feel very well,' she says softly, and then lets out the hugest, most resonant belch Brian has ever heard. It sounds like the devil talking through poor old Sissy Spacek's mouth in *The Exorcist*.

Rob snorts with instinctive mirth, and a corner of chicken sandwich pops out of his mouth and lands in Donald's lap.

'Thanks, mate,' chortles Donald.

But Brian's not laughing. He should have stopped Livvy from eating that damned thing. Jesus, if she gets sick . . . he resolves to sue the fat bastard in the van.

'Are you OK, sweetie?' he enquires softly. He's kind of hoping the burp has lanced the boil, so to speak, and she might be OK now.

She nods pathetically, her big round eyes still fixed on him. She doesn't look convinced, and nor is Brian.

'Do you need to go to the loo?' he asks.

She shakes her head.

'Do you want a sandwich?'

Another shake.

'Here, have some water.'

Brian hands his daughter a cold bottle of Evian and she sips it tentatively.

Maybe she'll be OK, he thinks.

The Guy is on the bonfire and he's going up a treat. Kids and adults alike watch, entranced, as he starts to crumple grotesquely, one arm suddenly pointing towards the stars before disintegrating spectacularly. Then he seems to look straight at them, as though desperately trying to hold on to his dignity until the inevitable happens. His head drops onto his chest and he lurches forward into the flames. Pure theatre.

It's a clear, cold night and Donald, Rob and Brian are cradling their beers through fingerless gloves, enjoying the fierce heat of the fire. Paul's on Brian's shoulders, his little fingers scratching at his father's woolly hat absent-mindedly, while Olivia is holding onto his left thigh. Emily has formed a youthful coven with a couple of other small witches, and the three of them are weaving in and out of the crowd, casting spells in high-pitched voices.

Now the fireworks are going, over to the right. Next to Brian, the reds, greens and bright white lights are reflecting in Rob's and Donald's eyes as the first set of bangers explodes into the sky. They are loving it, and so is Brian. He is loving being a dad, looking after his children, protecting them in that big, bear-like, masculine way that dads do. Brian's not built like a grizzly, but that's the feeling invoked when he's assuming the role of guardian to these small people he's been instrumental in creating. It's primitive. It feels like an entirely new sensation, but more likely it's been there all along and he didn't recognise it because he wasn't around enough to soak up his children's natural warmth. And when he feels this way, he has this sudden need for the whole family to be together. Tanya should be standing next to him, and they should be marvelling at what they've created together.

Brian does a quick 360-degree scan, and can see that virtually the entire crowd is made up of dads and their children, plus the odd enthusiast like Donald. There's hardly a mum in sight. Why? Who knows, but Brian guesses the combination of fireworks and camping earmarks this event as the father's job in most families. Brian looks at the faces around him: satisfied faces, mostly around the same age – maybe a little younger – and he wonders if they are all earning BlokeMiles in their own intense little worlds. Of course they are. They just don't know it.

There's a pause in the pyrotechnics while the organisers prime the big rockets for the grand finale. It's getting seriously cold, and Brian's starting to look forward to tucking the kids up in their sleeping bags and sitting round the gas heater drinking beer with the lads and talking about tomorrow's Wales game.

'Daddy . . .'

It's Olivia, and the voice is faint. Brian looks down and, shit, she's been sick. There's quite a lot of it, and most of it is on the poor kid's ghostly sheet.

'Oh, baby. Oh . . .' Brian hoists Paul off his shoulders and crouches at his daughter's level. Her face is white as the sheet she's wearing. Brian touches her forehead and it's clammy and cold. She looks terrible.

'I think I need a poo.'

Brian's brain whirs, and he turns to Rob and Donald.

'Er, guys, would you mind looking after Paul for a minute? Livvy's just been sick and I've got to take her to the loos.'

Donald picks Paul up and slings him on his shoulders, while Brian escorts Olivia away from the fire towards the Portaloos. Her sheet is beginning to reek appallingly.

They start queuing amongst the dads and their wee ones, but Brian can see Olivia's in discomfort by the way she keeps flexing her knees and gasping. He marches her to the front, saying 'excuse me' and people part to let them through. Their predicament is obvious.

The moment Olivia sits down, her insides explode. She's crying now, sitting on this horrible, alien plastic seat in the middle of a field, her face ashen, clearly feeling desperately ill. Brian's heart is bursting for her.

He knows as he carries her down the steps back towards the crowd that he's got to take her home. Even if this is the last of it and she starts to feel better, he can't make her sleep in a cold tent. She needs her own bed, the warmth, the familiarity, her cuddly toys, and she can wake up with both her parents able to care for her.

'I want Mummy,' Olivia mutters.

'I know you do,' whispers Brian. Of course she does.

The guys turn to meet him as he approaches. They know what's coming.

'I've got to take them home,' Brian says, his voice sounding breathless.

'OK, mate,' says Rob.

'Leave your tent, Brian,' says Donald. 'We'll pack it up and bring it back tomorrow.'

Friends. What a marvel. You think no one's noticing your distress, but friends always do. Brian feels a surge of gratitude. He expected this from Rob, but Donald? He should have expected it. Donald is a kind, generous-hearted guy. Brian has sometimes felt there's a distance between them, but he doesn't feel like that now.

Rob and Donald begin ushering the posse towards the tents.

'You guys stay here,' Brian protests. 'I'll take Paul.'

He reaches out to take his son from Donald, but he's having none of it. 'No, no, no. Come on. I'll get him in the car for you.'

They are walking in procession now. Faces are both serious and sympathetic. Even the children have caught the mood, although they turn to see the rockets explode into the sky. Two, three, four huge bangs, and multi-coloured, concentric circles light up the field.

Brian quickly gets Olivia out of the sheet and into her warm pyjamas for the journey home. She feels limp in his arms as he carries her to the car. Donald straps Paul in, and Brian shakes hands with his friend.

'Talk to you tomorrow,' he says.

'Hey, at least you'll be able to watch the game, you lucky bastard,' says Rob grimly.

'Devious plan,' says Donald, smiling, but with sad eyes.

'Chance would be a fine thing,' Brian sighs, and they're off, snaking their bumpy path round the edge of the field, out onto the black road.

Brian spends the first half of the journey fretting about whether he should be taking Olivia home or to the hospital. He keeps telling himself it's just a nasty tummy upset and she can sleep it off. He's sure that's right but there's this anxiety that maybe he's just being a bit too much of a male and taking the easy way out instead of grasping the nettle. But by the time he comes off the motorway, twenty minutes from home and about the same to the hospital, both kids are fast asleep. In the mirror, he can see the reflected light of passing cars crossing their innocent faces. He's certain now that he just needs to get them both in bed, top Olivia up with fluids, and she'll be just fine.

He pictures Tanya in his mind: beautiful, vulnerable. He feels full of regret. Regret that he wasn't smart enough, sensitive enough to see what was happening to his wife after the birth of their children, that she was suffering, depressed, lonely.

She needed love. She needed him, and where was he? Buried in his career, that's where. He was a single-minded working male, so shallow you could barely see him if he stood sideways on. Then he learnt about his kids, and became two-dimensional. Now he can see the potential of having a mother and wife integrated into the whole, wondrous package. He's in danger of being three-dimensional.

Brian is not sure how much to trust what he is feeling. He is looking for some kind of eureka moment, where it becomes clear what he must do to move his life forwards. Only days ago, maybe even hours ago, he felt his marriage was on a knife edge. Now, driving in the dark with his daughter asleep and sick in the back of the car, he sees life very differently. So wild are these swings, he daren't rely on them absolutely.

Brian starts to rehearse the conversation he intends to have with Tanya once they have settled Olivia. It's time to start again. Dust themselves off and move on. He will make commitments, as he's done before, but this time they will be real, and Tanya will know the difference. He has butterflies in his stomach. He doesn't know for sure how she will react, but he thinks she'll be thrilled. Hopes she will be.

Brian swings the car round the final bend and does a double take. There's a set of headlights poking out of the driveway, the nose of a car emerging from between the rhododendron bushes like a meercat sticking its head out of a burrow. Brian approaches slowly, and comes to a stop about ten yards from the entrance to the drive. There's a man in the driver's seat. Dark hair and glasses, and he looks straight at Brian, his face illuminated crudely by the BMW's halogens.

It's a surreal moment for both of them. Brian doubts the stranger knows who he is at first glance, but he can probably see the silhouettes of two children slumped in their seats, and his brain will tell him that this is Tanya's husband and those are her two kids in the back. Brian sees what looks like an embarrassed smile flicker across the man's white face, then he looks the other way, pulls out and drives away, the red lights fading rapidly into the distance.

Brian slips the car into neutral. He's not sure what he feels. Is this what it looks like? Perhaps he knew already. Perhaps he was in denial. Does this explain why Tanya lied about being with Judy? Of course it does. But such is the numbness, the shock that makes him feel cold on the surface of his skin, that he is compelled to just sit there for a minute, waiting for his heart to start beating again.

Chapter Sixteen

Brian waits for the anger to come, but it doesn't. He waits for the shocked numbness to wear off, but it doesn't. Rationally, he understands his predicament absolutely. He was about to make a massive personal commitment to help repair his creaking marriage with Tanya, and instead he has seen his wife's lover leave his house. While he has been agonising over his own failings, his wife has been cuckolding him behind his back.

Still, he can't summon the rage. He puts the car in gear and slowly rounds the corner onto the gravel drive. Of course, Tanya will be caught on the hop. Perhaps he should have called to warn her they were on their way, but he was too full of his own thoughts.

He opens the front door quietly. He can hear Tanya upstairs, humming busily to herself.

'Hello?' calls Brian. He has no wish to walk into the bedroom and catch his wife changing the sheets, or washing off the scent of him.

'Brian?' Tanya sounds predictably shocked, and appears at the top of the stairs. Her face is pale and worried. Her hair is dishevelled, and she's wearing white leggings and a loose pink sweatshirt. Convenience clothes.

'Olivia's been really sick. I had to bring her home. They're both asleep. Can you help me bring them in?'

'Yes. Sure.' She hesitates, looking over her shoulder towards the bedroom before coming down the stairs.

'Is she OK?' she asks, whispering, as she reaches Brian. She pecks him on the cheek.

'I think so. It was pretty bad, but she's slept all the way home. Just needs to sleep it off, I think.'

'How did she get sick? Was it something she ate?'

'No,' Brian lies. 'At least I can't think of anything. We had sandwiches.'

'Oh, the poor thing. Let's get her in.'

The two parents wordlessly transfer their children from car to bed. Both are heavily asleep and neither stirs.

Brian pours himself a brandy and slumps on an armchair in the lounge while Tanya puts Olivia to bed. The emotional part of his brain seems to have just shut down altogether. He doesn't know what he's going to say, but he does know it all has to be said.

Tanya sits on the sofa, still looking rushed, though she's brushed her hair. 'Poor little love. I hope she's OK. She's quite clammy.'

'She'll be fine.'

Tanya pauses. 'Are you OK?' she says. 'Why are you sitting over there?'

'Who was that bloke you had in here?'

Brian sips his brandy and looks at his wife with a level gaze.

'What?' Tanya shifts uncomfortably on the sofa and runs her hand through her hair. 'What are you talking about?'

'I saw him come out, Tanya. He left as we arrived.'

'Oh.'

Brian watches his wife's mind contort itself, working through the emotions, desperately looking for an escape route and finding none. She doesn't know what to say. She crosses and uncrosses her legs. She looks at the floor, then at Brian, and back to the floor again. He actually feels sorry for her.

'Who is he?'

'He's . . . um . . . a yoga instructor.'

'Your yoga instructor?'

'Yes.'

'Are you having an affair with him?'

Tanya winces at the question, as though she's been

whipped across the small of the back. Her eyes quickly fill with tears.

'I don't know. I don't think so.'

'YOU DON'T THINK SO?'

Ah, there it is. The anger. The reassuring rage. It's here at last, erupting without warning, threatening to wipe out everything in its path.

'Come on, Tanya, you either are or you aren't, and by the look on your face, and the fact that you've quite clearly thrown those clothes on, and the fact that you're probably embarrassed about the state of our bedroom – *our* bedroom – I'd say you are. Should I go upstairs and take a look now, just to put you out of your misery?'

Tanya shakes her head.

'So there we are,' says Brian softly, suddenly weary. 'There we fucking are.'

He pours down the rest of the brandy, letting it scorch his throat. Tanya is sobbing into a cushion, pressed hard against her face. She is rocking gently to and fro.

The confusion in Brian's mind is already beginning to blunt his anger. There's a strong instinct compelling him to walk over and embrace his wife, to comfort her. But how can he? She has been with someone else. An image of his wife, naked, with the dark-haired yoga instructor thrusting himself into her, forms itself in his mind. He feels sick. Surely there can be no turning back from this? He came close with Suzi but somehow didn't sleep with her. He was convinced that it was *his* behaviour that would decide their future. *His* ability as a male to control his carnal instincts and stay loyal to his wife. *His* ability to resist temptation. It never occurred to him, not for a second, that it could be his wife who would pull the trigger on their marriage.

'I'm so sorry, Brian,' sobs Tanya. She has put the cushion on her lap and is looking at him through tortured eyes. 'I felt so lonely, I . . .'

And the tears flow again, drowning her attempted words. Brian waits for her to compose herself.

'I didn't want to. I know it sounds stupid. I didn't want to.

It was horrible. I mean . . . I never wanted to. I don't know why I did. It was a . . . cry for help.'

'A cry for help? To who, Tanya? There was no one else here.' There's an edge to Brian's voice.

She shakes her head again. She has no answer.

'You don't know what I've been through,' she says, this time with more strength in her voice. 'You have no idea.'

'You didn't tell me.'

'You never *asked*,' she snaps, her voice suddenly shrill. 'I gave up my job. I missed it. Badly. Did you ever think about giving up yours? No. Course you didn't.'

'I couldn't have. How would we have paid the mortgage?'

'I know, I know. You can always hide behind that. And you're right, you did need to work. But you didn't have to abandon me.'

Brian is silent.

'Brian, I don't know what it would have taken for me to make you realise I needed help. Still need help.'

'You could have told me.'

'I shouldn't have to tell you, should I? Isn't it obvious? Isn't it painfully bloody obvious? I'm a mess. Look at me!'

Brian does as he's told, and realises he's been looking at her but not seeing her. He's admired her beauty, but failed to see the torment inside.

'I don't know why I did this,' she says, gesturing up the stairs. 'But I know I wish I hadn't.'

'Yeah, well, it does seem to have brought things to a head, doesn't it?' says Brian. He examines the bottom of his glass, then puts it down and stands abruptly. He's had enough of this. Has to leave. It's over. But he has nowhere to go. To Rob's place? Rob's in a tent in a freezing field in the middle of nowhere. Where Brian's supposed to be.

'What about *your* affair, Brian? Do you want to tell me about that?' Tanya's voice is soft, but challenging.

Brian hesitates, and then sits down.

'I didn't have an affair,' he says.

Tanya holds his gaze, but says nothing.

Brian sighs. There's just no point in hiding anything at this stage.

'A woman at work. Suzi. She came on to me after the party—'

Tanya's raised eyebrows throttle his self-deceit at source.

'OK,' Brian continues. 'I played my part. We ended up in my hotel room. But I didn't sleep with her. Couldn't sleep with her.'

'But you wanted to.'

'No. No, I didn't, and that's God's honest truth. I thought I did but when it came down to it, I wanted to run a mile. Why do you think I came home at 3 a.m. or whatever it was? I needed to be at home.'

'Were you naked with her?'

'Oh, come on . . .'

His reaction to the question is irritation. The details are irrelevant. Why does she want the details? His wife is watching him. She says nothing, but waits. He knows he can't brush away what happened. He can't trivialise it.

'Yes, we were naked.'

'You . . . touched each other?'

'Yes.'

'Well, don't you think that constitutes an affair?'

'I didn't sleep with her, for God's sake.'

'Does that make it so different, Brian? You were with someone else. Intimate with someone else.'

Brian takes a deep breath. 'So we both had affairs. But you slept with him.'

Tanya doesn't answer.

'Did you?'

'Yes, I did! I committed the great sin that will send me to hell while you can polish your bloody halo. I did it. And I hated every bloody second of it. Wished he'd leave. It was awful. Unsatisfying. Unfulfilling. I felt cheap, dirty, like I was letting you down, letting Olivia and Paul down. He knew it so he stopped, and I told him to leave. He wanted to stay, but I needed him out.' Tanya is sitting upright, her chest heaving, face red. She is staring at the fireplace.

The thought, the reality, of Tanya with another man – *having sex* with another man – hits Brian hard for the first time. Whatever the mitigating circumstances, no matter what rational sense of responsibility Brian feels for the situation he and his wife are in, none of it matters at this moment.

'Well, that's it, isn't it? I mean, sure, we both got ourselves in situations, but I didn't fuck anyone, did I? Huh? I stopped. You didn't. So what was he like, Tanya? Did he have a fit, fucking yoga body? A six-pack? Could he touch his toes while he was shagging you? Did he give you multiple-fucking-orgasms? Did he?'

Brian stands again. He wants to walk out and slam the door.

'Are you finished?' Tanya is calm now, looking at him levelly. 'If you must know, he is small, doughy, has horrible bad breath, and I hope I never see him again. I made a mistake. But so did you.'

Brian sits down heavily. He has an overwhelming need to sleep. But where is he going to sleep?

'I was hoping we could fix things,' he says quietly, as much to himself as to Tanya. He doesn't look at her, but can feel her eyes on him still. 'I thought maybe we'd blown it but then I remembered how we used to be. How happy we were. And I saw for the first time how I'd deserted you. When Olivia was born. And again with Paul. When you needed me, I—'

Brian can feel emotion welling up out of nowhere. He chokes back tears. He wants to keep control. 'I wasn't there.'

Tanya runs her long fingernails under her eyes, sniffs, and waits for her husband to continue.

'I was thinking maybe we could . . . rewind the tape and record over it all. Go and talk to someone. Start supporting each other and being a family instead of a bunch of disconnected bits.'

Tanya shakes her head and puts her hand over her mouth. She and Brian stare at each other.

'I'm sorry,' she says, and looks at him imploringly.

'I'm sure you are. And so am I. But like you said the other night, being sorry isn't going to help us.'

Tanya quickly walks to the liquor cabinet, pulls out the brandy and fills his glass. She puts the bottle down on the table and briskly walks from the room. Brian can hear her

running up the stairs, and then moving around in the
bedroom.

Later, they are both awake in the dark, in the guest bedroom,
lying on their backs with a small gap between them. Both are
wearing pyjamas.
   'Brian,' whispers Tanya.
   'Mmm?'
   'What do we do now?'
   'I haven't a fucking clue.'

Part Three

DONALD

Chapter Seventeen

Poor old Brian.

Donald is dismantling Brian's tent, and it seems somehow symbolic of the state of his friend's life just at this moment. His daughter's sickening is the tip of the iceberg. Donald zips up the bag, taking small satisfaction from the fact that he is doing something vaguely useful, albeit nothing that will particularly enhance Brian's existence in the grand scheme of things. He'd rather have his marriage than his tent.

At the thought, Donald winces. He's been carrying the awful weight of knowledge these past weeks, and it's not sat easy with him. Knowing that your friend's wife is having an affair, and he has no inkling, is tough to deal with. He found out because Tanya confided in Judy, and she told him. In some ways he wishes she hadn't. There's nothing he can do to help, so he'd have been better off in blissful ignorance.

And both of them fear the worst. Most men would have an extreme reaction in such circumstances, and Brian is no exception. He'll flip, and it's hard to see how the relationship can weather the storm. Blokes don't seem to be as naturally durable as women, so if they get hurt they don't heal. Not that a woman wouldn't walk out if she knew her man was cheating on her. But women are capable of more control in how they react. Donald recalls being jettisoned by a girl at school and crying about it for days. Then he got angry, and started haranguing her over the phone. It's an eye for an eye for men, and it's all rather childish.

Donald slings Brian's tent over his shoulder and wanders over to where Rob is loading up the jeep, his creased old white T-shirt riding up his back, his head buried in the boot. He's never lost his student look, and it seems that extends to not being able to afford a jumper. Donald hands over the bag and Rob slings it in the boot. They're ready to roll, except for the fact that Emily has disappeared off with her fancy dress friends of the evening before. Donald can hear them screeching somewhere. He looks at his watch and realises just what an early start they've had. It's only 7.15.

'Rob.'

'Donald.'

'I just realised something.'

'What's that?'

'If we leave now, we could be home in time to watch the rugby.'

'I thought it was a half seven kick-off?' says Rob, grunting as he heaves his trussed-up tent into the boot. Judging by the speed of his response, it's something he's already considered.

'Nope. Eight.'

Rob straightens up and looks at his watch. His dark hair's even more random than usual.

'Shit,' he says. 'I just promised Emily a McDonald's breakfast.'

Donald chuckles. 'You're going to get serious Cold Tongue Pie from Clare if she finds out!'

'Well, I don't intend for her to find out, do I?'

Donald can feel saliva rushing into his mouth. Awful as it is, the idea of a sausage-and-egg McMuffin is extremely appealing at this precise moment. It always is when you've had a few beers, as though it might just absorb the last of the alcohol from the system and leave you feeling sound again. As if.

'I, er, I could be up for that,' he says, with pretend hesitation. 'How about if we stop at Macky D's for a quick brekkie and then hack over to my place to watch the rest of the game?'

'Yeah, why not?' Rob slams the boot shut. 'Clare wasn't expecting us till late morning, anyway.'

So there it is. Donald's been thinking about this game on and off all night. A quarter-final against Wales. It's a mouthwatering prospect, made even more so by the fact that really England ought to win, and then it's the semis, most probably against France. One more victory at that stage, and the boys are on for the weekend of a lifetime. He gets goosebumps just thinking about it.

But first they've got to get past Wales. England haven't had any problems with the Welsh for a few years, and thrashed them with a B side in the warm-up game, but Wales are playing out of their skins. The way they took on the All Blacks and almost sprang an upset ... well, it's made this look like a real contest. It's unthinkable that England could lose to Wales, of all teams. They'd never live it down. But they've not really played well at all thus far, there are injury worries, and the Welsh have no pressure on them at all. It's a real one-off.

By the time they've corralled Rob's children the game's starting, so it's going to be first half on the radio, quick breakfast, and home for the second. Fair enough, really, given Donald wasn't expecting to watch any of it.

By the time they pull up beneath the Golden Arches, the omens aren't good. Wilkinson has popped over a couple of nice penalties, but it sounds as if Wales are outplaying the English. Radio is a lousy medium for rugby because you don't get a sense of the physical battle and who's pressuring whom up front, but as Rob reluctantly switches off the ignition, and the radio with it, it seems to be all Wales.

Rob flashes Donald a worried look. It now feels almost sinful to be heading into the restaurant to sit down, while the men in white are backs-against-the-wall in the World Cup quarter-final.

'Drive-thru,' says Rob, gesturing towards the big red sign directing traffic round the back of the building.

'Brilliant,' says Donald, and they duck back into the jeep and get the radio back on smartly.

Things are getting worse. Wales score a try. England seem to be suffering a series of brain wobbles. Tindall kicks the ball aimlessly in no particular direction, and Wales launch a counter-attack and score. It sounds like an absolutely awesome try. Shit. England can't possibly lose this, can they? Penalty to Wales. They don't kick it. Try. Shit! Missed conversion, but it's half time and Wales are seven points up.

What happens if England lose? Donald thinks to himself. Will they still go to Sydney? Surely not. He wouldn't want to go to the other side of the world to watch a bunch of Antipodeans play France in the final, for goodness' sake, or, worse yet, watch England fight it out in a meaningless third place play-off. And yet he very much doubts the flights are refundable. They'd be able to flog the tickets without a problem, but the flights . . . unlikely.

But Donald still doesn't believe England will lose. They've underperformed in the tournament so far. They were level with South Africa at the halfway point, down against Samoa and they're down again today. And so far, somehow, on each occasion they have come through reasonably comfortably in the end. These are battle-hardened old war-horses out there. Gnarled professionals who have learned how to win even when things aren't going well for them. And they'll do it again. Won't they? Surely.

Donald leads the column into his and Judy's house, kicking off his shoes and listening out for his wife. To his huge surprise, he can hear the telly. She's watching the rugby! What a dark horse! Donald was convinced her interest in the tournament, which was purely romantic anyway, had been snuffed out when England beat Samoa. But no, she's watching, and he is gobsmacked.

'Hiya,' she calls out jovially. 'Good timing. Second half's about to start.'

'I know. We've been listening.'

The word 'we' provokes Judy to turn round in the armchair, and she can see Rob and his kids getting un-shoed.

'Hi Rob,' she shouts.

'Hi Judy. Didn't know you were into the rugby.'

'Neither did I, but I must admit it's quite exciting.'

Donald shakes his head at Rob, and they both smile.

'Women! I don't know . . .' Rob says.

'Clare's watching it too, you know,' says Judy happily. It's as though there's something conspiratorial going on.

'You're kidding me!' Rob seems genuinely surprised.

'Nope. Anyway, come on in and sit down. Fancy a coffee?'

'I could murder one,' says Rob.

'Mmm,' Donald adds. He didn't risk a McDonald's coffee for fear of scalding himself, so he's gasping for one.

'Donald, would you?' Judy is looking up at him with that girly, sheepish look she adopts when she's trying to bribe him, and he knows he's going to have to give in.

'Good God, what's this?' he protests lamely. If she starts watching sport *and* soaps, he's in trouble.

'It's going to have to be instant, OK?' he announces, as he quickly slips out to the kitchen and pops the kettle on.

'Oh, come on, Wales!' shouts Judy, and then smiles impishly at Rob and Donald, who are sitting next to each other on the couch.

Judy's half Scots, but she's far more nationalistic about her Samoan heritage, and as a rugby fan, she'd probably quite like to see England beaten by whoever plays against them. Donald can't quite work out if she's at all serious this time, though. She's probably winding them up. She can see they're a little tense.

But England have come out strongly after half time. Woodward has brought Catt on and pushed Tindall out to the wing. Interesting choice, and one that Rob thinks is utterly daft. Donald's not so sure. Wilkinson looked uncharacteristically shaky in the first half, and with Catt's experience, he might just settle down and play a bit.

Then Robinson gets the ball, and he's away. Ripping the Wales defence open like a sharp knife slicing through a chunk of Emmental. Brilliant. They've got to score! He slings it out to Greenwood and . . . YES! Greenwood's in! The two men explode.

'YEAAAAAAAAAAAAAAAAAAAAAAAAAAAAAAAAAAAAAH!' they scream in a stereophonic, guttural roar, and jump spontaneously to their feet.

Emily appears in the doorway to check out the noise. Judy

is looking at Donald and Rob with a slight frown, rather as David Attenborough would if a giant anteater stood up on its hind legs and lit a fag.

'Steady on,' she says.

She doesn't get it. Donald knew she didn't, despite her apparent newfound love of sport. This is important. Seriously important, and it would be even if they didn't have the carrot of watching England in the final dangling tantalisingly in front of their eyes. There is just no way women will ever care about sport as much as men. It's just not in their DNA.

Wilkinson converts brilliantly from the corner. One of those laser-like kicks he does where, from the camera angle behind him, you can tell it's going over from the moment his boot makes contact. So can he, and he's picking up the tee and chucking it to the sidelines before the ball is halfway there.

Nerves are calmed, and it seems the natural order of things has been re-established. England are in control, and Wales are struggling to hold on. Possession, that's the key. England have got it, and the Welsh haven't, and the penalties are starting to come. Wilkinson isn't one to look gift horses, blah blah blah. Pop. Pop. In what seems like the blink of an eye, England are up by six points.

Pop. Pop. With a quarter of the match left, England are twelve up. They've scored twenty-two unanswered points and it looks reasonably safe at last. Donald looks over at Rob, who's biting his nails. He notices Judy watching him, still with a look of some bemusement. What's her problem? he thinks, but doesn't say anything.

Oh bollocks. Wales score another try, and much to Donald's annoyance, Judy yelps with delight and bounces up and down in her chair. Maybe she cares after all, but why the hell is she supporting Wales?

'Do you have some Welsh blood you didn't tell me about?' he says angrily.

She says nothing, but settles down.

Wales pressure, but no score. Minutes left. Jonny drop-goal. England are safe.

When the whistle goes, Rob and Donald shake hands. They give each other a look full of relief and excitement about what's to come. Judy's watching them again.

Chapter Eighteen

It's always a very special, tender moment. Donald is lying in bed with Judy's tousled, dark head on his chest. They have just made love and a wonderful peace has descended. They are wordlessly enjoying each other, the warmth, the familiarity, the oneness that one can just about get without sex, but that sex is uniquely able to perpetuate.

Sex is the subject of much banter between the three men – always has been – but as they get older, the conversations are more revealing, more honest, and it becomes clear that they all have problems from time to time. It's not as easy as it's supposed to be. Donald often keeps his confidence on such occasions, primarily because he has no wish to rub the others' noses in it. For whatever reason, and the most likely reason is that he and Judy have never had to deal with the all-absorbing, fatiguing experience of parenthood, they have never had a problem with their sex life. That is, apart from the month or so after he lost his job, when he lost both his desire and his ability to get involved. They still make love pretty much every night, and Donald is quietly relieved that he seems to be doing considerably better than either of his two close friends.

Judy's breathing is deep and regular and Donald is wondering if she's nodding off. His mind keeps flitting back to the rugby, like a bird building a nest. England are in the semis, and it's France. They'll have to step up a gear, but Donald thinks they will. They really will.

Suddenly Judy shifts her position in bed, clearly awake. 'Donald, I need you to hold my legs up.'

'What?'

'Oh, and can you grab that cushion off the chair and put it under the small of my back?'

'What? Judy, what are you talking about?'

'I just realised, it's the perfect time of the month. Perfect, to the day. And the book says if I put my legs up now for half an hour I think it is, it gives us the maximum chance.'

'Of getting pregnant,' Donald says. He knows, of course, but there is irritation in his voice.

'No, of winning the lottery, dummy. Now come on. Please?'

Donald slides out of bed and grabs the cushion off the wicker chair in the corner of the bedroom, and Judy arches her back, allowing him to slide it into a supporting position. She pulls up her knees.

'OK, so if you just gently push my legs up now and hold them there, the sperm – '

'All right, all right, spare me the gynaecology lesson.'

Donald lifts his wife's legs and gently pushes in, as though he's helping her through a pre-match hamstring stretch.

'Hey, hold on. I'd like to be able to breathe, please,' says Judy, her voice somewhat strangulated by the angle Donald has created.

He eases off.

'Judy, we just had sex,' he says.

'Yes, love, and it was super, but we are trying to get pregnant, aren't we?'

'Yes, but . . .'

'But what?'

'But . . . don't you think we might be trying too hard?'

'Darling, I'm not sure I understand what trying too hard means. We want kids more than anything, we've been working at it for nearly a year, so now we have to work a bit harder. It's obviously not going to just happen by us clicking our fingers. So we need to give ourselves the best possible chance.'

'I'm sure it will happen when it's meant to happen. We should just enjoy sex and let the biology take care of itself, don't you think?'

Judy lets out a yelp.

'I've got cramp in my foot. Give it a squeeze! No! Not that one, the other one!'

Donald massages Judy's contorted foot until she stops wincing.

'I just think the more uptight we are about getting pregnant, the less likely it is to happen.'

'Donald, that's psycho-babble,' says Judy. 'I'm thirty-eight years old and not getting younger, and I need to get on with it. If we can't conceive naturally, we may need to look at IVF or something, and I'd rather know sooner than later. Can't you see that?'

'Yes. Yes I can.'

Donald sighs and Judy shuts her eyes and tries to relax, despite the unnatural amount of blood circulating around her skull.

Secretly, Donald has been having second thoughts about having children. Yes, they were desperate, but the charade about his and Judy's modern decision not to have children has become tiresome. It's a heavy lie to have to keep telling. And when Donald looks at what has recently happened to Brian and Tanya, and the gradual degradation in their relationship since Olivia was born, it makes him wonder. He and Judy have a wonderful, sound, supportive relationship. So why tamper with a magic formula?

Of course, he doesn't mean it. Not really. Donald has always wanted children. But his ego has taken enough of a beating recently without being told he's sterile. OK, it may not be him – Judy may have some problem – but it's a distinct possibility. Donald has always felt that sex is something he's good at. He can't bear the thought that even in that sphere of his life he falls short. Please God, no.

'OK, love, that'll do,' says Judy, and Donald gently lowers her limbs to mattress level.

She gently takes one of his hands and places it on her warm belly. She makes to say something, but stops.

'I just felt something kick,' says Donald.

Judy takes his hand away and gives it a good-natured slap.

She reaches for the bedside light and turns it off, and the two of them lie in silence.

'When were you going to tell me?' Judy says, her voice just louder than a whisper.

Donald is trying to think what she means. It sounds like the conversation they had about him losing his job all over again, but it can't be that. He's flummoxed.

'Tell you what, love?' he says, with genuine innocence in his voice.

There's a pause. Not pregnant, exactly, although you never know.

'That you, Rob and Brian are going to Sydney to watch the final of the rugby?'

There's something in the way she's said it that makes it absolutely clear she knows. In other words, there's no point in Donald playing innocent. But how the fuck did she—?

'I found your tickets. To the game.'

'What the hell were you doing in my underwear drawer?' Donald asks, indignantly. It's an automatic response. 'I threw all the briefs out – the ones you thought would make me sterile. I told you that.'

'I was packing for your camping, remember? And as you know, I prefer it when you don't wear your pants for three days before throwing them in the wash.'

Donald is chastened. Her voice isn't antagonistic, which is good, but he's at a loss to really work out where she's at. She ought to be pissed off with him, but she isn't. So he's not sure how to play this. He can feel the initial shock of her discovery wearing off and a familiar gnawing churn of guilt beginning in the pit of his stomach. It's not that the tickets are a particularly big deal in their own right – it's a minor deceit – it's the bigger theme of Donald holding things back from Judy. Big things. Huge things. They haven't talked about it much recently, and he doesn't feel like talking about it now. It's still too painful.

'I was going to tell you, love,' he says, pathetically.

Her head's still on his chest. He is staring at the ceiling.

'That's good of you, Donald.' There's sarcasm there, but not biting. Her voice is still soft, too.

'We've been trying to get enough BlokeMiles, you know.'
She chuckles. 'You men are pathetic, you know that?'
He nods in agreement.

'I mean, for God's sake, why didn't you just ask? Because by being all sneaky about going to the final, you've screwed up the whole BlokeMiles idea. It's like you just created it as a sly way of getting what you wanted. The whole point was that we'd all be more open with each other, and yet you've ended up not being open at all. Why, Donald?'

Donald sighs. On the matt white ceiling above him, he can almost imagine a multiple choice of potential answers appearing. Something like:

a) We were worried you'd say no, and even if you said yes, you'd lay a big guilt-trip on us that would weigh us down for weeks afterwards.

b) We wanted to wait to see if England reached the final.

c) It's the BlokeMiles pitch.

He takes a deep breath and goes for c. 'I think the whole idea behind BlokeMiles has been this feeling that we shouldn't really have to ask.'

He needs some eye contact for this, so sits himself up, switches on the bedside lamp and manoeuvres Judy so she has to prop her head up on her arm. He looks into her brown eyes and plunges forward, like an explorer hacking his way through a jungle with a machete, not sure if he's going to find a clearing or get bitten by a deadly viper.

'I mean, asking you for permission is a bit like a schoolboy asking his mum if he can go out to play with his mates. And that's sometimes how it feels for us. It's not your fault or anything . . . It's more us. We still want to be blokes as well as husbands. But without the guilt.'

Just as he's getting going, getting a real head of steam up, starting to sound convincing, he's hit a wall. Judy's got him fixed in her gaze, sharp as razor blades, unblinking. 'Right, and me, Clare and Tanya all thought it was a great idea. We understood, you silly oaf. But . . . and I know this is difficult, but you have to admit you are in a slightly different category. Don't you? I mean, you can see how Rob and Brian have to be fathers as well. It's just . . . and don't take this the wrong way, but BlokeMiles does seem to be more designed for the others rather than us.'

That hurts. It's not what Donald wanted to hear. That basically he's been tagging along with BlokeMiles despite the fact he doesn't have the same excuses Rob and Brian have. He considers his defence. No, she's wrong. BlokeMiles isn't just the domain of couples with kids. The point is, couples need to be individuals too. They need space to be themselves. All true, but does the trade-off need to be institutionalised?

Judy sits up and puts a hand through her husband's hair and then rests it on the back of his neck, gently rubbing upwards against the grain of his hair. She seems to be on his side. Which is nice.

'It's OK, love. BlokeMiles is a fun idea. And it's not irrelevant to us. It was wonderful that you went on the camping trip in the end. Apart from anything, you were a great help to Brian.'

Donald is deep in thought. He can see now that BlokeMiles is really designed to untangle complex scenarios, where couples can lose track of who they are, can forget what it's like to be happy, can become cast adrift from the way they used to be. Of course, it can happen without children on the scene, but their arrival is the most common catalyst. No doubt about that.

'You know,' says Donald, sighing and scratching his chin. 'I really think one of the reasons I wanted to be part of the BlokeMiles thing was that I knew we were trying. You know, to have kids. I've seen how tough it is for Rob and Brian, and I wanted to experience it for myself somehow. In case we have kids ourselves.'

'What do you mean, in case we have kids? We are going to have kids.'

Donald looks at his wife and smiles. 'I know we are, love.' *Please God, make it true.*

Chapter Nineteen

Donald's redundancy came completely out of the blue. He was running a successful branch of a provincial chain of estate agents serving the well-heeled Surrey commuter belt around Guildford and Dorking, and his bosses – whom he rarely saw – were mild-mannered baldies in their late fifties. His business was doing reasonably well – they'd had a drop-off over the previous quarter, but nothing to panic about – but they sat him down and told him they were closing it down. Nothing personal, they said; he'd done a good job, they said; but there was a squeeze coming, they said; and they were consolidating his branch into the Dorking office. Donald remembers thinking, briefly, maybe he could run the new, enlarged business, and then he realised he was looking at the man who was going to do that. A partner in the firm. And although he appeared relatively healthy, those dusty brown brogues he was sporting bore all the hallmarks of Dead Men's Shoes.

Donald has since considered how Rob and Brian would have handled what he went through. Rob, he's not absolutely sure about. Maybe he'd have shrugged his shoulders and found something else in no time at all. He has this uncanny ability to land on his feet even when he's been tossed a mile in the air. It seems to come to him with minimal effort, though Donald suspects that's something of an illusion. You make your own luck.

Then there's Brian, who has actually suffered humiliation after humiliation at his workplace. OK, he's not been made redundant, but the powers that be in that firm – crusty old sods, from what he says – expect blood, sweat and tears, and yet dish out ladles of pious contempt in return. He's had promotions promised and then withdrawn, he's had his pay cut when the business was struggling, he's been hauled into an oak-clad office to be dressed down like an insubordinate school kid . . . so what, Donald thinks to himself, has kept Brian bouncing back?

The most likely answer is rage. Brian seems to have a healthy current of raw anger that lives only just below the surface of his skin. And rather than get him in trouble, as you might expect, it protects him. How? By arming him with this drive to prove the fuckers wrong. He doesn't feel used. He feels he's sticking two fingers up, and that keeps him sane.

There was no such anger for Donald, and that was his undoing. He was shocked, mystified even. But it was quite clear that this was non-negotiable. They offered him a reasonable, if not exactly generous redundancy package, so he cleared his desk and walked out. He felt almost no emotion at all. It was as though he'd agreed to have a small piece of his frontal lobe sliced off as he left the building.

He got home as usual, kissed his wife, ate his dinner, and went to bed. Judy surmised, after her enthusiastic frottage had failed to produce a reaction, that he wasn't in the mood for sex, but didn't think anything of it. Donald slept surprisingly soundly, and the next morning got up, put on his jacket and tie, and left the house, like a robot mindlessly following its program.

Despite the outward signs of denial, Donald knew what he was doing. He consciously compared himself to stories he had heard about Japanese 'salarymen', who do something similar when they've been fired, or laid off. They just keep coming into work, pretending nothing has happened, and the rest of the staff play along with it. It's a face-saving thing, designed to buy them time to work out what to say to their wives.

Donald's recollection of that morning is hazy. He walked for miles, stopped and had breakfast somewhere . . . then the rest is a blur.

It's as though he had a chance. There was a window to get

mad, get angry, get even, and he missed that one, so was consigned to a world of numbed feelings. And there was a window for him to tell Judy what had happened, get it all out there and get on with his life. But he missed that, too – walked right by both open windows – and suddenly found himself in a very frightening world that he didn't know. A lonely place where he felt as though his friends were cardboard cut-outs and his wife and his future with her was kind of make-believe. He couldn't be sure it wouldn't be snatched away at any moment.

And so it went on, until midway through the second week, when Donald woke up on one of those autumn days when the sun was on strike. It was windy and drizzly, and he felt as though he had to stretch his eyelids to attract sufficient light in. He couldn't face leaving the house, so he told Judy he was feeling under the weather. She left for work, and Donald was alone.

At least leaving home every morning, sitting in the library or just walking, got him out and about and helped create the illusion in his mind that he was doing something. Alone in the house, he felt as though the walls were closing in. He had no idea what to do with himself. He paced from room to room, unable to escape the sense of claustrophobia and panic. His head was imploding and he felt shaky, on the verge of tears. Technically, he was probably having some kind of nervous breakdown, or possibly he'd been experiencing a kind of slow-burning breakdown for the past ten days and this was just the culmination. The overwhelming sensation was that he didn't deserve to be alive.

Well, what to do? A suicide attempt? It was a ridiculous notion. How on earth could he consider ending it all when he had Judy? His rock. His wonderful rock, who had got him through everything up to now. But something felt different. His tank of self-esteem – always susceptible to random evaporation – seemed to have run dry this time.

I've got Judy, yes, but she's too good for me. I'm dragging her down with me. I am unworthy of her. I'm impotent, consigning Judy to a life without children. I'm overweight. I'm a loser. An underachiever. I'll never be able to change.

What's the point? Even my father, my stupid fucking father, had a successful career before he threw it all away.

Donald hadn't thought of his father for a very long time. Andrew Lewis had been the perfect role model while Donald was growing up. He was the chairman of a large London law-firm. He was tall, confident, wealthy, and Donald revelled in his father's sheer invincibility, until the day he self-destructed.

The firm had suffered a series of major public embarrassments, including an over-zealous defence of a politician accused of paedophilia. The man was later convicted, and Donald's father's firm was discredited to the point of ruin. Andrew was voted off the board of the company he had run for the best part of twenty years. It seemed to him like the ultimate betrayal, and it destroyed him. Within a week, he had hanged himself in his office. There was no note.

Donald had been seventeen years old at the time, and such had been the depth of his shock, he wasn't even able to cry. His mother had tried to encourage him to grieve for his father, but the teenager's only way of dealing with the tragedy was to pretend it never happened, to wipe it from his memory.

When his mother died two years later, Donald's tears flowed. But still the part of his brain where his father's memory lay remained locked away, the secret combination lost.

Until the day Donald wondered if suicide might be the answer. He looked at himself in the mirror, and saw his father staring sternly back. He wondered what his father would have made of him. He'd been average at school, a solid worker, decent O-levels, but nothing special. His incredible water polo success had come well after Andrew's death – perhaps he'd have approved of that. And his career? An estate agent? How his father would have scoffed.

But if his father could commit suicide, after all he'd achieved, then maybe it was good enough for Donald. *Suicide. It's in the genes. Judy will understand. Like father, like son.* But how to do it? His father had hanged himself, but that was far too gruesome for Donald. The idea of being found like that was abhorrent. No, it would have to be some other way.

Suddenly he was businesslike. Judy had the Saab, but the little Honda Civic was in the garage, where it had been for months, more or less untouched since they bought the new one. They tried selling it but couldn't get a half-decent price. He rummaged around in the garage looking for something he could use to divert the fumes from the exhaust in through the rear window. Where was the garden hose? Shit, he'd lent it to Brian. He racked his brains. Surely you didn't have to go to Do-It-All and tell some spotty youth that you needed a hose long enough to fill the interior of a Honda with deadly gas? Surely people who decided to take their own lives just did it? Surely it didn't need advanced planning? He was starting to feel even more inadequate, if that were possible.

He went back in the house and consulted the mirror again, but this time he saw something different. It was a sad face, framed with glasses, but there was something else there. Courage. Some kind of inner strength. Honesty. Integrity. He saw himself. Donald Lewis. A good man. Judy's husband. And he began to cry. How could he throw it away? *I am not my father*, he said to himself. *I am not suicidal*. He sobbed. Uncontrollable, heaving sobs, tears flooding down his face. He cried for himself, but most of all, he grieved for his old man.

Donald wonders if Rob quite realises how crucial a contribution he made to his life when he found him breaking down in the back garden that evening. He was so low, he had become irrational. He felt utterly alone, because not only was he harbouring a terrible secret, but he was nurturing the idea that Rob and Brian were thick as thieves and he was the outsider. It's true, he does feel that from time to time, because he isn't quite carved from the same stone as those two. First off, he went to public school, and whilst people tend to think that public schoolboys create an exclusive life club for themselves, Donald has found quite the opposite to be true. If anything, he tries to keep his schooling quiet, lest it turns people against him. With Rob and Brian, of course, there's no issue. Their friendship cuts through all the crap, though Brian does occasionally get hung up on the idea that a privileged education gives people a head start. Probably something to do with the plonkers he has to work with.

There's also the sport thing. They're both slim, athletic types who can eat copious quantities of junk food without appearing to put on an ounce of weight. Donald considers himself a bit of a fat bastard – well, perhaps not fat, but shall we say endo rather than ectomorphic – and he does bugger-all exercise these days, but he's always had a very natural residual strength. It annoys the others that despite their laudable discipline in going to the gym on a regular basis, Donald can still lie down and bench-press considerably more than either of them. And arm wrestling's no contest.

But the fact is, Donald thinks the two of them have a lot in common and sometimes, just occasionally, he feels as though he's on the outside looking in, rather than the other way round.

And that night, what with the weight of shame he was already carrying, the feeling of exclusion drove him right to the edge. He was standing on the precipice looking straight down when Rob appeared out of nowhere and yanked him back. It was like a hypnotist clicking his fingers to wake his subject. He was suddenly aware, and he talked to Judy that night. He sat her down the moment the front door had shut and their guests had left.

'Judy, there's something I have to tell you.' Donald ushered his wife into the sitting room and sat her down.

'What's that?' She sounded worried, probably because of the look on his face.

He cleared his throat and sat down next to her.

'I lost my job.'

There. He'd said it. His ears rang with the deafening silence, as though the words were just hanging there in the thick atmosphere.

Judy looked at him, her eyes watery, and then enveloped him in a huge hug. It wasn't quite what he was expecting.

'Oh, Donald. You poor thing.'

He cleared his throat again.

'Er . . . I . . . lost my job. It happened . . . about . . . a month ago.'

She pulled away sharply and stared uncomprehendingly at him. And another silence, even heavier and much more awful than the last one, began to settle. Donald couldn't take it.

'I couldn't face telling you. I couldn't face telling anyone. I've been leaving the house every morning in a kind of daze.'

He could feel tears welling up now. Judy was still staring straight ahead, and he could see she was crying quietly, strongly, keeping it inside.

'And then,' he gasped. 'When I didn't tell you, I felt even more rotten about myself. I wanted to. I really, really wanted to.'

Judy let out a huge sob. It burst out of her, and she threw herself into Donald's arms. She seemed to be fighting a cocktail of emotions. Sad, for her, for him, but angry too. Her hands on his back kept alternating between gentle strokes, agitated scratches and the occasional full-blooded, hollow-sounding thump. They both cried into each other's faces, each other's hair. For minutes. It felt like days. And then they both regained control, their bodies stopped shaking, their breathing deepened, and they loosened their vice-like grips on each other.

'Why? Donald, why on earth didn't you tell me?' she whispered, looking straight at him, her eyes red-rimmed.

Donald knew it was the million-dollar question, and one he'd already asked himself countless times. Why didn't he?

'I felt worthless,' he said, feeling his way. 'Worse than useless. A failure. I felt as though someone had reached inside me and ripped out my . . . myself. Me.'

'Oh, Donald,' Judy breathed, putting her head in her hands.

'I should have just told you straight away, but when I didn't, every time you kissed me goodbye and said have a good day . . . and, even worse, every time you left to go to the office yourself, I just . . . I felt I had failed you, failed everyone, really.'

Looking back, Donald is sure Judy was really angry with him, but she didn't show it, and she hasn't since. Most likely, this is just the strategy she's adopted to try to help him through it. She must have felt massively betrayed. Probably still feels it. And God only knows what she'd feel if he'd told her he'd seriously considered suicide.

That was also the part he neglected to tell Rob. Perhaps he'd have come clean if he hadn't made such an embarrassing hash of it.

Chapter Twenty

Donald is sitting on a worn leather armchair, and the woman opposite him is not unattractive. Her dark hair, tied back in a ponytail, frames a pretty, round face with alabaster skin. She has intelligent, hazel eyes, magnified and intensified by the thick lenses of her rimless glasses.

'Does your wife know you're here?'

'No.'

'Lie down,' she says softly.

'What?' Donald had no idea what to expect before he entered the austere Victorian terrace, but he's taken off-guard.

'Please,' she says again, gesturing towards a matching sofa, the shine of the leather long since eroded by the constant pressure of prostrate bodies.

Donald hesitates. It's a little soon. He hardly knows this woman.

'All right, if you don't feel comfortable, that's fine. It's generally better on the sofa, but you do have to be relaxed.'

Donald sighs. 'OK,' he says. 'I'll give it a try.'

She doesn't move to assist him, just sits in her chair and watches him. Donald slowly rises and sits on the edge of the sofa. Dr Berkova nods. He swings his legs up and lowers himself until he's lying flat on his back. He feels vulnerable, and glances over at her again.

'Close your eyes. Don't worry; I'll just stay here.'

For the first time, Donald picks up the trace of an accent.

'Why did you feel such a failure? I know it must have hurt,

but being made redundant is not that uncommon. It happens to many men like you.'

Donald squeezes his eyelids tighter. 'It wasn't just that. I . . . I suppose I've always felt I've underachieved. Estate agency was such an easy option for me. I studied land management. But I was better than that. I should have done more. My father was chairman of a law firm. My friends . . . I just knew I should have had more ambition. I was too damned comfortable.'

Donald is suddenly deep in his own mind, unaware of his surroundings. He has forgotten he's lying on the couch in a Harley Street psychotherapist's front room.

'Plus we've . . . Judy and me . . . we can't seem to have a child. I don't know if it's me, but maybe because I'm a bit overweight, and . . . I don't know, it would just kind of finish me off if I was sterile as well.'

'You don't feel you're being a man?'

'No, of course I don't.'

'Or perhaps you're not fulfilling the role you believe a man should play.'

'I want to provide for a family. Be strong. Be solid. Reliable. But Judy is the strong one. She keeps me together. And we don't seem able to have a family.'

'You don't consider you and your wife a family?'

'I . . . well, no. Yes. We are, but we want children.'

'Of course. But at the moment, your wife is your family.'

'Yes.'

'And she helped you through your job loss, once you told her about it?'

'Yes. She did.'

'And what do you think Judy would say if she knew you were here?'

Donald shuts his eyes again. He hadn't realised they'd opened, but he'd been mesmerised by the ceiling rose. What would Judy think?

'She'd think it was a good idea, but . . .'

'But she'd be angry you didn't involve her?'

'Yes.'

'So why didn't you?'

'I don't know.'

It's not good enough, and Donald knows it. Dr Berkova knows it too, judging by the silence. She's good at silences. They aren't passive. They seem to possess their own sense of urgency.

'I think she deserves better than having to deal with a basket case. I want to sort myself out, but I don't want to drag her along while I do it.'

'Can you do it on your own?'

'Yes. Absolutely.'

'But wouldn't she rather be there, supporting you?'

'Yes.'

'And wouldn't you rather have her by your side?'

'Yes.'

'You see, in some ways you are being very selfish here, Donald. I know that is precisely the opposite of what you are trying to be, but by excluding your wife, who you have already said is a great source of strength, you are pushing her away. You are indulging yourself in your self-pity.'

'That's not what I want to do.'

'Exactly. You want to put the self-pitying behind you and find a way to move on. Right?'

'Right.'

Donald takes a deep breath, and sits up on the sofa. He feels momentarily dizzy.

'So should I bring Judy next time?'

'I think you should discuss it with her, and if she's happy, yes. Or she can come and see me herself. Eventually it's better that you come together.'

Dr Berkova gets up from her seat, walks to a huge mahogany desk and begins to leaf through her diary. Donald is startled to see her move. She'd almost become some kind of abstract entity to him.

'Er, Dr Berkova, can I ask you one more thing?'

'Of course,' she says, her back still turned.

'There's lots of stuff going on. The guys . . . my friends, they are just sort of getting on with things. Watching the rugby. Even planning a trip to Sydney for just the three of us.

We've got this BlokeMiles thing . . . But at the moment, I just can't let myself go. It doesn't feel right.'

'Why not?'

'Because of what's gone on.'

'That means you can't enjoy yourself? You're not allowed to be happy?'

Donald reflects on what she has said.

She approaches and stands opposite him, diary in hand. She is taller than he realised, only an inch or two shorter than he is.

'What does your wife think? Does she approve of you doing things with your male friends? Or does she want you to herself for a while?'

'No, no. She's fine with it. I think she just wants me to be happy.'

'Well, I think you have all the answers, Donald. But you must start involving your wife. Right now, you are pushing her away for some reason. You think you want to stop hurting her, or letting her down, but the way to do that is to embrace her into how you feel. Let her help you. She can help you better than I can.'

Donald nods. It is all making horrible amounts of sense. Why has he been so bloody stupid? He's confided in Rob. Poor old Rob. It must have been a nightmare for him. This isn't what male friendships are for.

'Do you want to explain . . . what did you call it, BoyMiles, to me? Is that what you said?'

Donald is surprised by the question, but it's one of the easiest he's had to tackle in the last half hour.

'BlokeMiles? It's just a way the chaps get to earn points so they can do their blokey things.'

'You scratch my back, I'll scratch yours?' There's a glint in Dr Berkova's eye.

'Yes. Sort of. What's so funny?'

She is chuckling now. 'My husband and I had exactly the same system in the Czech Republic when our children were smaller. We called it Chlåpske Mile. Kind of AirMiles for Men. It worked very well.'

'Now.' Dr Berkova is businesslike. 'How would Friday the twenty-first be for you?'

'What, November?'

'Yes.'

'Christ, no!'

Dr Berkova tilts her head quizzically, surprised by Donald's sudden animation.

'I'll be in Sydney!'

Chapter Twenty-one

With a doctor's note empowering him to lighten up, Donald has discovered a hitherto untapped entrepreneurial streak, and has become obsessed with the idea that BlokeMiles has some kind of commercial potential. He thinks most couples will relate to it, but particularly those with young kids. This idea of trading with each other so you can keep your own identity instead of letting it become subsumed by the pressures of parenthood: it resonates. So what if, say, there was a BlokeMiles credit card, maybe one for Him and one for Her. And both sides can earn and redeem points by spending money in certain establishments. Say, for instance, there's a chain of health spas that recognises BlokeMiles, so if Donald were to book Judy a day of luxury like the one the girls enjoyed a few weeks ago, and he used his special credit card to pay for it, he would accrue points. Or miles. And perhaps a deal could be struck with a chain of pubs so blokes get drinking vouchers in return for BlokeMiles. Interflora; there's another obvious target for the supply chain. Donald can envisage a little 'BlokeMiles recognised here' sign on the door of a flower shop, or a restaurant.

On the other hand, maybe the credit card idea is overcomplicating matters. Perhaps, instead, Donald should take advantage of his flair for computing – he's something of a self-confessed geek – and build a little software tool that couples can use at home. Just a little program that helps you keep a BlokeMiles balance, and illustrates how blokes can accrue miles in a way that will please their partners –

customizable, of course – and spend them in ways that satisfy their need to, well, be blokes.

His enthusiasm for BlokeMiles the Venture is tempered by the dull nag of pragmatism. He knows he should be shipping out CVs to estate agents instead of wasting time and energy on this. But he feels as though something's changed. He's somehow moved on, and his next career move needs to reflect that change. Bugger estate agency. Boring load of toss, anyway. And in many ways, he'd be making more appropriate use of his degree than he did with his old job. He certainly knows how to write a business plan, not to mention designing software using C++, and he resolves to do both when he gets back from Sydney. He's already registered the websites www.blokemiles.com, and www.blokemiles.co.uk. Just in case anyone tries to claim the idea for themselves.

Back in the real world, however, Donald is becoming increasingly worried that the BlokeMiles concept has been irrevocably soiled by the blokes' failure to come clean about the planned trip to Sydney. He's been thinking about what Judy said, and knows she's right. What were they so scared of? The whole bloody idea was that they stop being afraid of doing the things they want to do, because it's all taking place in a world where both sides are aiming to achieve a balance. And if going to Sydney happened to shift that balance too far in their favour, then they'd need to put some effort in on return to get things back in equilibrium. Big deal.

Despite all the good intentions, and the supposed epiphany they have all had about their lives, and their need to be blokes and good husbands – and fathers in some cases – at the same time, they still copped out hugely when it came to the crunch. They have all but proved the theory that there are two types of males: the bastards, who do what they want and sod the consequences; and the wimps. And there's this nagging sense in the back of all their minds that women, ultimately, find the bastards more exciting.

Donald is surprised how unfazed Judy seems to be about the big trip. She's hardly mentioned it since she told him she knew, and he's assuming that the unspoken agreement is that she won't tell Tanya or Clare. So he's not planning to tell the guys she's found out either. What's the point?

It's semi-final day, and it's non-negotiable. Not that any of the men needed to negotiate. After all, their wives know they love their rugby – always have – and that the business end of the tournament has arrived. Donald suspects they are quietly into it themselves, though they do their best to suppress it. Must be a female thing.

They are all round at Rob's – all meaning the entire extended family of parents and kids. Rob and Clare's tends to be the default destination for major sporting events, since he has the biggest telly.

The smell of coffee brewing and croissants warming has, over the last few weeks, become just as evocative as that first pint of ale in a smoky pub before a Six Nations game. Nine in the morning is an odd time to be watching rugby – or any sport, for that matter – but they all seem to have adjusted to it quite comfortably. And it's nice not to have to fritter away the morning, glancing impatiently at one's watch. You get up and you're right into it.

Rob and Brian are jumpy as all hell, not just because of the monumental importance of the game, but because there is unending traffic in and out of the lounge. The women are taking an unhealthy interest in proceedings, and of course children naturally follow. It actually doesn't bother Donald – he's one of those lucky few capable of enjoying a game regardless of potential distractions like screaming children. They are glancing anxiously around the room and at each other, and pretty soon something is going to be said. The players are lined up for the national anthems . . .

And then, as if by magic, a hush descends as the game is about to start. Startled, Donald looks around, and sees that Judy and Clare are perched on the other sofa. There are no children in sight. Tanya appears to have whisked them away to the playroom so the rest of them can enjoy the game. Miracles never cease.

It's a filthy evening in Sydney, by the look of it, with rain sweeping across the ground. And although it's not the done thing to admit it nowadays, there's no doubt in Donald's mind that this will help England, not France. They're fair-weather players, whereas our boys are perfectly happy to drown in mud for the cause if that's what it takes. He has a good feeling about this match, in stark contrast to his gloomy prognosis in this same room a few weeks back when he predicted a French victory. He can hardly bear to think about the demons he was grappling with such a short time ago.

Richard Hill has returned to the fold for the first time since being injured in England's opening match, and his absence has been sorely felt. Mike Catt is in for Tindall. Donald isn't quite as convinced of the wisdom of this decision, but either way he's feeling significantly more relaxed this morning than he has done before either of the last two England games.

Tanya slips into the room quietly and squeezes in between Clare and Judy. She looks absolutely stunning, wearing jeans that make her long legs look endless and a tight-fitting white T-shirt that accentuates her . . . figure. She's got a maroon cardigan draped over her shoulders, but it doesn't get in the way of the T-shirt, Donald observes thankfully. He doesn't think about Tanya sexually, of course, but objectively he considers her by far the most beautiful of the three wives. This objectivity mustn't be misconstrued. Judy is his woman, and she does it for him, with her incredible vibrancy that radiates out from her lovely face like a beacon. But she's quite large in the hips, so she can't quite glide the way Tanya does. Clare's gorgeous too, but she's tiny and Donald has a penchant for taller women.

'Everything OK?' whispers Clare.

'Yep. For the moment,' says Tanya, and the three women settle back to watch the game.

Donald notices that Rob and Brian are also watching the ladies. They're all a bit stunned, really, but nobody says a word and the game clicks into motion.

The French score a try, and the mood in Rob Pearson's lounge darkens. The try was a bit soft, but it's a big blow. In wet conditions, with two evenly matched sides, there aren't going to be many try-scoring chances, so this is not good.

It's also not a great time for Emily to enter the fray. She immediately makes for Rob, who recoils just for a split second before letting Emily climb up onto his thighs.

Michalak misses a couple of penalties, and Rob, Brian and Donald exchange nervous, wordless looks of relief. Then Wilkinson notches a penalty and England are only a point down. Then a drop goal – his second – and a huge penalty just before half time. Up by five points, having had the worse of the wind, and Donald is comfortable that England have a powerful grip on the game.

It has been the quietest forty minutes of rugby they have ever watched together. Perhaps it's the presence of the ladies. Maybe it's because this is the World Cup semi-final, and the team is in sight of a shot at a glory that no English man or woman has experienced since 1966. Maybe it's because the boys have got plane tickets and seats for the final burning holes in their consciences.

Even now, not much is being said. Rob disappears and then re-emerges with three cold lagers.

'Sorry chaps. Forgot to get Guinness.'

Brian and Donald shrug and accept the booty happily.

Judy gets up from the couch and heads for the door. Donald looks up at her and reaches back to touch her hand as she passes. Their eyes meet.

'I'm on second-half duty,' she says, heavily. 'Drew the other short straw.'

Donald wants to ask why she should have to caretake other people's children when she'd rather be watching the game, but realises it's a selfish line of thinking, and it's up to her anyway.

But he's struck by how organised they are. They genuinely want to watch this game, so they drew lots to see who'd be on kiddie duty – or rather, who wouldn't. Tanya did the first half, but got off lightly. Judy's going to have her work cut out. And Clare just looks smug, curled up on the sofa, watching the TV intently. It's a revelation.

The England players emerge from the tunnel looking confident. The French look a little rattled, and a few of them glance up at the skies as they run onto the pitch, as if cursing their luck, or maybe checking their alibi for an excuse when the match is finished and they're being asked if the conditions were the reason they lost. Bloody French. No guts. No stomach for the fight.

'We've got this, you know,' says Brian.

'Don't say that!' snaps Rob quickly.

'You're tempting fate, Brian,' Donald agrees.

It's a complete role reversal, of course. Brian's normally the one preaching the hackneyed platitudes that you must always respect your opponents, no matter how useless they might be. No game is won until it's won, blah blah. And yet here he is, on an occasion when the stakes are out of sight they're so high, and he's jumping to dangerous conclusions.

But he doesn't back down.

'No, really. Our forwards have got this completely under control, and the French know they're beaten. Look at their faces.'

They all do, and see the hard, gnarled, grim faces of the French forwards. They don't look beaten to Donald.

'The only chance they've got is if they score a lucky try in the next five minutes,' Brian carries on.

Rob mumbles something under his breath as the second half kicks off.

Maybe Brian's right. Wilkinson misses a couple of penalties, but then Betsen has a rush of blood to the head and pole-axes the England number ten after he's kicked for touch. Well after.

'Oi, you can't do that!' shrieks Clare, bouncing animatedly.

'Is he all right?' says Tanya softly, as they watch Wilkinson flat on his back, catching his breath. He gets slowly to his feet.

'Tough little bugger, isn't he?' says Judy. Donald hadn't even noticed her come back in.

'Send 'im off!' shouts Clare.

'Off, off, off!!' chant the three women in almost hysterical unison.

The referee has called Betsen over, and the rugged

Frenchman is doing his best to look incredulous. It's that uniquely French expression, with the lips pouting, eyes wide, the hands out, palms pointing to the sky, shoulders hunched in a disbelieving shrug. But the truth is he's culpable as hell, and he knows it. The tall, balding referee brandishes the yellow card and is clearly heard to say 'that's absolutely crazy, he got the kick away', and Betsen trudges to the sin-bin, ripping off his head-guard in disgust. He slumps onto the bench by the side of the pitch.

'I thought he was going to the sin bin,' says Clare, her forehead creased with puzzlement.

'He is. He has,' explains Rob.

'Oh,' Clare says, sounding like a disappointed child unwrapping yet another dull book for Christmas. 'I thought they had to go to a special room or something. I mean, I can't believe he's just allowed to sit there and watch the game!'

Donald watches Rob to see if he's going to go on the attack, but he's smirking at his wife. He's going to spare her a real lashing, if not let her off scot-free.

'So what did you think, love? They have to go and cool off in a padded cell?'

Brian can't resist. 'Or they're suspended in a chair with the flames of hell licking their arses, while the devil prances about in front of them.'

Judy and Tanya turn and microwave him with their best withering looks. Oops. Clare just looks sorry for herself.

'Why's it called a sin bin then?' she says, but the joke's over.

'We should win now, shouldn't we?' asks Tanya quietly.

Donald realises she's looking at him, and it's a genuine question. She clearly sees him as the authority, which is quite a responsibility.

He clears his throat, but Brian answers.

'Yep. That's it now. They've blown it.'

It's all very weird. Normally the room would be full of familiar male banter, but today most of it is coming from their wives, who are taking an interest in the rugby for the first time, and yet seem unfeasibly into it. And Brian is being uncharacteristically gung ho, while Rob and Donald struggle to get a word in. Very odd indeed.

Another penalty, another drop-goal – perhaps Wilkinson is practising for the final – and the French are in disarray. Michalak misses another penalty and is substituted. The much-hyped battle of the fly-halves is over. The pretender to Wilkinson's throne has been vanquished. He'll have his day, but this isn't to be it. Donald allows himself, for the first time, to acknowledge that it really is over for them. There's even a pang of sympathy, but he quashes it quickly. After all, this is the French we're talking about. Would they feel sorry for us? Would they hell.

Tindall is on. Another penalty and the whistle goes. England are in the final.

Donald is on his feet, hugging Brian, then Rob, and there's a knowing firmness in those hugs. It's like they're saying IT'S ON! And then they spectate, jaws bouncing off chests, as they notice that their wives are jumping around the sofa, yelping and hugging. Then they approach the men, and it's all convivial hugs and kisses and *ooh, isn't it exciting* in squeaky voices. It is utterly bewildering.

Not surprisingly, no one has been in a particular hurry to leave. More Stella has been opened, and the girls are drinking wine. The kids, whose behaviour has been stellar, are now milling in and out of adult legs happily. Clare has ordered some pizzas, Rob has just gone to see if he's got any champagne . . . it's a party atmosphere, make no mistake.

There is indeed a supply of champagne and Rob starts filling ice buckets. Brian and Donald join him in the kitchen.

'Er, guys,' says Donald. 'You do realise we're flying on Wednesday night?'

Rob looks up sharply. 'Christ,' he says.

'When are we going to tell them?' asks Brian.

'I think now,' Donald says. 'Today, while we're all on a high. I mean, they seem just as excited as us. I don't think they'll be too worried.'

'Apart from the fact we've had tickets all this time and didn't tell them,' says Brian sullenly.

'Fuck it. Let's get it over with,' says Rob, grinding a second bottle of Waitrose bubbly into its nest of ice cubes. 'When we've all got champagne. We'll announce it as though it's a nice surprise, rather than something we feel shit about.'

Brian shrugs. Donald nods, but of course it's not really his problem. His wife already knows. He's thinking about what he'll pack. Thinking about the flight. Thinking about the hotel Rob managed to get them into last week in some seedy part of town called Surry Hills. Through luck rather than judgement, Donald has already confronted the awkward moment now facing Brian and Rob. He feels for them.

It takes a while for the champagne to reach an appropriate level of chilledness, during which time a small island of pizza has been consumed, a couple more lagers necked – glasses of chardonnay for the ladies – and the group has further settled into a lovely warm, hazy cloak of collective bonhomie. Rob has decided the time is right, and he's brought in a tray of twinkling, full champagne glasses, each shrouded with a crisp mist of cool condensation. Everyone takes a glass, and Rob steadies himself, shooting one final reassuring glance towards Donald and Brian. Fair play to him, Donald thinks. He is always the one to step up to the plate at times like this.

'Well,' he starts, choosing his words carefully. 'We're in the Rugby World Cup final!'

There's a spontaneous cheer, and they all chink their glasses. Nobody drinks, though, because Rob clearly hasn't reached the punchline yet.

'And there's something we – myself and my two old mates, Donald and Brian here – want to tell you.'

A hush falls, and Donald looks around at the faces of the three women. There's nothing too alarming. Clare has one of her quizzical expressions, Judy looks blank, and Tanya's head is tilted expectantly. No rats have been smelt yet.

'A few weeks ago, one of us – I can't remember who – came up with the idea of the three of us going out to the final in Sydney to watch England bring home the trophy.'

Judy is now sporting a smirk. So is Clare. Her eyes are saying don't you dare! Tanya's face hasn't changed.

Rob's hesitating, and Donald can almost see his brain getting hot with the effort of finding a tactful way to say what he has to say.

'Our idea was, we'd earn a stack of BlokeMiles, and wait to see if England made it to the final. And there didn't seem much point in worrying you about it, in case they lost and the whole idea was null and void.'

Clare puts her champagne glass down on the table just slightly too aggressively. Tanya is gently shaking her head.

Oh shit. Donald has no idea where Rob is going with this, so he fixes his eyes on the little bubbles in his champagne glass. It's kind of interesting watching them pinging to the surface.

'But, of course we had to make provisions. Which we did. We managed to score tickets to the final, and get cheap flights and accommodation. And we're off on Wednesday night.'

Donald has a huge amount of respect for Rob. He's a wordsmith by trade, and he has a knack with the language, no doubt about it. Usually his little speeches are beautifully constructed and Donald is left thinking, *Christ, I could never have done that.* But this one's different. It's a dog's breakfast. He has cocked it up well and truly, and instead of the rapturous applause that wasn't exactly likely anyway but you never know, there is a rasping silence. It's as though he got halfway through that sentence and then panicked. Or maybe he just got tired of trying to find the right words, so blurted out the truth: unspun, naked and vulnerable.

'Hope you don't mind,' says Rob, lowering himself into the coffin and pulling the lid shut. 'Cheers,' he adds, half-heartedly holding up his glass and taking a large, windy slug before anyone's had a chance to say anything.

Donald swallows, briefly letting the bubbles burn the back of his tongue before gulping the champagne down. Brian is sipping his and shifting uneasily from foot to foot. The silence is painful and embarrassing, and it feels as though it's going to go on for ever.

'Well,' sighs Clare. 'It doesn't sound as though we have a great deal of choice.'

'Oh, I don't know,' says Rob. He's already pouring himself

another glass, impatiently waiting for the froth to subside before filling himself up to the brim. 'You could always say, "There is absolutely no way you are going to Sydney for the weekend." '

Donald can't believe his ears. Nor can Brian, from the look of him. His mouth is hanging open spastically. But Donald can see now that Rob has that rebellious look in his eye. The one he gets when he's half cut. The one that occasionally requires his friends to extricate him from hairy situations with thugs who will break every bone in Rob's body, and his and Brian's to boot.

'And what response would I get?'

Clare's ill advisedly rising to the bait, but then again, these two love these little ritual fights.

Rob looks drunkenly defiant, but there's a smile somewhere in his face.

'I'd say, I'll see you, baby!'

'Shakin' that ass,' mutters Brian quietly, ostensibly to himself.

Judy snorts a mouthful of champagne painfully out through her nose and shrieks 'Ow! Fuck!'

The ice is broken. The rugby gods, the marriage gods, the BlokeMile gods or whoever, but someone, definitely, is in a benevolent mood.

Tanya starts giggling, then chuckling, then she catches Clare's eye and they're both laughing hysterically.

They're all doing it. Guffawing painfully, clutching stomachs, trying not to spill champagne. Children are appearing, like little angels summoned by the spontaneous outpouring of mirth, and they are looking up at the grown-ups with concerned faces. In their worlds, they must be seeing their parents going completely mad. And they're not far wrong.

Chapter Twenty-two

The boys are flying to Sydney this evening. Donald has frittered away the day, packing, unpacking, thinking. And repacking. And rethinking. He has a nervous, hollow feeling in the pit of his stomach. It's not a fear thing, more an anticipated sense of longing. He can remember the same sensation, aged fifteen, the day his first ever girlfriend moved to the States. They spent a day together, killing time, hardly speaking. After she'd gone, of course, he just cried. But the worst feeling of all was waiting for it to happen.

That feeling has returned today and Donald is trying to work out why. After all, he's about to go to Australia with the boys – what a blast! He should be thrilled. But he's afraid of leaving his wife alone, not because he doesn't believe she can take care of herself without him, but because he feels so incredibly close to her right now. Their relationship feels so precious and delicate, he wants to treasure every moment, so whilst he's looking forward to the trip, he feels sad at the same time. He and Judy have shared so much that it seems to have brought them closer, if that were possible. And Donald is equally convinced it has made their desire – their need – for a child even stronger.

His thoughts have been swinging wildly between the emotions of the recent past and the excitement of the next few days, which should be massively enjoyable, not a little drunken, and thrilling to boot. Being in that huge stadium, amongst the gold paraphernalia of the Aussies and the white of the England fans, watching history being made ... it brings him out in goose bumps. And now that it's just one match, it really does feel monumentally significant. Can they do it? Can they hold their nerve? England should really win – they've beaten Australia something like four or five times in a row. But in a way, that makes it worse. What if they lose? How will they cope with the scorn of the Aussies? Donald has never been Down Under, but it's not difficult to see how cocksure they are as a sporting nation, and just how much they love putting one over on the Poms. They'd be insufferable.

Judy arrives back from work at around 5 p.m. and immediately picks up her husband's mood. Strangely, there seems to be very little to talk about.

'I felt like shit today,' she says, and idly starts unpacking Donald's suitcase.

He's a little taken aback, as he thought he'd done a pretty good job of it, and had been especially careful to ensure that the top couple of layers of clothes were neatly folded. But Judy knows better. She picks off the shirts at the top and exposes the rest as a complete shambles.

Donald has particularly big feet, so packing shoes is invariably a headache for him. Shoes and sponge bags. Judy quietly gets on with reorganising his possessions, whilst in some kind of trance. It occurs to Donald for one cynical moment that she might be looking for yet more hidden clues, things he's not bothered to tell her about. Tickets to lap-dancing clubs, that sort of thing. But fortunately, on this occasion, he has nothing to hide.

'You do look a bit pale,' he says at last, and it's true. Judy is one of those people who usually shines with good health all the time, even first thing in the morning.

'Yeah, I think I've got a bug coming on. I had to sit down a couple of times today and take a few deep breaths.'

'Shit. What will you do if you get really sick?'

'I'm sure I won't. And anyway, my parents are coming down for the weekend.'

The Samoan-Scots combination strikes again. Donald's pleased. He didn't know Judy had asked them down, but it makes him feel altogether better about leaving her on her own in the house, because she won't be. And if she does come down with something, she'll have her own little support network on site.

Judy replaces the neatly folded shirts and gives them a little pat of reassurance, but she doesn't zip the case up. That's a boy job. Donald's suitcase is now properly packed. Hell, there's even room for a few bottles of plonk for the homeward journey.

She sighs. 'So, what time are you flying?'

'Ten o'clock.'

'And who are you flying with? Singapore, isn't it?'

'Malaysian.'

'Hmm. And what time's the taxi coming?'

'Seven. We wanted to get there in plenty of time. Make sure we get decent seats.'

Judy looks at her watch and sighs again. She's treading water. Donald doubts she even heard his answers to her questions. She looks a little sad, and the fluttering sensation returns to his stomach. His throat feels dry. She looks up at him and speaks softly, almost in a whisper.

'You just go and have a good time, OK?'

Donald nods. He can't speak right now.

'And when you get back, things are going to change. For the better.'

He nods again. 'Yeah.' He wants to say more, but simply can't.

Donald climbs up into the people carrier and sits down. Rob and Brian are already in the back, and they smile cheekily at him, their faces glowing in the light of the street lamps. He can see Judy's silhouette framed in the doorway, getting ready to wave, and his stomach lurches again. He has to swallow to stop himself from crying.

The noises of their departure slam into the night. His suitcase is hurled in and the boot bangs shut. The driver slides the passenger door – thunk – and then jumps in, pulls his own door shut and slips the car into gear. Donald leans forward and waves as they move off. Judy waves back and then she's gone.

Not a word is said for the first five or ten minutes of the journey. Odd, since they have just embarked on a pretty major boys' tour, and they ought to be gibbering like excited idiots. But they each seem to be lost in their own little worlds. Donald looks round at his mates. Rob smiles but says nothing. Brian is gazing out of the window, deep in thought, his elbow on the armrest and chin in hand. He sighs heavily, and Donald can't help wondering what kind of goodbye Brian just had with his wife and kids.

Part Four

ROB

Chapter Twenty-three

The mood begins to lift at the airport. We try to get ourselves an upgrade, despite our motley appearance. The Malaysia Airlines lady – who looks exotically Asian but speaks with a Scouse accent – is having none of it. Brian and I are giving her hell in a good-natured kind of way.

'Don't you know who I am?' I say.

'He's a very famous man, you know,' says Brian, putting an arm round me. 'Your bosses will be most upset if they realise he's been flying with you and you didn't upgrade him.'

'And his mates,' Donald chimes in.

'Donald, show her your false leg,' I say. 'At least let's get the bulkhead seats.'

She indulges us with a patient smile, letting our pranks wash over her. But she taps her keyboard. 'I may be able to get you the seats by the emergency doors. There's a bit more leg-room there.'

'Good on yer,' says Brian in his best Australian.

'Bonza rippa tucka,' I add.

We emerge from passport control into the huge Terminal Three lounge. It's basically an enormous shopping mall. We hover, looking around.

'So, does anyone need to do any shopping?' I say. Well, someone has to take charge.

'No, but I fancy a pint,' says Brian.

'What an absolutely sensational idea,' adds Donald.

Bloody hell.

By nine o'clock, although the flight is still an hour away,

we're well on our way. Whatever our complex domestic obsessions might have been an hour or two ago, they have faded to grey for the time being. Now it's boys on tour, and time to have a laugh. We are letting go, free of the constraints of home, free of responsibility, and free of any sense of self-preservation. We have a twenty-four-hour airborne ordeal ahead of us, and we'll be starting it with hangovers. Marvellous.

Having said that, I am beginning to think we should slow up. We've had four pints of wife-beater, as Stella Artois is affectionately known, and I can already feel the very faint pounding of an embryonic headache.

'Lads,' I say. 'Shall we go for a wander? We should probably stay sober, at least until we're on the plane.'

'Yeah, fair enough,' says Brian, and we gather our bags and stroll out into the bright lights of the terminal building.

The blinking TV screen is now saying GO TO GATE 16, so we turn right and start ambling in that direction.

'Hey, look!' shouts Brian, pointing. 'Who's that?'

He's pointing at a woman with straight blonde hair, borderline peroxide, wearing bright pink trousers. She's with a friend and they are looking at jewellery in the Cartier shop. There's an over-eager salesman prancing about behind them, visibly drooling with excitement.

Donald recognises her instantly. He's wagging his hand enthusiastically, but the alcohol is befuddling his recall.

'Oh, that's ... um ... Emma whasshername,' he says.

'Noble,' says Brian.

'Noooooo!'

'It's fucking Baby Spice!' I say.

'What's her surname?' Donald asks. 'Emma ... Bun ...'

'Who cares? Emma Bum-fluff,' says Brian, slurring slightly.

'Hey! Let's get our picture taken with her,' I say. I don't know what's made me think of it – I'm not big on British celebrity culture – but what the heck.

'Don't be daft,' says Donald.

But there's no stopping me now. I'm not too concerned about the consequences of my actions – for instance, how she might react to being approached by three thirty-something blokes, half cut, smelling of beer and second-hand cigarette smoke – only the actions themselves.

'Follow me,' I say, and I start walking towards Baby Spice. I suppose it's more stalking, actually. I'm in a slight crouch, and I'm looking animatedly from side to side as though checking for enemy snipers. Brian and Donald follow at a safe distance, and I can hear them giggling.

I'm there. Rob Pearson. Man with no fear, or perhaps man with no self-awareness. I've walked straight into the shop and right up to Baby Spice – whatever her name is – and I'm brandishing my camera at her.

'Excuse me,' I say, as politely as I can, being careful to iron out any slurring. 'Can me and my two mates have our picture taken with you?'

The look on her face is priceless, like something out of a silent movie. She is aghast, her eyes staring at me in disbelief, her nose turned up slightly, and her mouth twisted into an expression of complete and utter disgust. She glances briefly in Brian and Donald's direction, then back to me. Her glossy, bubble-gum, Baby Spice lips move slightly, and then her friend is hauling her away. Emma Bum-fluff is dragged to safety, away from the madman, but she can't tear her eyes off me. She looks as though she has just witnessed an act of perversion. I might as well be an eighty-year-old flasher who's just exposed his shrivelled member. She's gone, and I am left motionless, hands petrified in mid gesticulation. The salesman, whose face is now beetroot with rage, points speechlessly to the exit.

I stroll back towards my friends, feeling a warm but evil smile spreading across my face.

'Bitch!' I exclaim.

'What did she say?' asks Brian, his shoulders beginning to twitch with mirth.

'Nothing. But I'd love to know what she was thinking.'

And we've lost it. We are falling about laughing. High pitched, hysterical, unrestrained laughter. I can't help wondering when the last time my mates laughed like that was.

We are still struggling, gasping for breath, when we get to the gate, nicely timed so we're at the front of the queue as the flight starts to board. We are fantasising about selling our story to tomorrow's *Sun*, coming up with the potential headline.

'Rude Spice Rejects Raunchy Rob,' says Brian.

'Excellent, and they can print a pic of me naked, next to one of her, so it looks as though I've just flashed her.'

'Snooty Spice Snubs . . .' Donald's off to a good start, but he's stuck.

'Sexy Sergeant!' I yell. 'We'll pretend I'm a policeman and I just wanted a photo to take back to the barracks.'

'Not the fucking barracks, you nob!' says Brian.

'Oh, whatever.'

We are on the plane now, edging towards our seats, and I am suddenly painfully aware that we are operating at much higher volumes than anyone else. The stewardesses are eyeing us suspiciously. I smile sweetly at one of them. She's an absolute beauty, and wearing a stunning traditional dress of some kind, turquoise with a floral pattern. All the staff are wearing them, and they look gorgeous.

The noise levels drop as we pull out books, newspapers, iPods and other miscellanea before stuffing our bags in the overhead lockers. I'm pleasantly surprised by the seats. Three in a line in the middle of the plane. I sit down and stretch my legs. Yeah. Not bad at all. It's a rare moment I am actually glad I'm not six foot four.

The lovely hostess reappears. Or is she a different one? I'm not sure. Regardless, she's a stunner, with satin black hair, incredibly soft-looking, creamy skin and wonderful dark, sparkling eyes. She bends to talk to us in just the same way you imagine geishas bend – from the waist.

'Can I get you gentlemen some water before take-off?'

Luckily, there's no Scouse accent to shatter the illusion this time. In fact, there is no illusion.

'Yes please,' I say. Time to be sensible.

'Got any beer?' asks Brian.

Chapter Twenty-four

'So Tanya's having an affair.'

An hour or so into the flight, and we've been waiting for food to arrive and watching a programme on the early stages of the Rugby World Cup. Brian's words pierce straight through the banal commentary as though he's reached over and shut off the volume. Both Donald and I pull off our headphones and look at our friend, sitting between us. He still has his phones on, ironically, and is staring at the screen, unseeing. I doubt he registers Jonny's last drop-goal; the one that sinks the Welsh.

'I suppose you probably knew,' he says, flatly.

We shake our heads furiously. Brian shrugs. I notice a woman sitting across the aisle who appears to be listening in. I look squarely at her and lower my brow, warning her off. She returns to her magazine.

'I walked in on her. I mean, he was there. When we got back from the fireworks.'

The woman's looking over again. I can feel her eyes burning into us. This time my gesture is less subtle. I glare at her and open my mouth to speak. Again, she turns her head abruptly away and resumes the charade of reading what I can now see is *Marie Claire*. If her ears could stick out on ninety-degree stalks, they'd be obstructing the aisle.

The problem is, Brian thinks he's talking quietly, but he's not. In fact, he's drowning out the rugby commentary that's being piped directly into his ear canal.

'Brian,' says Donald.

'I mean, I didn't walk in on her exactly. He was just driving out when I got there. I stopped short of the driveway.'

'Brian!' Donald raises his voice this time, and gestures for Brian to take off his headphones, which he does, his expression forlorn. He'd clearly forgotten he had them on.

I snap my head to the side and, sure enough, the nasty gossip is ear-wigging again.

'Hey!' I shout, angrily. I can feel my face flush. I am genuinely tempted, just for a split second, to get out of my seat and make my feelings even more obvious than I already have. Shove the stupid magazine against her nose. But I think I've probably made my point. Her face goes cranberry red and she looks flustered and frightened. And hopefully, Brian's volume is under control now.

'Christ, Brian,' says Donald softly.

We're both watching him, not sure what to say. Unable to express ourselves physically either, because blokes don't do a lot of hugging, and planes aren't very tactile environments.

Brian suddenly looks desperately tired. He takes a huge breath that makes his shoulders go up and then slump down. He looks as though he might cry. Brian? No. No way. I've seen Donald cry and that was weird enough. But not Brian.

'So what happened? What did you say to her?' I ask.

'And do you know what?' says Brian, ignoring my question. 'I was all set to tell her I wanted to sort things out. I was even going to suggest we went to see someone together.'

I catch Donald's eye across the back of Brian's head. This is turning into a stream of consciousness, so remaining silent is the best policy. Let it come out. Brian is deep inside his own thoughts now, his eyes staring straight ahead. And then suddenly he's shaking his head and rubbing his eyes, then dragging his fingers down his face, pulling his skin so he looks momentarily like a pink-skinned Basset Hound.

'I can't stop thinking about the fucker. Stupid . . . fucking details, like . . . he's a yoga teacher so I bet he's fit and toned. And maybe he's hung like a donkey. And the thought of him touching Tanya, and her touching him . . . and maybe he made her come, although she said she hated it and got rid of him, but how am I supposed to believe that?'

This isn't good. I've got to get Brian off this subject somehow. It's hideously painful for him, and not terribly productive.

'I'll tell you what,' says Brian, his voice rising in volume again. 'The fucker is lucky he left when he did, because I don't know what I would have done if I'd caught him at it.'

Brian's more or less shouting now, and his face is red with anger. His fists are clenched tight. In his mind, I'm pretty sure he's about to use them. I glance over to check the eavesdropper's not with us again, because there's no way she's not hearing this now, but her face is buried deep in *Marie Claire*. A stewardess is walking by slowly, though, and she glances at Brian with a concerned expression. I smile at her and raise my eyebrows reassuringly. She smiles back. My knees go weak.

'So, Brian. What did you do? Have you left her? What did you say to her?'

I reckon bringing him back to reality will move him off this violent train of thought. Plus, I'm trying to imagine myself in the same predicament. I walk in and see Clare with another man. My woman. Touched by someone else. I'll be honest, it makes me feel physically sick. My heart goes out to Brian.

'Actually, I do know what I'd have done.' He's not heard me. 'I'd have smashed his fucking head in, that's what. I'd have broken my hands on his face, I'd have hit him so hard. I'd have dragged him down the steps by his hair, opened the front door, lined him up and kicked his fucking yoga arse down the steps.'

The stewardess is there again. 'Er . . . sir.' She reaches over and taps Brian on the shoulder. He looks shocked. His face goes Welsh-rugby-shirt red. 'Could you keep your voice down, please?'

'Yeah, sorry,' says Brian, scratching his head with embarrassment.

'Shit,' he adds softly, when the stewardess has swished through the curtain dividing us from business class.

'So . . . mate. What actually happened?' Hopefully he'll hear my question now.

'I was all ready to fly into a rage, scream at her, punch the walls and then storm out. But in the end, I . . . well, I haven't got a leg to stand on, have I?'

Brian turns and looks at me knowingly.

'Suzi?' I say. I knew there was something more than Brian had let on.

'Yep. I didn't screw her, but it was bad enough. I told Tanya. Had, to, really. So we're sat there, I'm wanting to scream at her, she's probably wanting to give me a slap, but neither of us can because we've both been at it.' He pauses. 'Except she just went and fucked the bastard, didn't she?'

Donald clears his throat nervously. 'Didn't you say she threw him out?'

Brian sighs and inclines his head to concede the point. 'That's what she said. She said she suddenly hated herself for it and just wanted him out of the house, so she . . .' Brian grimaces at the images in his head. '. . . stopped and told him to leave.'

'You don't think she was lying, do you?' I say.

'No. No, I don't.'

'How did you leave it? I mean, coming on this trip.'

Brian shrugs. 'Just kind of in limbo. We both know we've screwed up, but it's too early to tell if we still have the stomach for picking up the pieces and putting it all together again. I guess in some ways we both need the space. A bit of time to think.'

He looks at me, then Donald, with a weak but embracing smile.

'So I'm blowing my BlokeMiles account just in case it gets shut down for good.'

It's a cue to laugh supportively, and we oblige. I reach across. Normally it would be a slap on the back, but it's difficult when you're strapped into economy-class seats, so it's a pat on the spur of the shoulder instead. Brian's body feels tense. He looks as though he's trying hard to keep his emotions in check.

It's agonising. In our three-in-a-row seats, there's nothing Donald or I can do to comfort our friend. There's no question now, he's fighting back tears, but the good news is he's winning. Thank God. I don't think I could cope with both my friends crying on me in relatively quick succession. I notice Donald shifting in his seat. Our eyes meet and Donald nods just slightly to indicate he has some kind of plan. The big man puts his hand flat against Brian's chest. I'm quite surprised by the intimacy of the gesture. Donald makes to withdraw it slowly, as though he's slightly embarrassed, but Brian grasps it. Donald looks momentarily startled – I sense this is a huge moment in the relationship between my two mates. They aren't so much holding hands as clasping them, as you do when your team-mate has scored a great goal. It's a grown-up handshake, but it's strong, it's static and Brian seems to be drawing strength from it. And soon, he gives Donald's hand a little, powerful shake to indicate that he's under control. And maybe to say thank you.

'Sorry,' he says

'Don't be stupid,' says Donald.

'No. I mean, I was going to tell you both, but . . . basically that's it. It's out now, and I don't want to talk about it again. OK?' He looks from side to side, accepting our nods.

'OK.'

'OK.'

'What a fucking mess, eh?'

'Yep,' we both agree.

'But now I just want to really fucking enjoy this trip, OK?'

'You're on,' I say.

Chapter Twenty-five

We're staying in a serviced apartment called Medina on Crown, in Surry Hills, a fairly unprepossessing suburb. The accommodation is pleasant enough, though. There are two bedrooms, both with twin beds, and I seem to have scored a room to myself. Top result, although I was surprised that Brian and Donald just wandered in and put their bags on the beds in the same room. Maybe it was in deference to the fact that I booked the hotel. Or maybe they are enjoying their new-found closeness, who knows? Either way, they seem happy with my choice of hotel. Not that I had much choice.

Before venturing out, duty calls. Time to phone home. I call Clare while Brian's in the shower and Donald is unpacking.

'Hello?' says a voice that definitely isn't Clare's. I'm taken aback.

'Mary?' My voice echoes back at me about a second after I speak.

'Yes. Is that you, Rob?'

'Yes. What are you doing there? Have you been co-opted?'

'Er . . . yes, actually, but it's always a pleasure! Did you want Clare?'

The older generation always think it's rude to talk on the phone for longer than ten seconds. Mary is Clare's mum. I didn't know she was coming, but ho hum, great, no problem.

'Yes please, if she's there.' *If she's there.* Of course she's bloody there.

'Actually, she's not. She's out with the girls.'

'What, Judy and Tanya?'

'Yes. They've gone out for dinner. She said if you called to give you her love. Apparently there's no mobile signal at all where they are.'

'Oh.' I feel rather let down, I have to say, for no particular reason. 'They're at the Crooked Billet then.'

'Yes, I think that's where she said they were going. Shall I give her a message?'

'No, it's fine. We're here safely. I'll leave her a message on her mobile.'

'Right you are, Rob. All's well here with the little ones.'

'Great.' Oops. It should have been the first thing I asked, of course. 'Thanks for looking after them.'

'Bye then.'

'Bye.'

Donald emerges from the bedroom.

'Ah. Call home. Damned fine idea.' He picks up his mobile from the kitchen counter.

'Don't bother. The old tarts are all out for dinner at the Crooked Billet.'

'Seriously?'

'Yep. I'm just going to call Clare's mobile and leave her a wee message of love.'

'I'll do the same.'

And we do. And so does Brian when we advise him. He seems almost grateful not to have to talk to Tanya.

If I'd been on my own, I'd have had a kip. No doubt about it. But collectively we drum up just about enough willpower to simply shower, change, don the shorts and sunnies, and head out into the summer we've been miraculously transported to. Sleep will have to wait, and then we'll have a chance of shaking off the lag before the big game, which has been catapulted forward by eleven hours in our confused internal clocks. It's tomorrow, for goodness' sake.

We walk up Oxford Street, and reckon it's just like, well, Oxford Street, but without the plastic sameness of every high street in the UK. Lots of clothes shops catering for young, slim, trendy people – quite an alienating experience, actually – so we decide to jump in a cab and go to the opera house.

Pathetically touristy, admittedly, but we have no idea where we are and decide that that most famous of Sydney icons is a better place to start our orientation. And one heavily tipped, irritable taxi driver and a minute and a half later, we are there. Literally. In Sydney. Arrived. Our mini holiday starts now, because the clichéd centrepiece of the city is anything but a cliché.

Sydney is a quite stunning place. Magical. It doesn't really hit you until you see the opera house glistening like a giant, fragmented pearl in the sunshine, and behind you is the Harbour Bridge, impressive but somehow intimate at the same time, and all around you is water, deep blue, gently lapping the squared-off walls of Circular Quay. You feel as though you've been superimposed onto a postcard.

The sun's warm, but there's a nice breeze keeping your sweat on the inside, and you become transfixed by the slightly comical, old-fashioned green and yellow ferries chugging around the harbour. Of course, there are tourists everywhere, many recognisable by their nation's rugby shirts, but what's striking is that this is a living city. The ferries are carrying real people to and from their homes, or their workplaces, and they sit on the benches that frame the decks, gazing out at the scenery from behind their sunglasses. As I try to take it all in, I'm pretty sure these people have absolutely no idea how incredibly lucky they are. Christ, can you imagine living here? And taking this for granted?

Of course, the first pleasant sensation a Pom feels on arrival in Sydney in late November is the warmth of the sun. It somehow slows you down, thaws you out, and gently infuses a sensation of wellbeing. We've strolled down the Quay to the opera house, done a circuit, taken in a corner of the Botanical Gardens, circled back all the way round to The Rocks area, and now we're back at the ferry terminal – or whatever it is they call it – and we're scanning the potential destinations. To me, they look familiar. Manly, Taronga Zoo . . .

'Darling Harbour,' says Donald to himself.

'What's there?' asks Brian.

'Dunno. Just heard of it.'

'I think it's a touristy area with lots of restaurants and bars,' I add. I was the only one watching the Sydney information video on the plane as we came in to land. So I'm the tour guide by default.

'Could go there for lunch?' says Donald, ever the first to think of food.

I look at my watch. Lunch hadn't even occurred to me, though now he's mentioned it my stomach's rumbling something rotten. Shit, it's nearly midday. They're both watching me. I just shrug.

'Could do,' I say. I feel so relaxed I could just lie down, right here, and listen to the ferries and the seagulls, and doze while the sun puts a little colour in my face and tourists step over my prostrate form.

'What about Bondi?' says Brian, scanning the ferry information anew.

Good point. The three of us search for Bondi, assuming that it must be there but we're too knackered to find it. It's not.

I notice the bloke in the ticket kiosk at Platform Four isn't serving anyone, so I quickly approach before a cluster of Japanese finish taking photos of each other prior to buying their tickets. I often think how mind-numbing it must be when they all get together in Tokyo and watch the slide shows. There's me next to the kiosk, ooh, and there's you next to the kiosk. And there's both of us next to the kiosk . . .

'Excuse me,' I say, aware that I sound rather British. 'Can we take a ferry to Bondi?'

There's a flicker of a smile beneath his grey moustache, and his eyes crinkle slightly.

'Nah, mate. Train to Bondi junction.' And he nods his head towards the train station, elevated above street level behind us.

'Right. Thanks mate,' I say, adding a slight twang to the word mate. I like to fit in.

Brian and Donald haven't moved. Lazy bastards. They're waiting for me to give them word, like a couple of little kids on holiday. I should be handing out lollipops.

'OK,' I say, surprisingly comfortable playing the parental

role. 'How about lunch in Darling Harbour, and then we'll take the train over to Bondi?'

We're on Bondi Beach, stripped to the waist, propped up on our elbows, soaking up the sun and enjoying the sights and sounds of Sydney's most famous bit of sand. It's a moment where I have to pinch myself to appreciate that I have, in fact, travelled from one end of the planet to the other, from winter to summer, from grotty old England to, well, paradise.

Despite my most twisted, innate British cynicism, I am impressed with what I'm seeing. What the hell was I expecting? Well, actually, I thought Bondi Beach would turn out to be a tasteless trap for back-packing Brits who want to hang out with other back-packing Brits. But it's not like that at all. It is a truly astonishing beach. Bigger than I had imagined, and beautifully shaped into a bay. I guess that's what creates the surf, and I'm spellbound by this most Australian of pursuits. I've never tried surfing – mainly because I'm a crap swimmer – but it does look like a mad laugh. The surfers all seem to be clustered at one end of the beach, their heads bobbing on the surface. And then each of them picks a wave of an appropriate size, and rides it in. Some are content just to maintain their balance and arrive in one piece. Others ride the wave as long as possible, weaving up and down the face, taunting the bubbling crest as it threatens to break, and then shooting up vertically into the air and landing the other side of the boiling broth as it crashes down. It looks both scary and exhilarating. Maybe I should give it a go.

I'm watching one bloke with much whiter skin than the rest, and he's wobbling on his board – clearly a beginner. I think he might have picked the wrong wave as well, because this one's still swelling, getting taller and taller, and more threatening, while the poor chap desperately tries to keep his balance. Now he's looking at the big brute of a wave as it rears up above him, and he makes a good call. He jumps off and disappears beneath the surf as the wave picks up momentum and thunders in to the shore. I watch for him to resurface, which to my relief he does, gasping for air and looking thoroughly crestfallen. On reflection, I'll give surfing a miss.

'Christ, did you see that?' I say.

'Yeah, it looks awesome. I think we should give it a go,' says Brian.

'You've got to be joking.'

'Oh, come on, we can't come all the way to Australia and not try surfing. What do you think, Donald?'

Donald is now lying flat on his back with a floppy white hat protecting his face from the sun. But he's awake.

'I'm game,' he says, his voice muffled.

'OK, well you two have fun. There's no way I'm trying that. You know how crap I am at swimming.'

'Rob, we're not going out there with the big boys. We'd die. We'll just hire boards and splash about on the beach break, all right? Let me go and ask someone.'

Before I can protest further, Brian is jogging up the beach towards the surf hire guys, conspicuous in their bright yellow polo shirts and red shorts.

'Donald, have you surfed before?' I ask, aware of just how nervous I sound.

'Nope. But from what I've heard, there's nothing much to it. We'll just splash about near the beach and fall off every now and again.'

'Guys!' Brian is bounding breathlessly towards us, barely able to contain his excitement. 'The bloke's going to give us a quick lesson on long-boards and then we're off!'

Brian looks at me. I am utterly terrified, and my face must betray as much.

'Rob, don't worry. He's going to point out where we can go. We won't be catching any big waves, and the lifeguards will be watching us the whole time. You don't have anything to worry about.'

I sigh, and stand up wearily. 'Do they hire out arm-bands as well?'

The surfing instructor is a cliché. He's called Shane, he's got bleached blonde hair, a mullet, and it's almost certain he has a bronzed six-pack under his short-sleeved shirt. He's lined up three long boards called Spongees, which are especially good for beginners because they are soft on top so you are less likely to break a limb whilst falling off. And from what Shane is saying, falling off is about all we'll do for the next hour or so.

'OK, goiys,' Shane is saying. 'Just stand there for a minute, feet shoulder-width apart.'

We do as we're told and Shane disappears behind us, only to shove Donald hard in the small of his back, knocking him forward.

'You're normal.'

He does the same to Brian.

'Normal.'

And me.

'And we've got ourselves a goofy. There's always one goofy.'

'Why am I goofy?' I ask. This is the last thing I need. Some kind of surfing defect.

'You put your right foot forward, so that's how you'll stand on the board, assuming you get to stand, that is. Right is goofy, left is normal, that's all. Nothing personal.'

Brian and Donald can't contain their mirth.

'Come on, Goofy!' says Brian. 'Let's be having you.'

For the next five minutes Shane has us lying on our stomachs, simulating paddling out through the surf. I can't suppress images of sharks mistaking surfers for turtles. It was on the Discovery Channel a week ago. Then he shows us how to hop up into a kneeling position, and from there to standing. It's hard enough balancing on the sand, let alone with the ocean underneath the board.

'Since it's your first time, you'll be lucky to get to a half-stance,' Shane is saying. 'And if you do, you'll probably just fall in. But that's completely normal, so no dramas.'

'So where's the best place for beginners?' I say. I'm damned if I'm taking the slightest risk here.

'OK, just stay in this area over to the left of the swimming flags. There's a nice even surf there. Don't go further left.' Shane indicates with his arm. 'You see where the waves are breaking real messy and then there's a little section where there's no white water at all? That's a rip-tide. If you get caught in a rip, you might find yourself a hundred metres out to sea before you know what's happened. The thing to do if you do get caught in a rip is don't fight against it. Let it take you out, and then swim round to the left and back towards the beach. But don't worry, we'll be watching you.'

As if I needed anything else to add to my fear and trepidation.

'If someone's already on a wave, it's his right of way . . .' Shane's still issuing instructions, but I'm barely registering them any more. I'm staring at the sea, watching the big waves rear up and crash down in spectacular explosions of white foam. I was enjoying watching them from the safety of land. But being amongst them . . . well, it's entirely unnecessary.

But we're off, boards tucked under our arms, stomachs sucked in, heading for the quieter water where a sprinkling of other beginners are splashing about. It's noticeable that not one of them appears to be surfing. Generally, they seem to be preoccupied with holding on to their boards as the water cuffs them about the head.

After ten minutes, I'm knackered. All I've succeeded in doing so far is paddle my board out beyond the first couple of breaks and get my knees up, only to get knocked off by the next wave, which decides to dump its load a little earlier than the first two. Brian isn't having much more luck, but seems to be enjoying himself, whilst Donald has already got himself into a standing position two or three times and is going well.

I make a decision to paddle out twice more and call it a day. This really isn't my idea of fun. I've worked out that my problem is I'm not quite going far enough out, which is why the waves are breaking on top of me. I need to get about twenty yards further so I can pick up the swell before the wave gets all white and angry. So off I go, working my arms, gritting my teeth and trying to convince myself that I, Rob Pearson, am a finely tuned athlete and if anyone can do it, I can.

I work my way to where I was before, and sure enough a big wave rears its ugly head. I decide to duck under it. I've seen a couple of other guys do the same. The wave whacks my head against the board, and despite it being a Spongee, it hurts like hell. But I emerge on the other side of the wave relatively unscathed, and paddle out a bit further. Yes, this is better. They aren't breaking here. Rather, I can feel them swelling under my board, like a giant breathing. All I need do now is turn toward the beach, pick a wave and try to get up as it picks up speed.

This is good. I've got the bit between my teeth now. A swell is building underneath me, lifting me up and easing me, slowly at first, towards the shore. I push up with my arms and pull my knees up to my chest. Is this what Shane meant by a half-stance? Either way, I'm in it, and it's the first time I've got this far. I make a spontaneous decision to go the whole hog and stand up. It's now or never. I drag my feet up as quickly as I can, goofy leg forward, and – holy fuck – I am surfing. I'm up, and for a split second I can see Donald, close to the sand but quite a bit over to the left. I try to wave at him but it makes me wobble, so I just grin in his direction. Donald's mouth is wide open, and he's making some kind of hand gesture towards me.

And the wave hits me. Another wave. Or maybe I wasn't really on a wave at all. But either way, I'm buried by a wall of water. I feel pain, as my knees, then arm, crash into the board, and then it's just me and the sea, and it's about survival. I am in a tumble drier, being turned around repeatedly. I wait for the churning to stop, so I can come up for air, but it doesn't. I begin to panic.

Now I'm being pulled, rather than tossed, but still there's no sign of the surface, and my chest is starting to burn. This is a rip. Shit. I'm in a fucking rip-tide. I remember Shane's advice not to fight against it, but I'm not strong enough even if I wanted to. The problem is I can't hold my breath for much longer. Oh Christ. I'm going to die. I think of Clare. Of Emily. Of little Ralph. And the world suddenly seems a very sad place. Sad, and getting darker.

There's a hand on my arm, pulling at me. It's incredibly strong, and the pressure and urgency of the hand pull me out of my stupor. The grip is actually causing me pain, but I now realise I'm being helped. And suddenly my head breaks the surface of the water. Everything explodes. My lungs grab at the air. The sunlight pierces my head. The swell of the ocean is lifting and falling, but out here there are no waves.

I'm looking at Donald. It's Donald who has grabbed me. His face looks white with shock and fatigue, but his eyes are strong. Steely.

'Hold on to me, Rob. The lifeboat's coming.' His voice is calm.

'Lifeboat?' I look back towards the beach, and it looks small. We are a long way out. Perhaps a quarter of a mile.

'What are you doing out here?' I ask, shivering now with shock and cold.

'What do you bloody think? I saw you go under and I swam.'

'Fuck.'

It's all I can say. My brain is trying to process what happened. Donald. Of course. The water polo player. The Olympian. But even so, he swam out here?

The lifeboat pirouettes alongside, and wiry, tanned arms pull the two of us aboard.

'He OK?' says one of the two lifeguards to Donald, nodding his head in my direction.

Donald nods. He looks too tired to speak.

'Jeez, just as well you saw where he went. We saw him go down but then lost him. Good on yer.'

'Good swimmer for a Pom, too,' says the second lifeguard. He pushes the throttle forwards, and the boat wheels towards the shore.

I can feel my brain beginning to function again, as well as my lungs, but my limbs are like jelly. I look over at Donald, who is breathing heavily. The sun is glistening on the drops of water on my friend's powerful body. To me, at this precise moment, Donald looks huge. His shoulder and back muscles are enormous, and I have this strange sensation that I'm seeing – really seeing – my friend for the first time.

'Thank you,' I say, just loudly enough to be heard above the roar of the engine.

Donald looks at me with fatigue in his kind eyes, and just nods and smiles slightly.

The nurse shuffles around me to get a better view of the wound on the top of my head. I can't help thinking this simply wasn't in the script. Just about now, on our first evening in Sydney, I reckoned we'd be sampling the local brews in some loud pub in The Rocks, or maybe gawping at prostitutes in Kings Cross, or who knows, maybe we'd have even had the bollocks to find a lap-dancing club. There's a first time for everything. But no. I had to go and drown myself, didn't I?

When we got back to the beach, I blacked out. Needless to say, I can't remember a damned thing, but apparently my eyes went up inside my head, my legs buckled, and wallop. Face down in the sand. The lifeguards took me to their first-aid shack to give me the once over, and discovered a nasty gash on my head where I'd been pummelled against the sand bank. I may have even hit a rock. So I was dispatched to a hospital in somewhere called Randwick for observation. I was diagnosed with possible concussion, with tests required to rule out a more serious head injury.

Nice work, Rob.

The nurse has finished her stitches now and is dabbing the area with some evil-smelling fluid.

'There you go, daarl. Good as new,' she says, smiling benevolently. 'The doctor will be in to see you shortly. He may want you to have a scan, I'm not sure. But you did take a nasty crack on the head, didn't you?'

'I don't know. I suppose I must have.'

The nurse pats me comfortingly on the shoulder, pulls back the curtain, and she's gone. Seconds later, Brian and Donald reappear.

'Tell you what', says Brian, perching on the edge of Rob's bed. 'I'm impressed with the nurses. Phwoaaaa.'

'Yeah, right,' I chuckle. The nurse who just attended me must weigh at least thirty stone.

'So how much longer are they going to keep you here?' says Donald, looking concerned.

'I'm really sorry, guys,' I say. 'Why don't you two just go out and have a few beers. I can always call you when they're finished with me.'

'Don't be a twat,' says Brian.

'Yeah, well put,' adds Donald. 'Anyway, I'm sure we'll find something open when we get out of here.'

'Kings Cross, maybe?' I say.

We all laugh, but there's no real humour left. The banter ran out about half an hour after we reached the hospital. My brave attempt at laughing off my horrific experience ran out of steam, as the reality of my near miss started to sink in.

The curtain swishes open again, and a young, dark-haired doctor strides purposefully up to the bed, his white coat floating on his slipstream. He glances at the case notes and then puts the clipboard back in its holder.

'I'm Doctor Sargeant,' he says, fingering my hair so he can take a good look at the wound. 'OK, that looks clean enough. Now, I bet you've got quite a headache, haven't you?'

'A bit,' I admit. 'Not so bad since the painkillers.'

'Mmm. You'll need to take those for a few days, I should imagine. Now, I know you and your mates want to get on – you're here for the rugby, aren't you? Should be a belter. So, what I suggest is we do a quick scan just to check there's no bleeding going on under your skull, and if everything's clear, you can be on your way.'

I nod. 'We were thinking maybe Kings Cross. Is that far from here?'

The doctor laughs. 'If you feel like drinking after what you've been through, you're a better man than me! No, I would strongly recommend sleep. And lots of it.' He smiles at me, then nods amicably at Donald and Brian. 'Right, someone will be down to get you for the scan in the next twenty minutes, half an hour.'

Sleep. Yes. I suddenly feel heavy. Tired beyond description, but also lonely. It's utterly daft, because I have my two best friends with me, but it's not them I need right now. It's Clare. My Clare.

'Guys,' I say, my voice sounding weak, 'I really need to speak to Clare. Do you mind?'

'Sure.'

'No worries. I might ring Judy, too.'

Donald pulls the curtain behind him, and I am alone. As I dial the number, I have to hold back tears. I know it must be the shock, but there's probably more to it. I nearly died, for God's sake. I nearly made my lovely wife a widow.

'Hello?'

It's Mary.

'Mary, it's Rob.'

'Oh . . . hello Rob. Are you OK? You sound all funny.'

'I really need to speak to Clare.'

I know instinctively she's not there. Clare is normally quick to pick up the phone, and conversely, Mary hates phones.

'Um, I'm afraid she's not here.'

'Again.'

'Yes. Um . . . shall I leave her a message?'

'Leave her a message? I'm on the other side of the bloody world, I'm in – ' I stop myself. There's no point in alarming Clare's mother, or indeed Clare. Imagine coming home to a note – ROB'S IN HOSPITAL – PLS CALL. No, that's just not fair.

'Oh, it doesn't matter.'

'I'm sorry, Rob.'

'That's all right. Not your fault. Um . . . Mary?'

'Yes, dear?'

'Is Clare away? Has she gone away for a few days or something?'

'Um . . .'

There's a pause.

'That's OK, Mary. I know you're not meant to tell me. Bye.'

And I hang up.

Brian ducks back in, shaking his head.

'Tanya not there?'

'Nope.'

'Did Donald get through to Judy?'

'Nope. He's just gone for a slash.'

Something very strange is going on. Donald slips past the curtain and can see Brian and me having a team frown. He joins in. Our brains, slowed by the fact that it's morning and yet it's evening and our body clocks are confused as hell, are telling us that something is amiss, and yet we can't quite fathom it.

'Do you think they've buggered off together?' says Donald. 'I bet that's it. They've decided if we're going to swan off to Sydney, they're going to have a girly weekend. Do you think?'

'Could be,' says Brian.

'I think you're probably right,' I say, and it's all beginning to make sense in my mind. I had a hunch they were up to something when I made my less than inspired speech the other day. They just weren't quite pissed off enough that we were going to Sydney without them.

'They're probably getting their own back,' says Brian. 'I reckon they'll be hanging out in wine bars hoping to get chatted up, or dancing around their handbags at discos, winking at teenagers.'

'And they'll have booked three strip policemen for later,' Donald adds.

It's gallows humour, but there's not much laughter, and yes, it does seem that our wives may have taken out a BlokeMiles-related loan, and reinvested it in some pleasurable female pursuit. They've plugged it into a fancy currency converter and miraculously have a sack-full of ChickMiles to spend.

'I can't fucking believe it, can you? Look at this. I'm in hospital, about to have a brain scan, and it could even be worse than this. What if . . . what if, you know, we really did need to get in touch with our families urgently? Why the fuck didn't they tell us they were doing it, instead of diverting their bloody mobile phones and pissing off for a girly weekend?'

'Like I said,' says Brian calmly. 'They're getting their own back.'

'For what?' I snort.

'For the fact we didn't tell them we were coming out here.'

'We don't have a leg to stand on,' says Donald, looking at me earnestly over the top of his specs.

'Jesus!' I'm feeling just a little emotionally unstable, and my anger is like a fast car caught in a cul-de-sac, revving pointlessly with nowhere to go.

The curtains are pulled open.

'Mr Pearson? Are you ready for your scan?'

I nod, sighing, as two nurses take the brakes off my bed and manoeuvre me into the corridor.

'See you shortly,' I say.

'Good luck,' says Donald.

Brian looks worried.

Chapter Twenty-six

It's Saturday, 22 November – a date that's been imprinted on our subconscious minds for months now, knowing it could represent a historic day for English sport, but not daring to take a thing for granted until we absolutely, definitively knew that the men in white would compete in the final.

And here we are.

Donald and Brian are having breakfast when I surface, and judging from their reactions, I'm not a pretty sight. Not that I'm surprised. It's not just the splitting headache – that was always on the cards – it's the fact that my whole body hurts. The old 'twelve rounds with Mike Tyson' cliché doesn't do it justice. I feel as though I ran a marathon before stepping into the ring. Every muscle in my body aches.

I drag my corpse to the kitchen table and pour myself a bowl of cornflakes.

'So how do I look?' I say.

'Great,' says Donald.

'Shit,' says Brian at the same time.

I chuckle, and wince as pain shoots across my rib-cage.

'Ouch. Fuck. I need some of those painkillers.'

'Don't worry, mate, we'll start drinking soon,' says Brian.

'They didn't say you couldn't drink, did they?' says Donald.

'They didn't dare,' I say.

The three of us eat our breakfast in silence, subdued by a potent cocktail of jet-lag, emotional scar tissue, and the fact that Sydney itself seems to have changed overnight. It looks altogether different, with light drizzle falling from a leaden sky, and the traffic shuffling listlessly at street level.

We've had a copy of the *Sydney Morning Herald* shoved under the door, and the back page pronounces that, in fact, this weather was forecast. The paper is full of the big match, and weather is taking centre stage. I suppose it's mind games again, but the general gist is that the rainy conditions are going to play right into England's hands, with our big old pack, dubbed Dad's Army by the Australian press. Of course, Woodward has come out and said that he doesn't want wet conditions any more than the Wallabies do, and in fact he thinks the rain will probably be a leveller, rather than an advantage to England.

Hmm. Sometimes the truth hurts, doesn't it? My first reaction – in fact Donald's and Brian's as well – is to come out in support of Woodward. The Aussies are just making excuses in advance, like the French. England can play the game any way they want. We can play it tight if need be, as we did against France when the heavens opened. But we can also run the opposition ragged if it's dry and fast, as we did to Australia last time we played them over here. It's just that . . . well, we haven't exactly been scorching over the turf so far in this World Cup. It's all been a bit of a struggle.

So the truth, unpalatable as it is, is that we do want rain. Lots of it. Heavy, wet, Mancunian and miserable. England have the shirts for it, too – the water will just pour from those sleek little numbers just as it does off a proverbial duck's back. By contrast, the Aussies' jerseys, old fashioned, cotton jobs, will become heavy, dragging their drooping shoulders down as Wilkinson pops over penalty after penalty. England's power in the scrum will have the Wallaby pack sliding backwards as though they're wearing roller-skates, and Vickery and co in the front row will take great delight in grinding their opponents' faces into their native mud. Marvellous.

On the other hand, purely objectively, we'd rather see a fantastic spectacle of running rugby, with tries galore, and our boys coming out on top in the end. That would live longer in the memory and it would shut the Aussies up with their bloody trumpeting about England's inability to score through any other means than Jonny's left peg. And our seats are out in the open as well. Did we bring wet weather gear? Did we hell.

Once we've exhausted the rugby conversation – and believe me it's taken some doing – we realise, on reflection, that we're quite missing our families. Why are we surprised? I don't know for sure, but I sense that we are each, in our own way, quite taken aback by the little pang of emptiness that seems to have hit us, more or less at the same moment.

'I wonder how Ralph's teeth are,' I say to myself.

'I was just thinking about kids myself,' says Donald reflectively. 'Well, babies, actually.'

There's a pause, while Brian and I digest what we've just heard.

'You two aren't trying, are you?' says Brian.

Donald nods and turns away, trying to dodge a moment of pain.

'Been at it a while?' I ask.

'Nearly a year,' sighs Donald. 'Feels like about ten.'

'She be roit,' I pronounce in my best Sydney accent.

There's a little silence, filled with collective rumination.

'Livvy's probably watching *Scooby Doo* on the Cartoon Network,' says Brian wistfully.

I sigh. 'Look, I know we were pissed off last night that our wives have buggered off somewhere, but look on the bright side. If they are having a hoot, and they've offloaded the kids, then we can really enjoy ourselves here, can't we? I mean, we don't have to feel guilty any more.'

'I wasn't feeling guilty,' says Brian.

'Nor me,' says Donald.

Bloody hell. Are they serious? Am I the only one with the guilt problem? I can't believe that, I really can't. Surely it's not only me who can't really relax and have fun because I have this inescapable, creeping, gnawing sense that I shouldn't be doing what I'm doing? That I should be at home, supporting my wife and being a father for my kids? That I'm an irresponsible, immature, selfish arsehole? Don't my friends share my inherent self-loathing? Isn't that why we spend half our time making our respective dog houses as comfortable as possible? I thought it was, but maybe I've just been assuming too much. Jesus Christ.

'Oh, come on. You know what I mean?' I look from Donald to Brian and back again, feeling just a little desperate. I really need a bit of support here. 'If we know they're off somewhere having a great time, it's ... you know ... comforting to know that, right? So you just relax a bit more than you otherwise would.'

'Yeah. That's fair,' says Donald generously.

'So we can get really shit-faced tonight,' says Brian, smiling. 'As opposed to, say, just a bit squiffy.'

'I think we'll be getting shit-faced, one way or the other,' I say.

And thankfully, our minds turn back to the rugby.

The rather moribund mood we've all woken up with clings to us like passive smoke to clothing. We've walked back to Circular Quay, drunk coffee, read the Aussie papers – which are arguably even more parochial than ours back home, if that's possible – and then wandered aimlessly around The Rocks, ducking in and out of tourist shops so as not to get soaked by the intermittent drizzle.

I find myself trying not to get upset about the weather. Rain on holiday is always doubly depressing, since it's precisely why you go away in the first place, but having said that we didn't come to Sydney for the weather, so why should we care? It's astonishing, though, the difference the sun makes. Don't get me wrong, Sydney is a fabulous place but, just like at home, when the weather's drab it coats everything with a grey sheen. The ferries, which I've fallen in love with, look murky green instead of bright and bouncy. The sea is gun-metal grey and dangerous looking, whereas yesterday it was deep blue and you just wanted to leap in. People are hunched and unsmiling and the taxis swish bleakly past.

There are lots of rugby fans milling about with no sense of purpose, mostly English. They all look apprehensive, and perhaps that's why we're a little down in the dumps. We're nervous as hell. You wait so long for an English team to get to a major final like this and, now the moment's arrived, the fear of failure is palpable. If it only happens every thirty-seven years, you really can't afford to blow it, can you?

We've stumbled into a pub for a drink, because we can't think of much else to do, plus we're hungry and there's an unmistakable waft of grilled food coming from the open door. And Donald has just announced that midday has arrived, and for men of our age, that's an acceptable time to start drinking.

We're not the only ones. The place is full of Poms, sitting, standing, drinking beer and killing time. The deal seems to be that you grill your own food, so Brian heads off to investigate this strange notion while Donald and I consider the drinking options.

'What beer do you recommend, mate?' I ask the barman.

He scratches his ginger goatee beard for a second whilst considering my question.

'Have you tried the Tazzie beers, mate? Boag's, or Cascade? They're probably the best. Got good water down there.'

'Yeah, all right,' I say. 'Three of those then, please.'

'Boag's or Cascade?'

'Whatever you think.'

Oops, that's thrown him. He's scratching the beard again and staring at the fridge, as though he's waiting for a bottle of beer to leap out, shouting Pick Me, Pick Me! Then he reaches in and pulls out three nicely chilled bottles of James Boag's Premium. It's a nice-looking bottle, with a classy label showing a lovely mountain stream.

'Ah, Tasmanian,' says Donald. The barman gives him an odd look.

'We didn't know what you meant by Tazzie,' I explain, and he nods.

I hand Brian his bottle as he reappears.

'It's brilliant,' he says, breathlessly. 'You choose your meat, stack up on salads, baked potatoes, that sort of thing, and then sling 'em on the barbie!'

'Bonza,' I say. I'm getting rather fond of that phrase although, worryingly, I've not heard an Aussie say it yet.

I throw down some pain-killers with my first slug of beer, and we follow Brian out through the door of the bar into a little patio that opens out into an eating area, partially sheltered by a trellis with ivy growing through it. There are two huge open grill areas, and overweight Englishmen dominate the scene. We find a table, deposit our beers and walk up the stairs to the counter, where enormous steaks, chicken soaked in BBQ sauce, and assorted salads are attractively displayed beneath glass counters.

I'm sorry to keep saying this, but the bloke in attendance at the food counter is blonde-maned, goatee-bearded and mulletted. The place is a cliché! But when he speaks, I'm relieved to hear he's South African.

'Can I help you guys?'

We're all eyeing the huge, succulent steaks. I can hardly speak for the saliva gushing into my mouth through all available sluices. It's head versus heart again. We desperately want steaks, but the old health bollocks is flashing green crosses into our minds. I would say it's the heart that wants the steak and the head that wants a nice cool salad, but I reckon one or two steaks of that size and the heart will pack up for the day.

'Fuck it,' I explain. 'I'll have a steak, please, mate. But . . . er, a smaller one if you can.'

The South African frowns and prods a few bits of meat. He picks up one that looks a little more modest than the others, but it's attached at the hip to another piece, about twice the size.

'Sorry,' he says, smiling sheepishly. 'They're all pretty huge.'

'Fine. Whatever,' I say.

In normal circumstances, I suppose, one person might cook all three steaks, but for us, the novelty of grilling your own food in a restaurant is too much to resist, so once we spot a gap we're all three standing over the heat, beers in one hand, prodding the slabs of meat with the other.

'I wonder what the girls are doing,' says Donald.

'I don't,' says Brian dismissively, but I'm with Donald. I've been thinking about Clare all morning. In fact it started at about four a.m., when I had a startlingly erotic dream in which Clare was ... oh, never mind. It was so real that it took me a while to realise I was alone in bed.

'You know, I've been thinking,' I say, and it's true. 'I think we made a mistake not telling the girls we were coming here.'

'Oh, that's bollocks, Rob,' says Brian. He's in an obstreperous mood. 'Don't you remember the very first time we talked about BlokeMiles? We said we wanted to get away from feeling we have to ask permission to do every last bloody thing.'

'No, we wanted to get away from the guilt,' I say calmly. I'm not in the mood for an argument. 'And anyway, this isn't really *every last bloody thing*. This is a trip to the other side of the world to see England in the final.' I flip my steak over and it hisses angrily.

'You're the one that said it's just a weekend away.'

'I know, I know.'

'I agree,' says Donald. That's what I like about Donald. He usually agrees, and when he doesn't, he keeps it to himself. For some reason, Donald's steak is almost ready. I think he's been flipping it more regularly than me or Brian. 'Judy actually said that to me. She said we were stupid not to be up front about this trip, because that's what they all thought BlokeMiles was about.'

'What?' says Brian, turning his steak over rather clumsily, to the extent that a small piece has got wedged down the side of the grill. He tries desperately to gouge it out with the tongs, but gives up and cuts it loose. 'I mean, what did they think it was all about?'

'Being more open and honest about what we want to do. They thought that with BlokeMiles, we'd stop sneaking off and doing things behind their backs, or more likely just whinging about not being able to do things.'

'Or feeling guilty about thinking about doing things,' I add.

'So when we didn't tell them about Sydney, they were pretty pissed off, apparently.'

'Wait a minute,' I say. 'They didn't seem that pissed off when I did my little speech. Is there something you know that we don't, big man?'

Donald's sliding his steak on to his plate now.

'Er, yeah. Judy found the tickets to the final in my pants drawer. They knew we were coming about three weeks ago. That's why they didn't hit the roof.'

Donald bestows a meaningful look on us, devoid of remorse, and heads for the table. Brian stares at me. Wow. That's a bit of a clanger. We both sling steaks on plates and hurry after Donald.

'Why didn't you tell us they all knew?'

I'm quite perturbed about this. We don't often keep things from each other, and the thought that Donald led me into the dragon's lair with that speech the other day, knowing that our wives were on to us anyway . . . well, I'm not pissed off yet – more confused – but the potential's there.

'I didn't know, to tell you the truth.'

Donald puts a large piece of meat in his mouth and masticates with great concentration, his brow furrowed as he takes in the taste. Brian and I wait patiently for him to continue. Eventually he swallows, wipes his mouth with his napkin, and looks up.

'At the time she found out, there were other things on my mind. You know, I mean, it was a pretty big deal that I lost my job and didn't tell Judy, so this was the same thing all over again. Well, it wasn't, but it could have been. I was shit-scared.'

Now Brian and I are chewing in stereo, while Donald takes a well-earned break.

'So, was she OK about it?' says Brian, putting his knife and fork down in a polite inverted 'V' formation.

Donald sighs. 'She was brilliant about it, and we just kind of agreed to pretend I'd told her and get on with BlokeMiles and all the good things about it. I didn't think she'd tell Tanya and Clare, but . . . I didn't really give it much thought. I was more concerned about you two finding out I'd blown our cover.'

'Same again?' says Brian, wiping a dribble of BBQ sauce

off his chin. He's only halfway through his lunch, but it's fair to say we need a refill.

'Yeah, cheers,' says Donald, relieved, and Brian collects the Boag's bottles and heads for the bar. It's Brian's way of shrugging his shoulders and saying *fuck it, there's nothing we can do about it now*. And he's right. We're here, in Sydney, what's done is done, and we have a huge day ahead of us. The thought of it sends butterflies flitting through my entire being, culminating in a contraction of the bladder that has me scurrying for the gents.

Chapter Twenty-seven

The Rugby World Cup final

The atmosphere's electric. As usual, the English fans are much more vocal than the locals, but they're still pretty quiet by normal standards. There are lots of gold Wallaby jerseys, scarves and flags, but the faces are taut. It's noticeable – naturally, I suppose – that the Aussie fans are more demographically diverse than the English. Let's face it, we're about ninety-nine per cent boys on tour, whereas the folk in green and gold include a remarkably high percentage of women and young kids. I guess rugby union is a family sport the world over – there's no hooliganism whatsoever, other than what you see on the pitch – but even then, this looks more of a family crowd than you'd get at Twickenham. It's nice to see.

There's always a moment at a sporting venue that takes your breath away, when you walk up the steps to the section where your seats are, and there's the pitch ahead of you, greener than is reasonable and illuminated by the floodlights. The stadium itself is enormous but the pitch is frighteningly small in comparison. In some ways, the surrounds reflect the monumental importance of the occasion, whereas the pitch is just a pitch. It's the same sport you and I played at school.

With the dramatic classical music being pumped across the ground, the atmosphere is unmistakably gladiatorial. Although there are fifteen men in a rugby team, it might as well be one huge Roman warrior against another in a fight to the death, the crowd baying for blood.

I find myself wondering what's going on down below in the changing rooms. Is Dallaglio pacing the perimeter of the room, chin jutting, thumping himself on the chest, issuing words of motivation to anyone who cares to listen? Has Johnson got the front five in a private huddle, in the shadow of the skipper's imposing black brow? Is Wilkinson sitting quietly on his own, taping up his socks slowly, deliberately, visualising his first drop-out? Is Greenwood cracking jokes to break the tension? Is Tindall lining up his first bone-crunching tackle?

I wonder how much fear there is down there. This is a hugely experienced bunch of players, familiar with winning in all sorts of circumstances, so they ought to be feeling pretty confident that they can do it again. But having reached the final, having put themselves only eighty minutes from glory, can they hold their nerve? Will the suffocating fear of blowing it at the last paralyse their minds and bodies?

I'm petrified as I stand in front of my folding seat and take in the scene. And I can see the same apprehension on the faces of the people around me, mostly Australians as luck would have it, but there's a sprinkling of white shirts as well. Our eyes keep meeting and we exchange nervous smiles. There's very little bravado, but equally there's not much banter coming from the locals, either. It's as though the time for all that crap is over, and now it's one team against the other and may the best win. That was the overall tone of the media today as well. Gone was the goading, replaced with a kind of stoic honour and respect for the opponent that I'd not seen before.

Will the best team win, I wonder? After all, England has, without doubt, the best team. They've earned that badge. But . . . I don't know. It's going to be a test of nerve. Here we go.

It's a relief when the game finally starts. We had the national anthems and we had the silliness of the whole stadium being drenched in gold glitter. Jeez, the things people will do to give their team an edge. Now we're underway and it's an awesome spectacle. Conditions are absolutely perfect. It stopped raining around mid afternoon and, after all the speculation, the weather looks unlikely to have much of a say in the outcome of the game.

So how's it going to pan out? There's some powerful running from both sides, solid tackling, astute kicking, but pretty much a stalemate. Both sides feeling each other out. I look across at my two mates, and can see them transfixed by the occasion. I do a quick 360-degree sweep, and the faces are all locked on the action. There's an uncanny quiet about the place.

But it doesn't last. The Wallabies are building some pressure deep in our twenty-two. Larkham has put the ball into touch rather than go for goal – twice, in fact – and that's got the crowd going. Suddenly Brian, Donald and I are huddled in the teeth of a storm, as the Aussies find their voices.

'AUSSIE AUSSIE AUSSIE!' someone shouts.

'OI OI OI!' someone shouts back. It's lame.

'AUSSIE AUSSIE AUSSIE!' He's not giving up that easily.

'OI OI OI!' Now there's a good few voices joining the rather pathetic chant.

'AUSSIE AUSSIE AUSSIE!'

'OI OI OI!'

I glance across at Donald and Brian. Donald raises his eyebrows. At first I think he's being disparaging, but then I realise it's a nervous gesture. We're under siege.

The Wallabies win the line-out. Larkham launches a steepling kick high into the night sky. We all watch the ball at its apex, then look ahead to what's happening beneath it. Jason Robinson's there, but so's Tuqiri, and he's about a foot taller than our man. Uh-oh. I can feel the whole stadium getting to its feet as the ball comes down from the heavens. Tuqiri's airborne. He's got it. He's over the line. Try. Shit. Not, like, SHIIIIIT, but just a quiet 'shit' muttered under the breath. No need to overreact.

The noise is deafening. I sit down, because frankly I don't see why I should stand up and celebrate an Australian try. But now all I can see is a row of bouncing gold jerseys, so I stand up again. Brian leans over to speak to me.

'. . . Robinson . . . Tuqiri . . . fucking . . .'

I nod, having got the general gist. Roughly translated, I think Brian was saying what the hell was Robinson doing one on one with Tuqiri under a high ball? Didn't they think that one through?

The crowd sits down as Flatley gets ready to take the conversion. He misses it.

'Yes,' I hiss quietly to myself.

And then, slowly, steadily, England begin to exert a grip on the game. It's quite clear, minutes after Tuqiri's try, that our boys aren't panicking. They never do, but everyone in the stadium can see our team go back to basics, work possession, gain field position, and start the long process of sucking the life out of the opposition. Penalty to England. Wilkinson will kick, of course he will. I can sense the Aussies around us groan. They know he doesn't miss these, try as they might to throw him off with their silly media antics. They had cut-out Stop Jonny Voodoo Dolls in yesterday's paper, and I wonder how many of them are being furiously poked and prodded at this moment. Not many, I shouldn't think, judging by the result. The ball sails through the posts, and we're on the board. We yelp our approval, clapping hands. But it's a muted celebration. We're still behind.

Not any more. Another penalty. This time we issue a sharp, unisonic 'YESS' and jump to our feet.

'Aw, the bastard's just gonna kick us to death,' whines a voice behind me. I turn to express my contempt, not through words but through one of my best snotty looks. It's a middle-aged bloke with grey hair and a walrus moustache. His eyes briefly meet mine and he looks away.

I find myself hoping upon hope that we do more than just kick goals, not for any other reason than I don't want the Aussies to be able to say, when the dust has settled, that the Wallabies tried to play running rugby and England just played for Wilkinson's penalties. I know it shouldn't matter, but it does. We need to win fair and square, with no arguments left to run.

Now we're starting to play. The Wallabies have sent on a replacement stand-off who looks about fifteen, wearing a head-guard, and the first thing that happens to him is he gets absolutely pole-axed by Wilkinson, who can clearly do more than kick. The ball is loose. We've got an overlap. Go. Go. Gooooooooo! Ben Kay, yes yes yes yes ... AND HE'S DROPPED IT! Oh my God. We're on our feet, but the hands that were about to be thrust into the air in triumph are forced to abort mission and grab clumps of hair instead. Kay has dropped the bloody ball over the line. Disaster. We won't get many better chances to score than that. Oh Shit. Oh Crap. Oh please God . . . I look to the heavens. I'm not the slightest bit religious, but just in case he's there ... it can't hurt, can it?

Another Wilkinson penalty calms the nerves a little. We're nine-five up and gaining the ascendancy. No doubt about it. We stretch our legs, taking it all in, when I make eye contact with the moustachioed Aussie again. This time he doesn't look away.

'Jeez, what would you boys do without that Wilkinson fella?' he says. It's one of those comments that's loaded with possible interpretations. It's a compliment, of sorts, but it's also a psychological ploy to prepare for losing. He's been watching the same game as us, so he knows we've been moving the ball around really nicely, trying to score tries. In fact we should have scored one. But obviously, we've got a class kicker and we aren't going to spurn opportunities to put points on the board.

So what this guy is doing is preparing his post-match spiel. *We played all the rugby but that bloke, he's just a robot. He kicked us to death.* I'm unsure whether or not to rise to it.

'We'd still beat you, but probably by a smaller margin,' I say. I've risen to it. But the bloke just laughs good-naturedly. His moustache curves up so the ends almost touch his ears when he laughs. It's quite endearing, actually.

'Ah well, I guess we'll never know. Let's just wait and see.'

I smile and turn back to the game. We're taking it to them. We're flowing. Forwards look really strong. Dallaglio's away, through the gap. Inside to Wilkinson. This looks good. Floated pass to Robinson and he's away ... he's in!

'YAAAAAAAAAAAAAAAAAAAAAAAAAAAAAAAAAAAAH!!!!!'

We're in a three-way embrace, yelling at the tops of our

voices. There's plenty of other English supporters doing the same. Now it's the Aussie fans' turn to soak up the punishment. There's just nothing you can say or do when the opposition's scored against you. You just have to take it on the chin, let the other bastards have their little celebration, and then move on. I can't help turning to the bloke behind me who said, or rather implied, that all we could do was kick.

'Fair play, mate. Great score,' he says.

Wilkinson's missed the conversion, but anyway we're fourteen-five up and although not a single, solitary chicken has been released, let alone counted, this does look good and it affords us just the tiniest little opportunity to contemplate, for the first time, that we could, even *should* win this match.

The half-time whistle blows and our players trot off with a decidedly jaunty look to their step, whilst the Wallabies look a little careworn.

Wow.

The players emerge from the tunnel, forty minutes from immortality. I wonder how much they are able to keep that thought out of their minds and just concentrate on the task ahead, which undoubtedly won't be easy. When you're fourteen-five up and playing well, one of two things will happen. Either we'll score a couple more penalties, or a try, relax and then just take the game completely away from them. Or they will claw their way back and it will be excruciatingly tense. I know what I'm hoping for, but I know what I'm expecting too, and they aren't one and the same.

I take a deep breath, and feel a tap on the shoulder. It's Merv again. I mean, he's probably not called Merv but it's definitely a Merv-style 'tash.

'Mate,' he says, and I see he's offering his hand. 'Good luck.'

I take his hand and give it a good shake. 'Thanks. You too.'

I cannot believe it's come down to this. The second half has been one of the most frustrating experiences of my entire life.

Every time we've looked threatening, someone's made a stupid mistake, knocking the ball on or giving away a penalty. Flatley has gradually kicked Australia back into the game. Wilkinson's missed another drop-goal, and now the referee has started penalising our scrum, despite the fact that we're quite clearly stronger than them in there. What's he on about?

Anyway, the upshot is that there's no time left at all on the clock, we're three points up, but Flatley has a kick to tie things and send the final into extra time. It's not an easy kick at all, but he's done brilliantly in this half to get his team back into it. As he goes through his routine, the tension is almost unbearable. It's probably worse for the Aussies, because if he misses it's all over. If he gets it, it's bad for us, but it doesn't mean we've lost.

Here he goes. Bosh. It's difficult to tell, from where we are, by watching the ball, so I cheat and look at the big screen over to my right. The crowd roars, and Flatley's body language tells me right away that he's nailed it. It's an incredible kick. Fair play to him. Fair play to them, as well. They just won't give up.

That's the generous bit. I'm trying to suppress my inner rage. So is Donald. Brian may have tried but he's patently failed.

'I don't believe it. We fucking blew it,' he moans, loud enough for our neighbours to hear. 'I've never seen so many bloody knock-ons.'

'And what was going on in the scrums?' says Donald.

The worst possible scenario now rears its ugly head in my mind. I can tell my friends have had the same thought. We're very subdued, to say the least. What I'm thinking is this. To have come so close, only to implode in a second half riddled with errors, to manage to get on the wrong side of the ref, to let the Aussies back in despite being the stronger team . . . to substantially blow a winning opportunity in a Rugby World Cup final. That might be our legacy. The legacy of this great team. The legacy of our brave trip. The legacy of BlokeMiles, who knows? Surely it can't turn out this way.

The locals are predictably cock-a-hoop. The gossip's going

round about extra time. It's ten minutes each way, and if things are tied after that, it goes to sudden death. And then, curse the thought, the World Cup will be decided on drop-goals.

It's *déjà vu* – there's about a minute left of extra time and we're three points up. Wilkinson nailed a huge penalty from the halfway line just at the end of the first period, and we've held on since then. Can we do it? Can we do it? Incredible drama. And ... no NO NO NO NO! It's a penalty to Australia. Dallaglio's the last to get up from the heap of bodies and he's shaking his head and playing the innocent.

'You DICK-HEAD!' screams Brian.

We've got our heads in our hands.

'Come on Flatters, do 'em again!' yells Merv. I turn round and he winks at me. 'Can you believe this?' he says.

'In a word, no,' I say.

'What a bloody game of rugby!'

But I can't speak. Flatley's lining it up. This is easier than the one he slotted to end full time, so mentally I just see the kick over. Looks like we're going to sudden death. Sure enough, he's got it. Elton Flatley, a bloke I'd hardly heard of, is the hero of all Australia, and quite right too. He's got some nerve.

'How much time's left?' I ask nobody in particular.

'About a minute,' says Donald.

Wilkinson goes long from the drop-out. I guess he doesn't want to risk field position for another Wallaby penalty, or maybe they're thinking more positively than that. Good pressure from the back row and the ball's in touch for an England line-out. The clock's ticking. Maybe there's time for one more drop-goal, or a penalty or something. I'm praying more than hoping.

We've got it, and we're attacking. We're in their half, in centre field but a long way out still. I can hear Merv muttering 'No, no, no,' under his breath. The ball's in a ruck and Wilkinson's dropped back. Dawson's ready to pass to him and ... Dawson's gone! Ducked under a tackle. He's made another ten or fifteen yards and we've got another ruck. Johnson's taken it on. We're close now. Close enough for . . . Dawson back to Wilkinson, on his right foot. It's wobbly but . . . it's THERE!

The rest is in slow motion. My brain has shut down and I haven't registered that that's basically it. There's no time left. But the roar of the crowd is deafening. Groans, cheers, screams, sighs. I can see the players' reactions. Wilkinson's arms are aloft, so are a few others. But there's time for a restart, and Johnson is desperately trying to get his players back inside their own half to reform. The golden-shirted Wallabies rush the ball back to the halfway line and get the ball back in play, but it's gone too far. Catt's got it, socks round his ankles. It's got to go out. It does. Catt hoofs the ball miles into the stands. I can't hear the referee's whistle but the players explode. They are embracing, leaping like idiots. The Wallabies sink to the turf, spent with their incredible effort. England have done it.

I turn to my two great friends – Brian and Donald – and we're all crying. We hug, speechless, and then we're shaking hands with complete strangers who suddenly feel like our friends. The Australians all around us want to congratulate us. This selfish, arrogant, ruthless sporting nation . . . well, the media, maybe, but not the ordinary people. They might be tough, they might be partisan, but they are fair and, tonight at least, they are generous in defeat. It's a moment that will stay with me for a long time, and change my view of Australians for ever.

Chapter Twenty-eight

We've found a pub in The Rocks that's open late, and not surprisingly it's now heaving with deliriously happy England fans, bedecked in white shirts with red St George's crosses. Most of the Aussies – and there were plenty for a while, gamely attempting to withstand the enemy's euphoria – have drifted away, tortured into distraction by decreasingly tuneful renditions of 'Swing Low, Sweet Chariot'. The atmosphere's been convivial, although the group that started singing 'three dollars to the pound' to no particular melody probably got a few local hackles up.

We've managed to find a table in a relatively quiet corner after standing for ages. Truth be told, we're absolutely shattered, but England's glory is still coursing through our veins, blending comfortably with about eight or nine bottles of Tasmania's finest and in my case a half dozen powerful pain killers, so we're not about to turn in for an early night. After all, we've said to ourselves that this is probably a once-in-a-lifetime thing, we're on the plane home on Monday and our normal lives will resume their respective mundane rhythms.

The mood's gone a bit reflective, though, with long silences developing and the small print on our cold bottles of James Boag's providing surprisingly compelling reading.

'Do you realise we've got to go home on Monday?' I say. It's not the most insightful contribution I've ever made, but I feel I need to get things moving again.

'Well, at least we've got tomorrow,' says Donald.

'So what do you think we should do?' I say.

'I know what I want to do,' says Brian. 'I want to go to the immigration office and make some enquiries.'

'You what?' I say.

'I could really live here,' says Brian quietly, intently peeling off yet another label from his bottle and adding it to the pile he's made.

'Brian, tomorrow's Sunday,' Donald says.

Brian looks up, realisation dawning. 'So it is.'

'So what's the deal?' I say. 'You're ready to give up your wife and kids for a bit of sun and sand?'

'I didn't say that.'

'You'd bring them out here?' says Donald.

Brian shrugs. 'Maybe. Could be a fresh start, don't you think?'

Neither of us feel authorised to agree or disagree.

'Blimey,' I say.

'What about your job?' asks Donald.

'Bugger the job,' says Brian, shaking his head and staring at his beer. 'It's complete shite. I can't believe how seriously I've taken it. How many years I've busted a gut for those prats. And you come here, and you see how people live, and for Christ's sake it doesn't matter what job they do, does it? I mean, can you imagine sitting on the deck of one of those ferries in the morning on your way to work? It wouldn't matter what happened from nine to five, would it? You'd just do your job and then head for the water.'

There's a strange, intermittent buzzing sound coming from somewhere. It's Donald's diminutive little phone, and it's doing engaging little pirouettes in a puddle of stale beer. Donald picks it up.

'Hello?' he says, and then immediately cups his other ear with his hand. It's obviously not a good line.

'Aw, hello love,' he says in a remarkably different tone. It's like his voice just unbroke itself and he went from baritone to mezzo-soprano. I guess we all have our sweetie voice, but it's astonishing hearing the instant change. Like a different dialect.

Donald's turned slightly away from us to give himself a

sense of privacy. Brian and I are silent, looking away, but our ears are tuned in.

'Have you? Oh, sorry. I suppose there are millions of people ringing at the same time. Yes. Yes. Absolutely brilliant. Did you? Brilliant. Amazing, wasn't it? Yes, we're in a bar in The Rocks. Sorry? Oh, the Lord . . . Lord something-or-other.'

'Nelson,' says Brian, still resolutely pretending not to eavesdrop.

'Nelson. Yeah, it's open late. Oh, well, I suppose we've had a few. Yes. A skin-full actually, but we're still going strong. Sorry? No, well, no I think we'll just stay here till they kick us out. Sorry? Bloody line's breaking up, Judy. OK love. I love you. Love you loads. See you . . . oh.' He looks up at us, eyes filling. 'Bloody mobile phones.'

I'm starting to get irritated. Christ, Donald's fighting back tears. What is going on? Our team just won the Rugby World Cup final and my two mates are all over the shop! I suppose they are both going through the mill a bit, but there's a time and a place, surely?

'What's up, mate?' I say, gently enough.

'Oh, nothing. It's just . . . hearing her voice. Today. The rugby. Everything . . . it just made me realise how bloody lucky I am.'

So why are you all chocked up? I think it. Wouldn't dream of saying it. But Brian and I just watch Donald. He's got it under control, but he's clearly been hit by a tidal wave of emotion. Tick, tick, tick. Big pause while Donald gathers himself and the embers of another round of beers hiss a slow death.

'I think it's my round, isn't it?' sniffs Donald. It's true, and we are fairly religious, in normal circumstances, about buying rounds in their proper order.

I just nod at him. I'm loath to offer to go to the bar myself, but I will if he's still suffering. He's not got up yet.

'You know, I thought quite seriously about trying to kill myself a few weeks back,' Donald says, looking from me to Brian and back.

'You did what?' says Brian, his face white.

Donald nods.

'You seriously did?' I ask him. I'm pretty blown away as well, but of course Brian didn't have the benefit of the conversation I had with Donald that night in his garden.

'Yeah, sorry, I left that bit out when we had our little talk,' Donald says. 'It was pretty pathetic. I mean, I went through the motions. I don't know what I was doing, to be honest. But . . . how could I have got myself in such a bloody state?'

'What . . . what did you do?' says Brian.

'Nothing in the end. But the plan was I was going to gas myself in the car.'

'What, with the Saab?' I say.

'No, the old Honda.'

'Even so.'

'What do you mean?' Donald's face is crumpled into a deep frown.

Brian and I glance at each other knowingly.

'They've both got catalytic converters,' says Brian.

'And fuel injection systems probably,' I add.

'So what's that mean?' says Donald.

'It means the emissions are too clean to top yourself,' says Brian. 'Best you could do is give yourself a nasty headache.'

'You picked the wrong technique, mate,' I say, sensing that Donald's really OK about this. 'And I'm glad you did, because otherwise I'd have drowned yesterday.'

'Now there's a thought,' says Brian, contemplating life without his two best mates.

Donald shakes his head, kicks back his chair so hard it falls over, and zig-zags drunkenly in the direction of the bar.

I love my two friends, Donald and Brian. And I mean that. I love them, in that male sort of way that women find hard to fathom because it doesn't fit within their frame of reference for what constitutes love. Male love is sort of bungling and awkward, unspoken and vague, fickle and moody, but as certain as Ralph's bowel movements and far, far more concrete. I suppose the eccentricity of male love – the friendship kind – is that we rarely talk about anything that gets too close to the bone. It's implied. We mostly talk complete rubbish, but somehow amidst the banality we communicate with each other what's going on in our minds and our lives. Brian tells me how he's feeling about Tanya by being in a bad mood, drinking a little faster than usual and looking at his watch irritably on a regular basis. I know Donald's in trouble because he'll call me when he normally wouldn't. In male terms, these are grand, cathartic gestures.

But much as I love them, they piss me off enormously from time to time. I know it's selfish, and maybe it's the beer talking, or the jet-lag, or the pills but for Christ's sake we've just witnessed England beating Australia to take the Rugby World Cup. I mean, honestly, is now the time to be confessing suicide attempts and planning emigration? Can't it wait? Jesus, maybe it's me that's the odd one. Maybe I should tell Clare I'm gay or something, just to compete. Fuck it.

I'm sulking. Donald's at the bar and Brian's taken to peeling off the Boag's labels again. The evening is in danger of grinding to a complete halt. Sometimes, when you're drinking, each pint lifts the evening on to a higher plane and by the end you're really flying, cracking jokes and laughing hysterically and finding innovative new ways of getting rid of hiccups. Other times, each beer seems to slow the flow of blood, the conversation stops and eventually you reach a complete, collective standstill. I can sense that happening to us now, and it's criminal, given the circumstances.

I'm not going to let it happen, dammit.

'Brian . . .'

'Mmm?'

. . .

. . .

. . .

. . .

'What?'

. . .

. . .

. . .

. . .

I am hallucinating badly. Three women have just breezed into the pub like a gust of fresh mountain air. Gorgeous.

They are giggling and looking around rather than going straight to the bar, like they are looking for someone. One of them is small but perfectly formed, wearing her brown hair in a neat bob; the other two are much taller, one blonde and the other brunette – both are striking. The petite one catches my eye and holds it, smiling. My stomach turns over as reality dawns. It's Clare. Tanya. Judy. They are here. In Sydney. The phone call . . . must have been from round the corner.

Cannot compute. Cannot compute. Cannot compute.

Brian has seen my face – God knows what it looks like, actually. I probably look as though my wife has just gatecrashed a boys' weekend on the other side of the world, breaking every rule in the book. In other words, utterly dumbfounded, my mouth hanging open spastically as I try to take in what I'm seeing.

Donald's stopped only feet away from our three partners in life. He's somehow clutching six bottles of beer – maybe he, too, sensed that the evening was dying so decided we needed more drink. Smart thinking. Or maybe he was in on this little conspiracy as well. Nothing, at this moment, would surprise me. Not any more.

It's not until the six of us are seated at the table that I can begin to digest what has happened. My head is pounding, which may have something to do with the volume of painkillers I have taken, and the fact that I've swilled them down with a dozen or so bottles of Tasmanian beer, but all I can really feel right now is a sense of outrage that so many of life's unwritten rules have just been broken.

'Just what the *hell* did you think you were doing?' I say. It's a strange feeling. I'm definitely fairly pissed, granted, but this is one of my typical mute monologues, except this time, it's on the outside. I'm not quite sure if I actually intended to open my mouth and speak, but dammit that's what's happening, and there can be no regrets. I'm addressing the three women, but mostly I'm talking to Clare.

'This was *our* trip. Us. The three of us. The lads. I know you think we're just pathetic little boys, but actually these things mean a lot to us. Spending time just us. Without kids screaming at us. Without . . . and we planned this for ages. This was a chance for us to do something a bit different. Watch England in the final. We fucking earned it.'

I'm on a roll, but I suddenly feel really drunk, or ill, or something. In fact, I'm struggling to focus, but when I do – just briefly – I can see that Clare's eyes have narrowed and her jaw is set. It looks as though Donald's mouth has dropped open, and Brian's eyes are wide and getting wider. What's the matter with them all?

'So why are you here?' I ask. I feel hostile. Awful. But brittle at the same time.

Clare remains silent, but her eyes narrow even further. I do the same with my own eyes, not to compete with her but to try to keep her in focus.

'I thought we had some rules of engagement with BlokeMiles,' I say, softly now.

'Uh-huh?' Clare agrees, arms crossed.

'It was . . . it was all about giving ourselves space. To . . . be ourselves. Do what we want to do.'

'Uh-huh?'

'And . . . not have to beg and feel so fucking guilty all the time.'

'Uh-huh?'

It's come down to a shoot-out between me and Clare, though I feel like a reluctant spokesperson for the male species in a universal game of boys versus girls.

'Rob,' says Donald sharply, interrupting the flow. 'Shut the fuck up, would you?'

I squint at my friend through stinging eyes. OK, so I've been sacked as spokesman. My head is beginning to throb badly. I look around the table, and there are sheepish grins. Nobody quite knows where to look. It seems such a dramatic reversal of roles, it's almost embarrassing.

Brian is on his feet. He steps round the chairs and gives me a hug round the neck. 'Mate, you're losing it. I think we need to get you home.'

The curtains of fog part briefly, and I'm aware that I've made a fool of myself. I don't really know what I've said or why I've said it, but there's a mixture of concern and embarrassed amusement on my friends' faces. And then I'm hit, hard, by a squall of emotion, and I have no choice but to cry. Everything is a blur again, and I'm vaguely aware that Brian has been replaced by Clare, and my wife is pulling my head to her breast. Her smell is wonderfully reassuring.

I keep my eyes shut tight until I've conquered the tears and my breathing steadies, and I can hear Donald recounting the story of the day before. I can feel Clare gently tracing the stitches on my head with the tips of her fingers. And when I look up, my wife is gazing at me with eyes full of love and sympathy. I don't feel alone any more.

I close my eyes again, and tune back in to the conversation. They are talking about the rugby now and the girls are eager to hear the first-hand accounts of the game.

'What was it like being there?'

'What about that Jonny Wilkinson!!'

'It must have been amazing . . .'

They are genuine, too, like excited schoolgirls. I would never have predicted that these three ladies would become such ardent rugby fans. Never.

'Well,' says Donald, during a momentary lull in the conversation. 'Here's to all of us.' They drink, and Donald lifts Judy's hand, the one he's been holding, and kisses it gently.

I've managed to haul myself into a sitting position. I had to, otherwise I'd have fallen asleep. I notice Brian and Tanya smiling at each other, each daring the other to say something or make the first move. Tanya slips from her chair and makes towards Brian, but he stands and meets her halfway. They kiss. A deep, passionate kiss that seems to explode whatever tension was left in the situation for all of us.

Donald pulls back from Judy. The two of them, and me and Clare, are transfixed by Brian and Tanya who, for their part, have been transported to some other world.

Finally, after what feels like minutes but is probably only seconds, the couple come up for air. They look round, dazed and slightly embarrassed.

'Sorry,' says Tanya, giggling.

Brian looks like a teenager who's just had his first blow-job. The two of them sit down, holding hands, unable to separate.

'Everything all right with you two, then?' I say.

They smile, and Brian gives me a V-sign.

'So can we have fun now?' says Clare.

'I think that's a damned fine idea,' I say, unable now to speak without slurring, and we chink glasses, or rather bottles, again.

Donald and Judy stand up together, still holding hands.

'We're just going for a bit of fresh air. Back in a second.'

'No worries,' I say. 'At least you've got the decency to go outside for a snog.'

'Oh,' says Clare, suddenly. 'I've got an interesting-looking letter for you.' She reaches into her jacket pocket, pulls out a crumpled manila envelope and hands it to me.

I recognise the handwriting. 'Hmm. It's from my agent.'

I tear the envelope open and pull out a word-processed letter with a flamboyant signature at the bottom. It's quite clear what the letter says, but it takes a monumental effort to digest it. Make sense of it.

'Holy shit,' I mutter.

'What is it, mate?' says Brian.

'My novel. My bloody crappy novel. I've got a US publishing deal!'

Clare squeaks with delight and throws her arm around me, kissing me on the cheek. 'I was hoping that was what it was. You are a STAR!'

Brian walks round the table and slaps me on the shoulder, then gives me a firm hug. 'Well done, fella. We all knew you'd do it. You just didn't know it yourself.'

I am stunned. It is dawning on me just how low my confidence and self-belief had sunk. I used to be a recognition junkie, but it's been so long since I really achieved anything, I'd stopped believing. Just kind of written off my career as a lost cause. Decided that careers don't matter as much as being a father and a husband – but somewhere deep inside I was pining desperately for that sense of worth that a career can give. That sense of being a proper bloke. I can feel the pilot light of accomplishment igniting itself again, spreading warmth through my being.

Donald and Judy return to the table, both grinning broadly.

'What's the letter, Rob?' he asks, and I hand it to him.

'He's got a publishing deal,' blurts Clare, unable to wait until Donald has scanned the page.

'Bloody well done, chap!' says Donald and shakes my hand forcefully. 'That is awesome news.'

Judy, too, gives me a hug of suffocating enthusiasm.

And so, the six of us – the three couples – appear to become a single living entity, changing shape as we move round the table, reconnecting with each other, sipping beer, sitting, standing, embracing, kissing. BlokeMiles has brought us together, but we aren't thinking about that now. England's rugby team have been crowned world champions, but even that has slipped our minds.

I am having a moment of quiet, private admiration for my wife. She has always encouraged me to stick with my writing. Not to give up hope, not to change direction or lose the faith. Her belief in me has never wavered. She has been my spine. Without her, I'd be nothing. I can suddenly see, with the last bit of startling clarity that my exhausted mind can summon, how women make men whole. They provide the rails that stop us wandering off into oblivion. They provide us with those crucial dimensions outside ourselves that make life worth living – I mean, really worth living – but they also help us look inside our souls and see something we struggle to see on our own. Something good.

'Where are you staying?' I say to Clare, although for some reason the question seems to have attracted everyone's attention.

'Same place as you.'

'Shall we go home?'

Chapter Twenty-nine

Nine Months Later

The woman at the bar is drop-dead gorgeous. Auburn hair, this time, tied back into a ponytail. She's leaning on the bar facing out, looking rather anxiously for someone and pretending she doesn't know she's being stared at. She wouldn't notice me and Brian, though, because we've become practised at enjoying the sight of a lovely lady without making it too obvious, and perhaps also because we are almost, but not quite, old enough to be her father.

'Did you see that?' I say.

'What?'

'She just looked me straight in the eye.'

'Yeah, yeah, yeah.'

'No, really!'

'Rob, I know. I saw it too. She clearly wants to make mad passionate love to you.'

'Blimey, don't know if I could manage it.' I smirk meaningfully at Brian.

'Seriously?'

'Yeah! We've got this new routine where we pack the kids off at seven exactly and go straight upstairs and get to it. Well, not every night, but the point is we can when we feel like it. It's all become possible again.'

The two of us chuckle and sip our Stella.

'Speaking of which,' I say. 'Are you and Tanya ... you know ... still ...'

'Yep,' says Brian, smiling smugly. 'Almost every night. It's bloody marvellous.'

'So that therapist helped then?'

'Her? Piss off. Total waste of money. We just remembered how much we fancied each other, that's all.'

'Hello, hello, hello?' The familiar resonance of Donald's voice interrupts the conversation. He's holding three pints of Stella and looks particularly pleased with himself, though there's no hiding the dark rings under his eyes.

'Donald!'

'Hey, you made it!'

'Never in doubt, chaps, never in doubt.'

Donald doles out the beer and sits down, but not before wriggling out of a rather nifty leather back-pack.

'You brought your laptop to the pub?' I ask.

'Yep. Don't worry, I'm not going to show you any more pics of Jack. Unless you'd particularly like that.'

Brian and I both hesitate. Donald chuckles.

'It's OK. There's something I want to show you, though. I've been mucking about with an idea.'

'So how did you get a pass?' says Brian.

'Christ, I've been working on it all week. I'm now feeding him with expressed milk every night at ten, getting up with him at five or six or whenever he wakes up, changing God knows how many bloody nappies ... I reckon I've earned a couple of pints with my friends, don't you?'

'And then some,' I say.

Donald inhales half his pint thirstily. 'Anyway, let me show you this thing, and then I'll just put it away for the evening.'

He takes out his tiny IBM Thinkpad and fires it up.

'So, do you remember I said I'd had this idea of how to create a little software tool for BlokeMiles? Well, I had a go at it.'

'When the hell have you found time to do that?' asks Brian admiringly.

'You'd be surprised. Judy tries to sleep when Jack does, and sometimes the place is like a ghost house for two hours at a time.'

'I used to sleep as well,' I say.

'I find I can't. At least not when they're both asleep. Anyway . . .'

Donald turns the screen towards Brian and me. I can see what looks a bit like a database input screen, except there's a little graphic of a harassed-looking bloke, hair all over the place, scratching his head.

'Is that meant to look like Rob?' asks Brian.

'Maybe,' says Donald, smiling.

'I'm honoured,' I say.

'Anyway, this is where you work out your BlokeMiles budget. You input the tasks you've agreed with your partner, like . . . so.' Donald clicks on the task window and a list of activities drops down. He's obviously designed this for his and Judy's predicament, because there are things like *wake up with Jack, Judy lie-in till 9 a.m.,* and *take Jack for weekend / expressed milk.* 'So each one has a value, pre-agreed, of course, and at the end of each week you just put in what you've done and the system keeps a balance for you.'

'How do you redeem them?' I ask.

'OK . . .' Donald quits out of the *Save* section and clicks on *Spend.* My original list, the one I showed Brian at the squash club that day last year – it seems an age ago – pops up on the screen, complete with an entry for lap-dancing, with a red stamp saying 'Banned' over it. Nice touch.

'The idea is,' Donald continues, 'you select from the list, and it sends an email to you and your partner, showing your new balance.'

'And do you have to wait for her approval?' says Brian. It's always been his big bone of contention with BlokeMiles and how it's implemented.

'I don't think so,' says Donald. Because you agree all the parameters up front, so this is just a courtesy of the system, letting both parties know the score.'

'Love it,' I say. 'But what happens if you don't have enough BlokeMiles in your account? Does it just tell you you can't do it?'

Donald smirks. 'Funny you should ask that. You can set the system up in either one of two ways. Either it just says *sorry, insufficient blokemiles available; go and do something nice, or . . .'*

'Or you get an overdraft?' says Brian.

'Not an overdraft, exactly.'

There's a pause while Brian and I try to work out what Donald's looking so smug about. And then a light comes on in my mind. I've got it.

'Is there a dog house in there?'

Donald claps his hands happily, and goes back to the laptop. 'Right, so you can see your balance down here. I've got ten BlokeMiles. I say I'm going to go on a boys' golf weekend . . .' He's clicking through the menus so fast now, I can't keep track.

'And . . .' Donald sits back and turns the screen so it's facing directly away from him and towards Brian and me.

The words and numbers on the screen have gone grey, and a large hut is appearing on the screen with the words DOG HOUSE above the door. The bloke who looks like me is skulking across the screen, opening the door and going inside. The door slams shut, and the face – my face? – is now peering mournfully out through the window.

'Brilliant,' I say.

'You're a bloody genius,' says Brian.

'Wait, wait.' Clearly, there's more.

And then the music starts up. It's some kind of heavy metal, and the dog house shakes to illustrate the extreme volume. The face looking out of the window seems to cheer up.

'So you can actually choose your own music for the dog house,' chuckles Donald proudly.

'And you can play it as loud as you want?' says Brian.

'Exactly. Which is more than you can do in your own front room, am I right?'

We're laughing. I think it's lovely. There's something very symbolic about the dog house to me. I sometimes feel as though I carry mine around on my back, like some kind of snail. It's a place where I can hide and lick my self-inflicted wounds. Not that I've had many to lick recently. My book's coming out in a few months, I'm working on a second, I'm loving my wife and my children, and I'm even reasonably fond of myself.

And I never thought I'd say that.